PROMISE AT PEBBLE CREEK

Books by Lisa Jones Baker

The Hope Chest of Dreams Series

Rebecca's Bouquet

Annie's Recipe

Rachel's Dream

Secret at Pebble Creek

Love at Pebble Creek

Promise at Pebble Creek

Anthologies

The Amish Christmas Kitchen
(with Kelly Long and Jennifer Beckstrand)

The Amish Christmas Candle
(with Kelly Long and Jennifer Beckstrand)

Published by Kensington Publishing Corporation

PROMISE AT PEBBLE CREEK

Lisa Jones Baker

ZEBRA BOOKS
KENSINGTON PUBLISHING CORP.
www.kensingtonbooks.com

ZEBRA BOOKS are published by

Kensington Publishing Corp.
119 West 40th Street
New York, NY 10018

All Kensington titles, imprints, and distributed lines are available at special quantity discounts for bulk purchases for sales promotion, premiums, fund-raising, educational, or institutional use.

Special book excerpts or customized printings can also be created to fit specific needs. For details, write or phone the office of the Kensington Sales Manager: Attn.: Sales Department. Kensington Publishing Corp., 119 West 40th Street, New York, NY 10018. Phone: 1-800-221-2647.

Zebra and the Z logo Reg. U.S. Pat. & TM Off.
BOUQUET Reg. U.S. Pat. & TM Off.

First Printing: May 2020
ISBN-13: 978-1-4201-4748-3
ISBN-10: 1-4201-4748-X

eISBN-13: 978-1-4201-4749-0 (eBook)
eISBN-10: 1-4201-4749-8 (eBook)

10 9 8 7 6 5 4 3 2 1

Printed in the United States of America

To John and Marcia Baker,
my two dearest friends

ACKNOWLEDGMENTS

First of all, I visited numerous sources to acquire information for this book, and any errors are mine and mine alone. Much love to my mother and father for their unconditional support the past sixty years. My wonderful, reading specialist mother has helped me to edit over thirty books, and without her, I would only be dreaming of becoming a writer.

To Vince Conlee for patiently assisting with this story's welding details. We are blessed to have you in our family. Thanks so much to June Morris of Salem, Illinois, for sharing your quilting talent with me. Huge appreciation to Margaret at Stitch and Sew in Arthur, Illinois, and to Elizabeth Chupp for sharing insider details on quilting. You are talented ladies. I'm greatly appreciative of Nolan Recker, Adult Ministries Pastor at Vale Church, for helping me to clarify my Scripture questions and for all you do for our church! I owe my junior high and high school English teachers, the late Helen Foltz and Dave Eatock, for sharing their valuable knowledge and for their superb ability to convey that information; your teaching trumped every college writing instructor I ever had. Thank you to my Amish go-to girl who carefully reads my books from start to finish to ensure I adhere to the Amish practices in

Arthur, Illinois, and who prefers to remain anonymous. I'll never forget meeting you over a decade ago. Since then, you have shared your life and your beliefs with me, and I'm blessed to know you. Lisa Nortato, true friend and confidante for thirty years; what would I do without you? Thanks to sharp Aunt Velda Baker in Lincoln, Illinois, who's always up for reviewing my stories before they go to edits, and to the Bloomington Geek Squad for salvaging my laptop issues. I'm grateful to my dedicated street team members and all my readers for your support and for constantly offering me valuable input to help my characters float off the pages and into the hearts of those waiting to see what's next. To *New York Times* bestselling author Joan Wester Anderson; you're a tremendous, unexpected blessing, who helped to launch *Rebecca's Bouquet* and my Hope Chest of Dreams Series, and I'm so grateful to you. I can only aspire to write as well as you. To my sister, Beth, and brother-in-law, Doug, I love you for everything you do!

Many of you are aware that my writing journey took twenty-four years to see my stories in print, but during that long, challenging time frame, I always believed that God tests our faith and our tenacity, and when I finally signed with Kensington Publishing in New York, the pieces that had taken years to cultivate were finally in the right places, especially fantastic editor Selena James, the entire Kensington team, and agent of the year Tamala Hancock Murray of the Steve Laube Agency, who worked with me for years when there was no guarantee of publication. Now, enjoy *Promise at Pebble Creek*!

Chapter One

Who is he? Hannah arched a curious brow as she hid her adventure book near the cash register and stepped to the entrance of Amish Edibles. *Of course, I don't know all my customers. Why would I be surprised that I've never seen him?*

The bell above the door chimed as he stepped inside. Outside, she glimpsed a white car. She certainly wasn't an expert on vehicles, but what he drove resembled a Chevy Malibu she'd ridden in with a neighbor to her doctor.

Lifting her chin a notch, she silently ordered herself to remember her manners. She smiled a little while she motioned him in and offered the taller-than-average man a warm welcome. In response, he nodded and gave a soft, friendly hello. His voice had a low timbre mixed with an odd combination of gentleness and ruggedness.

When he glanced to his side, she motioned to the shelves of edibles. Homemade breads, jelly, egg noodles, spices, dolls without faces, and miniature hand-carved hope chests made by Amish workers prompted a satisfied smile.

Horses, buggies, and delicate-looking sachets created

by Rebecca and Mary Conrad filled the shop with pleasant floral scents.

"Feel free to look around, and if I can help, let me know."

He narrowed his dark brows. "I'd like something for lunch sandwiches. Peanut butter and jelly?"

The request automatically lifted the corners of her lips. *So, this rugged-looking man likes peanut butter and jelly.* She quickly decided on a response. "There's a store in town that sells peanut butter. But . . ."

When he eyed her to continue, gray flecks danced on beautiful jade-green eyes. The shade reminded her of summer grass after the first mow.

"I'd recommend that you buy the bread and jelly here."

He offered a nod. "I'll take that recommendation."

She lifted her chin with sudden confidence and pointed to the selection of homemade loaves. She repeated the motion of her hand when she turned to the shelves of jelly. "Over here."

The soles of his worn leather boots made a light sound against the cement floor as he strode to the part of the shop where different flavors of jelly were lined up. As he bent to check out the lower shelf, her curiosity kicked into higher gear.

No, I shouldn't be surprised I've never seen him, but he just doesn't look like other customers who come here. She considered her realization and added, *In fact, he's far from it.*

As the battery-powered fan's large metal blades whipped around and offered relief from the hot, early

July temperatures, Hannah stepped closer to him while he pulled a container of strawberry spread from the shelf.

"Strawberry's *gut*. But if you want my honest opinion . . ." He looked up at her while she tapped the toe of her sturdy black shoe against the floor. "Raspberry is my utmost favorite. And this year, they have an unusually sweet flavor."

"Thanks for the tip." He winked, grabbing the raspberry. "My decision's made."

As he smiled at Hannah, she automatically smiled back. But to her dismay, it was hard to look away. She was fully aware that her last intention was to stare, but her unusually keen curiosity took over while she took in the set of broad shoulders and the fit build of the above-average-height stranger.

She'd always been taught to focus on a person's heart and not their physical appearance. But she couldn't help but appreciate his handsome ruggedness.

A short silence ensued until he offered her a half smile and extended his hand. "Marcus Jackson."

In embarrassment, she tried to stop the warm blood that rushed to her face. Obviously, she'd been staring, even though her intention had been not to. "Hannah Lapp." She shook his callused hand.

"It's a pleasure to meet you."

Trying to hide her keen interest, she forced her most casual voice. "You're new to the area?"

A quick nod provided her answer. "I just came into town. From Chicago. Starting tomorrow, I'll be working at a chemical company near here."

She looked at him, waiting for him to go on.

He waved a dismissive hand. "Anyway, it's a long story. I won't bore you with it."

She tried to hide her disappointment that he didn't offer more details and spoke the first thought that came to mind. "Country life must be far different from what you're used to."

Hannah knew about everyone in the Arthur-Arcola area, even the *Englisch*. At one time or another, most had come to her shop for her renowned jelly, especially around Thanksgiving and Christmastime.

She had a knack for recalling faces and names, and she was sure she would have remembered this soft-spoken *Englischer,* whom she guessed to be about twenty-five, five years her senior. His gray T-shirt fit his body loosely, revealing muscular, tanned arms.

His blue jeans were a loose fit, too. But what piqued her interest was the way he smiled at her. His expression had seemed genuine enough, but his dark jade-colored eyes hinted at excitement and adventure. At the same time, she thought she noted a shadow of sadness in the haze around them.

Automatically, she tried to imagine what could have brought him so far from Chicago. *There I go again. I wish my imagination would rest. I'm being nosey. Maemm's always reminding me to mind my own business.*

His attention suddenly turned to the back room. She followed his gaze, which landed on her quilt in progress. The door was opened, offering a glimpse of her work.

He softened his tone. "You quilt?"

"*Jah.*" She offered a quick nod. "It's one of my passions." She deliberately neglected mentioning that her other was reading *The Adventures of Sydney and Carson*, her favorite book series.

When he didn't inquire about the others, she sighed relief. Of course, there wasn't anything wrong with enjoying adventure stories. Not that she knew of, anyway. But she loved them so much, and the way they challenged her imagination, that she preferred to keep her secret.

Oftentimes, Maemm had voiced her disapproval . . . that perhaps Hannah could do something more productive with her time . . . so Hannah kept her stories out of sight.

When his gaze lingered on the quilt, she stepped closer to him. "Would you like a better look?"

He nodded. "That would be nice."

With a wave of her hand, she led him into the back, where he stood very still and took in the material that was stretched out on top of a wooden frame. The pieces of material showed the back side. Multiple pins around the sides attached it to the stand. Spools of thread lined the end of the table. There were thimbles. A sewing box. A ruler.

She suddenly realized how unkempt the scene in front of them must look. "Sorry for the mess."

"No need to apologize. It looks like a lot of work. But it's already beautiful. Even with the wrong side showing." He let out a low whistle. "I can only imagine what it will look like when it's done."

"*Denki.*" When he continued gazing at it, she decided to tell him a bit about it. Her heart warmed at his obvious interest. At the same time, she was even more curious about the *Englischer.*

It was unusual for men, especially someone so

outdoorsy-looking to express such a sincere interest in something that was so feminine.

The expression on his face was so endearing, she felt compelled to tell him as much as she could. In a soft voice, she fixed her attention on the squares that had already been sewn together.

"I helped Maemm with them when I was little. When I got older, I started doing my own. Usually, I make them for newborn babies. Or newlyweds. Oh . . ."

She gestured with her hands. "The last one was for a lady who goes to our church who was hospitalized."

"Who's this for?" He ran a finger gently over one of the squares.

She lifted her palms to the ceiling and offered a slight shrug. "I'm not sure."

He looked at her and smiled appreciatively. "I don't know a thing about quilting, but there's one thing I can tell you with absolute certainty." The corners of his lips curved in a combination of amusement and seriousness. "Whoever gets this will love it."

Hannah beamed and drew her hands to her chest with great affection. In a voice that was barely more than a whisper, she said, "*Denki*, Marcus."

He continued to look at the quilt, slowly bending to run his tanned hand over the soft cotton fabric. While he did so, she took the opportunity to study him. When he stretched out his arm, his T-shirt revealed more muscle.

Short, jet-black hair framed a confident-looking face. She couldn't see his eyes now, as he bent to study her project, but she'd noticed the unique shade as soon as he'd entered the shop.

Finally, he drew in a breath and smiled a little.

"Thanks for the look at your project." Automatically, she began to return to the main area of her shop, and he followed. "Nice shop."

"*Denki.*"

His lips curved in an amused smile. "I suppose you're wondering why I'm so intrigued with your quilt."

She lifted a brow for him to go on.

"My mom used to sew. My late mom," he corrected.

She softened her voice to a sympathetic tone. "I'm so sorry." She hadn't missed the emotional catch in his throat.

"Thank you." He waved a dismissive hand. "It's been about six years since I lost her. But there's one thing I'll never forget about my childhood, and that's the blanket she sewed for my sixth birthday. It was three shades of blue that are nearly identical to your quilt."

Right then and there, Hannah knew why Marcus Jackson was so interested in her quilt. It was because it struck a happy chord. Apparently, the memory was a strong one.

Immediately, Hannah experienced a strange connection to this man. Oddly, she'd never felt such an emotion. But no matter where he came from, no matter his circumstances, she wished him the very best. In fact, tonight she would begin praying for *Gott* to bring him happiness.

He paid cash; she gave him change, which he accepted in the large palm of his hand. His attention shifted to the metal horse to her right that was separated from the buggy.

He picked up the two parts and eyed her. "I can fix

this for you." After a slight pause, he added, "Do you mind if I take these with me?"

"Of course not. In fact, I'd very much appreciate it."

"One more thing. I was wondering: you don't know of anyone who needs a renter, do you?"

She offered an eager nod. "*Jah*. My brother." She quickly went for a piece of paper, wrote down his name, and handed it to him.

He eyed it. "Is there a number where I can reach him?"

"He has a phone in his barn."

A surprised expression filled his eyes.

She quickly explained. "We Amish usually have phones in our barns or sheds."

She took the paper from him, wrote down the number, and handed it back to him. "But it might be easier to reach him at work. He's a welder at Cabot. Not far from here."

Marcus flashed her a smile. "I'm headed there next."

When she parted her lips in surprise, he added, "After several phone interviews, they hired me." A sigh of relief escaped his throat. "Everything seems to be falling into place. Thanks, Hannah."

She offered a nod and added, "It's my pleasure. I hope you like the jelly."

As the door shut, the plastic sign hanging on it moved up and down, making a clicking sound, until it finally landed back in place. Hannah glanced at the wall clock inside Amish Edibles.

The time showed ten thirty. So far, only one customer this morning. Marcus. Of course, it was always quiet this time of year. For some reason, customers were few and far between at the start of July.

But today, that was fine with Hannah. She smiled a little and shoved a loose strand of hair back under her *kapp*. The welcome free time offered her the opportunity to sew some more on her most exquisite project: her king-size quilt.

In the back room, she got down to work, admiring the vegetables in her small garden on the other side of the window. While her scissors snipped the material, the ceiling fan circulated all sorts of earthy aromas throughout the shop.

There was the smell of oak from the wooden, hand-carved buggies she'd recently set out on display. She breathed in the fresh, familiar smell and smiled.

There were sachets. A cinnamon candle. And the heavenly aroma of fresh bread that Hannah had baked and wrapped very early that morning.

She focused on her quilt. She bunched a small square, gathered the material, and inserted her needle and thread, and began connecting the pieces to another square.

She stopped a moment to organize the numerous spools of thread in her large, compartmented organizer, breathing in the pleasant aroma of the spice. She sold it in small containers, but this particular scent emanated from the homemade burning *kandl* near her cash register in the middle of the shop.

After sighing satisfaction, she eyed the wooden organizer that had been last year's Christmas gift from her brother, Ben, and his wife, Ruth.

As Hannah ran her gaze over the enormous piece of material stretched out on her wooden frame, she pressed her lips together thoughtfully. She could hear the tin pans on both sides of the garden as the light breeze caused them to meet.

The large faux owl perched on top of one pole had been given to her by her *daed* when he'd learned that Hannah's garden appeared to be a popular gathering place for rabbits. A faux snake on the outskirts of the rapidly growing plants served the same purpose. Past experience had taught her that the movement helped to keep away insects and rabbits.

Because she preferred things natural, she didn't use pesticides. Beyond the garden, the county blacktop went on for miles throughout the Arthur-Arcola countryside. Every once in a while, she'd glimpse a car or a horse-drawn buggy traveling the narrow, uneven road.

Anxious to proceed on her project, she refocused her gaze in front of her and smiled with satisfaction. Automatically, past projects flitted through her mind. The navy-and-white quilt she'd completed a couple of months ago for Ben and Ruth, to celebrate the large home they'd purchased. The creamy shades of white she'd done six months ago for a friend's wedding.

She parted her lips in awe as she recalled their simple yet exquisite beauty. Then she assessed the piece in front of her and narrowed her brows. This one differed in many ways.

And there was a plausible reason why. She'd routinely designed her quilts for certain people. But this time, amazingly, there was no recipient, yet, for her most beautiful, special work. Because of that, she'd chosen her personal favorite colors, three hues of blue. The blend that she would select for herself.

A nature lover, she had always been taken in by the sky's different shades. Especially deep blue, which reminded her of a cloudless summer sky. As she created the quilt, she dreamed of eventually presenting her very best work to someone so extremely special and watching that person's expression while they unwrapped it. *Who will it be? Who is special enough for this gorgeous work?*

A reddish-brown face appeared on the other side of the glass. A scratching sound followed. Hannah immediately went to unlock and then open the back door.

As usual, the stray kitten stepped inside. Hannah closed and locked the door behind her, bending to stroke the soft fur. "Scarlet, you're lucky I adore you." She wagged a finger at the cat. "But don't you dare tell Maemm I let you in."

The feline made its way to the small pillow Hannah kept in the corner of the room. Following normal protocol, Hannah proceeded to the nearby bathroom sink, where she filled a small plastic container with water and placed it in front of her furry friend.

Back at her project, she glanced at the corner before cutting a piece of thread. "Come lunchtime, I'll share my chicken salad with you."

A meow followed. With great care to make her lines even, Hannah hand-stitched the fresh pieces together. In the back room of Amish Edibles, she smiled approval at the beautiful material in front of her while she enjoyed the warm breeze from the ceiling fan's blades. No doubt someone would most likely store this quilt in a large hope chest.

She turned to the corner to check on her friend, who

had made herself comfortable on the soft cushion. "Or maybe, Scarlet, they'll decide to snuggle up under this warm, thick cotton fabric every night."

After a light shrug of her shoulders, she went on, as if the cat could understand everything she said. "Whatever the case, I have no doubt that this project will bring joy to somebody."

Her beloved hope chest immediately popped into her mind. The mere thought of it brought a warmth up her arms and landed comfortably in her shoulders. For a moment, she gently closed her eyes and enjoyed the sweet sensation.

Her hope chest had been designed by the well-known late Sam Beachy. Maemm and Daed had given it to her shortly after Sam's death. It had been her eighteenth birthday, and they had planned to invite Old Sam to their home for dinner that night.

Old Sam had been down with pneumonia and had eventually passed on to heaven. Hannah appreciated every bit of love and creativity the famed hope chest maker had invested in her unique wooden piece of art.

He'd been blessed with great creative talent; everyone around had heard of his work. He'd skillfully carved the Ten Commandments into the lid of her particular chest.

The needle stuck Hannah's thumb. "Ouch." She gave her finger a quick shake to rid it of the pain. "That will teach me to pay attention to what I'm doing."

But as she continued working, the miniature hope chest, which she kept beside her bed, remained in her thoughts. The inside of the oak structure had enough room for the things Hannah considered special enough to put in it; at the same time, it was small and light enough to easily move across her room.

However, so far, the chest was empty. Even so, Hannah enjoyed the woodsy oak scent. She also loved touching the deep-blue velvet that lined the inside.

Definitely, she planned to save her most valuable possessions for the chest. Things that Maemm would pass down to her, and that she, in turn, would pass down to the daughters she planned to bear.

But she was selective, and so far, nothing qualified to be in the most special gift she'd ever received.

After admiring the beautiful colors, she measured another square with a ruler, and her heart picked up a notch of speed. But not because of the particular passion in front of her. No. The upward curve of her lips and the excited skip of her heart was brought on by her other love.

The Adventures of Sydney and Carson.

She'd often imagined herself as Sydney, and Mary Conrad's brother, Jonah, who worked with his *daed* at Conrad Cabinets, as Carson. Oddly, at that moment, she had no interest in Jonah.

Hannah hummed under her breath as she tidied the pile of backings before stepping to the cash register area, where she pulled her most recent adventure stories from near the cash register, sat down, and began to read.

As she did, Hannah couldn't stop thinking about Marcus Jackson as she held *The Adventures of Sydney and Carson* in front of her, resting the paperback on the area that housed the cash drawers. She bent closer to the pages, reading faster and faster while the two fictitious characters sought shelter from a fire that had seized the Grovers' home.

She imagined someone with strong arms, arms that could lift huge, heavy bales of hay and carry her away from the fire. For some reason, she now replaced Jonah with Marcus. She raised an inquisitive brow. *Probably because I just met him*, she reasoned. *And because he was so enamored with my quilt.*

On the printed pages, the flame grew. The fire was catching them. As she imagined Marcus carrying her away from a blazing fire, the crunching of gravel interrupted her. She stopped and looked out the window. Automatically, she did what she always did when there was a customer.

She pulled her homemade bookmark from its spot beneath the cash register, stuck it in her paperback, closed the cover, and shoved it on the shelf to her right.

Her pulse pumped to a nervous beat and her hands shook a little, not just because of the excitement in the story, but also because the sound had caught her off guard, and she did her utmost to keep the series she loved top secret. She did so for two reasons.

The first was because Maemm had made it clear that she disapproved of fiction. If Hannah was going to spend her *Gott*-given time reading, Maemm preferred the print to be the Holy Bible. Secondly, Hannah intended to keep her dream of being in an adventure story to herself. The stories were so precious in her own imagination, sharing them would surely spoil some of her excitement.

Because of those two things, the books were her secret and hers alone.

When she glanced out the front window for the source of the crunching sound, a car appeared to merely turn around. She smiled satisfaction when it was back on the blacktop.

With the exception of a couple of slow weeks, summer was a busy time for Amish Edibles. Tourists interested in the Amish frequented Arthur for buggy rides, tours, and other things. But the three weeks prior to Thanksgiving and the month leading up to Christmas were by far the times she and Maemm did most of their business. Most of the time, Hannah manned the shop she owned with her parents.

Fortunately, the Welcome Center offered flyers that advertised Amish Edibles, as well as sign-ups for Amish homecooked meals, buggy rides, and shops nearby that sold beautiful handmade furniture.

Nine of her ten brothers and their families were well-known in the area for their family store, Lapp Furniture. Her *daed* had started it years before and was in charge. And they also carved special trinkets for interested visitors who craved Amish handmade goods. Ben was a welder at Cabot, the company that apparently had hired Marcus.

Conrad Cabinets had recently expanded their inventory, too, and people from all over the United States went there for custom-made furniture and cabinets. Fortunately, there was plenty of business for everyone.

Hannah's thought drifted back to Marcus Jackson. Fully aware that she'd just met him, she acknowledged that she indeed considered him a friend. Talking about her quilt and his late mother had somehow struck a bond between them. And Hannah couldn't wait to see him again.

Chapter Two

Outside Amish Edibles, Marcus enjoyed the warm breeze that fanned his eyelashes. As he turned around to get another look at the small shop, he could see beautiful Hannah as she headed back to her cash register.

His eyes followed her as he considered the young woman he felt he'd known all his life. He glanced down at the paper she'd given him before putting it in his pocket and getting into his car. Ben Lapp.

But his thoughts immediately returned to Hannah and her warm smile. He wished she hadn't been wearing a head covering so he could've checked out her chestnut-colored hair. Automatically, he wondered how it looked down, and if it went lower than her shoulders.

And her bland navy dress and sturdy black shoes. He lifted a curious brow as he turned the key in the ignition and pressed two levers to lower the front windows. He had already learned that the Amish called themselves the Plain Faith, that their less-than-flattering clothes weren't designed to make the women beautiful, but that the purpose of their bland dress was so people would appreciate them for their inner beauty.

He noticed the lone Standardbred and the black shiny

buggy, a sharp contrast to the small, cluttered parking lot of the busy Citgo Mart where he usually bought his lunch in the city. As he pulled out onto the blacktop, he eyed the openness of the vast countryside.

As fresh air came in through the windows, he considered the fields of corn and soybeans on both sides and thoughtfully compared it to his former surroundings. Here, it was . . . quiet. There was so much space. He pressed his lips together thoughtfully because he wasn't yet convinced that was a bad thing.

In the vast countryside of winding roads, two-story farm homes, and crops, this was the first shop he'd come across that sold food. At least, the words "Amish Edibles" had indicated that there were things to eat.

As he drove in the direction of Cabot, with the help of his GPS, his thoughts quickly returned to Hannah. And he'd, hopefully, get a chance to speak to her brother about his rental.

This young woman's enthusiasm and kind effort to help him told him that she definitely possessed inner beauty. And as far as exterior beauty? His smile widened a notch. God definitely had been generous to her. He'd noted chestnut-colored wisps that had carelessly escaped her head cover. Her eyes were the same shade, only a slightly richer hue. What piqued his interest, though, wasn't her outer appearance, but the genuine enthusiasm and energy evidenced in her voice.

He didn't know much about her, but what he was sure of was the memory evoked by the three shades of blue in her quilt. Amazingly, the gorgeous hues were a reminder of a blanket his late mother had sewn for him.

He blinked at the salty sting of tears. He swallowed an uncomfortable knot in his throat.

But the special gift from the person he'd loved most in the world had been much more than merely a soft bedcovering to clutch in his hands and hold close to him. The shades represented what his mom had referred to as the three parts of life. The lightest, she'd told him in her clear, teacher's voice, represented a person's young years.

The medium color represented middle age, and the darkest, the color of a stormy summer sky, one's final years.

Marcus blinked at the emotional sting of tears. Only God could create such colors in the sky. At that moment, the miracle of what had happened to him only a month ago stirred in his head until unexplainable joy filled him. The amazing, unexpected moment he'd accepted Christ as his Savior rushed back to him, and his heart warmed. The moment's stress quickly evaporated, like steam from a teakettle.

Despite his fears and uncertainty, he immediately ac-knowledged that there was much to celebrate. One by one, he ticked off what came to mind. His excellent health. His energy. That he'd had the best of the best as far as recommendations to step into a new job. That his cash should last about three months.

He quickly straightened in his seat and squared his shoulders. *Stay tough. Like Dad taught me. I'll fit in here. God will set me on the right path because I'm doing what my mom always taught me, to follow my heart.*

* * *

That evening, inside her family's kitchen, Hannah contemplated her new friend as she sprinkled flour on egg noodle dough and continued to gently roll it out into a square that reached all four corners of the cloth sheet. Maemm had always stressed rolling as little as possible so the dough wouldn't be tough.

And she heeded her role model's advice. Because Maemm was considered one of the best cooks around. When the mixture reached all sides of the pastry cloth, she put down the roller, rinsed the flour dust from her palms, wiped them on a hand towel, and proceeded to cut the dough into lines. Because they preferred thick noodles, she made generous spaces between the lines.

Why did Marcus leave the city? Why did he choose Arthur as his new home? Would he rent her brother's small house?

In the background, five of her nephews chased one another in a game of tag. The laughter became so loud, Hannah knew she had to quiet them before Maemm strode down the stairs.

Letting out a sigh, Hannah squared her shoulders, turned, and proceeded toward the group, but before she got out a word, Maemm's stern voice commanded the kids to stop running in the house.

Immediately, the room quieted, and the children stopped in their tracks. Afterward, Maemm stepped into the kitchen, and the boys rolled out of the side door, where they continued their game. Hannah could hear their happy voices and see the sets of bare feet running in all directions in the large yard. A wide dirt path led to the old red barn.

Before continuing her noodles, Hannah stepped to

the large battery fan to get relief from the intense summer heat. She closed her eyes a moment while the blades whipped around in circles and the air gently caressed her forehead and cheeks.

Maemm's voice prompted Hannah to open her eyes. "Sure is turning out to be a hot summer."

"*Jah.*"

"And the forecast says no rain for another week. But *Gott* will make sure our vegetables make it."

"He always has."

The unexpected snapping sound made Hannah jump. When she saw the source of the noise, an amused smile tugged at the corners of her lips.

"Got 'em!" Great satisfaction edged Maemm's voice as she looked down at the floor where she stood, fly swatter in hand. Past experience had taught Hannah that any fly her mother targeted was doomed to die.

And Hannah guessed Maemm's mission wasn't complete. She was fully aware that swatting flies was common. But to Maemm, ridding the house of flying insects seemed to be a sport.

When their gazes locked, Hannah offered a nod of congratulations. "*Gut.*"

As Hannah had been about to tell her mother about the *Englischer* who had been at their shop, Maemm quickly became distracted by another buzzing insect that circled her head.

Hannah was convinced that Maemm loved swatting flies every bit as much as Hannah enjoyed *The Adventures of Sydney and Carson*. Imagining herself in the female role, with a hero who helped her to save and protect, made her happy. It offered her a great sense of satisfaction, even if her role was fictitious.

Hannah was fully aware that *Gott* had created everyone with different interests. And her role model's was definitely keeping the house free of flies. Which was difficult, considering the large number of times the side door was opened throughout the day.

A sigh of acceptance escaped Hannah's throat while she continued cutting noodles. At the same time, the delicious aroma of baked chicken floated through the kitchen. Hannah could use the bags of noodles she'd already dried out. In fact, she'd learned that they sold quickly in her shop, and that homemade noodles were every bit as popular with the locals as they were with tourists.

But this time, she preferred a fresh batch. She arched a curious brow. Automatically, she wondered if Marcus cooked. What he did in his spare time. And what on earth he was doing in this neck of the woods. Hopefully, eventually, she'd find out more about him.

Maemm stepped up behind her to return her purple fly swatter to its place above the refrigerator. "Oh, I forgot to mention that Ben just rented the small house on his property."

As Maemm stepped to the hall, her voice floated back to Hannah, who could hear water running in the small bathroom. When Maemm returned to the kitchen, rubbing her hands together, she grabbed a small dish towel, dampened it, and began cleaning the countertop area closest to the refrigerator. "Um-hum. A fellow from Chicago needed a place to live right away. The same guy just got hired on by Ben's company as a welder."

* * *

Inside his new place, Marcus took in the simple blue curtains that covered the windows. To his pleasant surprise, a light in the middle of a gas line running across the ceiling illuminated his kitchen at night. He was fully aware that some Amish didn't have that, and it was an advantage to those who lived closer to town. A gas stove and refrigerator sat to the left of a large sink.

If he looked out of his front door, he could see Ben Lapp's large two-story house and the dirt path in between their two homes. Marcus had very little to do with him, and for some reason, he felt as if he belonged in this modest dwelling.

Bringing his focus to the broken horse and buggy he'd offered to repair for Hannah, he smiled a little. He barely knew Hannah Lapp. Still, he already liked many things about her.

For instance, her enthusiasm about her shop. Her quilt. Her smile. The way she seemed . . . nonjudgmental. Of course, if she knew about his brothers and their run-ins with the law, it would probably frighten her. He hoped she wouldn't think less of him because of his relationship to them.

If she had any idea that they'd tried to get him to join in with their thefts and that the very reason he'd come here was to get away from them and start a Christian life, she'd be astounded. The corners of his lips began to drop.

As he placed the horse and buggy, now in one piece, on the countertop, he smiled with satisfaction. He'd fixed the display. It was a small favor for a pretty

Amish woman; at the same time, it was a big thing to do. Small because the job had taken a mere fifteen minutes. Big because this presented another opportunity for him to see her.

As warm summer air came in through his two screened windows, he recalled the project she'd shown him in the back of her shop. To Marcus, working with needle and thread was a talent he much respected. Not only that, but the moment he'd glimpsed the large piece of blue, his heart had floated back to a wonderful time in his life.

He stopped for a moment and arched a brow. Then he realized the true reason he wanted to return to Amish Edibles. It was to see Hannah.

Chapter Three

A few days later, delicious-smelling potpourri scents that had just been dropped off by Rebecca Conrad, the area's well-known florist, filled Amish Edibles with the most sensational fragrance.

At her shop, Hannah stood hunched behind the counter breathing in the delightful aroma of mixed flowers and holding *The Adventures of Sydney and Carson* so close to her face, the paper touched her nose.

The sound of the entrance bell startled her, and the paperback dropped to her feet. Without wasting a moment, she bent to retrieve it and quickly slipped it back on the shelf to the right of the cash register.

When she looked up, she smiled at Marcus Jackson. The slow speed of her pulse immediately picked up.

"Morning, Hannah."

She smiled back, trying to keep her voice from giving away her sudden happiness at seeing him again. She loved the sense of safety and calmness he exuded, not to mention the way he spoke to her, as if they'd been friends forever.

"Marcus, it's *gut* to see you. I hope everything's going well. I hear you're in Ben's house."

"Thanks to you." As he stepped toward her, he drew his right hand up in front of him. When he was directly opposite her, he held out the horse and buggy for display.

She couldn't stop the excited breath that escaped her throat as she drew her hands up to her chest in great appreciation. "You fixed it!"

Without responding, he carefully placed it next to the register. She slowly reached out to take it in-between her hands, then scrutinized the beautiful, one-piece horse and buggy. After glancing at Marcus, she proceeded to turn it from side to side, upside down, and right side up, squinting to find where he'd welded it. To her surprise and happiness, there was no visible sign that the piece had ever been broken.

Darting him a grateful smile, she carefully placed it next to the register and lifted her chin to his face so that their gazes locked. "You did this?"

He offered a modest nod. "It was an easy fix."

She continued looking for visible signs of the repair and finally gave up. "You must be very talented to have repaired this without a blemish."

He bent at his waist. "Thank you, Miss Lapp. But I have a confession." He paused, and she looked at him to continue.

"What I really came back for is more of your delicious raspberry jelly."

Hannah led him to where it was. Of course, he already knew. Still, it gave her a further opportunity to make conversation with him.

"So, how do you like Arthur so far?"

He plucked a purple container from the shelf and

looked at it before turning his attention back to her. "I feel right at home here."

Hannah beamed. "That's *gut*."

"Oh, and by the way, your brother Ben's a great guy. In fact, I think we'll end up good friends."

Just like us.

"Not only am I living at his place, but we're also working together now."

When he started toward the cash register, Hannah stepped to his side. Happy to see Marcus again so soon, she tried to control the obvious excitement that edged her voice. She hoped they'd talk more before he checked out.

He pulled his wallet from his pocket, but she stopped him with her hand. "This one's on the house."

He hesitated. "But if you give away your jelly, you don't make money." He gave a shake of his head. "And I'd hate to see this lovely shop go out of business."

She lifted her chin. "I don't think this one item will set me back. Besides, I'm grateful that you fixed my horse and buggy."

"Hannah, it's my pleasure."

A short silence ensued while he looked as if he couldn't decide whether to go on. But he did, and she listened. "When I was young, my mom asked me to promise something."

"What?"

"To follow my heart. That's what I'm doing here. I'm starting a new life here. As a Christian."

* * *

Hannah blinked as the Saturday morning sun beat down on her while she traversed Ben's yard. Outside the back door, as the screen sprang shut, she stopped for a moment to appreciate the delicious aroma of chicken and dumplings that floated deliciously out of the open windows. Hannah was sure the large barn raising crew would love the lunch she and Maemm had helped Ruth make.

She could also smell the fresh peach and apple pies that were almost ready to remove from the oven. There were fifteen place settings at the dining room and kitchen tables for her brothers and the neighbors who had come today to help with Ben's barn raising.

Hannah smiled inside. She always loved it when everyone got together to help someone. Working for a *gut* cause made her happy.

Mary Conrad was on her way with homemade sponge cakes. The thought of the community plant guru prompted the corners of Hannah's lips to pull upward into a wide smile. They'd grown up together. And the beautiful floral arrangements Mary created with her *maemm*, Rebecca, fascinated Hannah.

Absently, she considered Mary's feelings for Wayne Miller. She'd loved him forever, it seemed, yet, sadly, Wayne had never asked Rebecca and William to court their daughter. Hannah wondered why Wayne hadn't done so. By now, he had to be aware of Mary's deep feelings for him.

Still, Mary hoped to someday be Mrs. Wayne Miller. Hannah stepped aside to avoid a pothole. Back on the dirt path, she considered marriage: finding the special person to spend your life with.

Hannah lifted the bottom of her dress to quicken her steps to the group of workers. As she stopped to tuck some loose hairs back under her *kapp*, she glanced back at the two-story house Ben and his wife, Ruth, had purchased in April. They'd been fortunate to move into this old country house with the large number of bedrooms they needed for their growing family.

Hannah pulled in a determined breath and resumed her walk to the barn that was being built. As quick strides took her across the two acres of yard, from her peripheral vision she noted the horses tied in a queue to the wooden fence that led from the winding blacktop to the dwelling. The deep, rich grass reminded her of a thick, velvety green carpet she'd once seen.

Black buggies lined the fence, too. The smell of freshly cut wood reached her, thanks to the light breeze. Pebble Creek appeared blissfully in the distance.

As she got closer to the barn in progress, the sound of familiar voices filled the air. She was near enough that she could easily identify the low, gruff voice of her *daed*, who was carrying a board to the main area of construction.

She also detected Jacob's argumentative pitch, countering Ben's easygoing voice. Jacob was the sibling closest to her in age. But one voice in particular immediately warmed her heart. It was the calm tone of Marcus Jackson.

Suddenly, her cheeks felt flushed, and she silently scolded herself. She wasn't sure why she reacted as she did whenever Marcus was around, but she soon reasoned that it was due to their immediate friendship, and that he'd opened up to her about the emotional reminder of the blanket his late mother had once made for him. Now, she even knew a new tidbit. That he was a Christian.

A honeybee buzzed around her forehead, momentarily distracting her from her thoughts. She kept going, careful not to step in a dip in the earth, as she gently swatted away the insect. But as she stepped closer to the men laying concrete, Marcus popped back into her thoughts. And when she spotted him emptying a bag of cement mix into a wheelbarrow while Ben stirred the mixture with a hoe, a warm smile tugged the corners of her lips upward. When he glimpsed her, he offered a nod of recognition.

"Lunch is ready! Come and wash up!" Hannah put her hands on both sides of her mouth and hollered.

Her *daed* waved to her. "Coming!"

Daed was a man who offered few loving gestures. But in her heart, she knew his tough exterior was a façade and nothing more. He'd done too many things for her for Hannah to think anything else. For instance, when she'd fallen ill with a sinus infection a couple of years before, he'd brought a bowl of Maemm's homemade vegetable soup to her room.

The memory nearly caused her to laugh with happiness. The recollection was funny to her because this particular display of love was so unlike him. And happiness because she'd never forget the worry lines around his eyes when he'd sat down on her bed and gruffly asked her how she was feeling.

Jah, she was Daed's girl. Hannah knew he loved her

brothers, but to her knowledge, he'd never offered them the patient, fatherly affection that, at times, he'd provided her. And there was no one here on earth Hannah loved more than him.

As she made her way back to the dwelling, she could hear her father convey that it was time to head to the house in a tone loud enough for everyone to hear.

A familiar female voice caught up with Hannah when she approached the house. "Mary!" They embraced before stepping inside together.

"I've already set out my sponge cakes in the kitchen. What a big crew!"

Inside, Hannah poured fresh lemonade into glasses and set them on the table. When the crew came in, they took turns using the hall bathroom to wash up before taking a seat. When everyone was seated, Hannah's *daed* gave the prayer.

After that, the three women helped serve everyone.

From her peripheral vision, Hannah watched Ben sit down beside Marcus. Her brother spoke to him in between bites of chicken. "This ain't your first rodeo, is it?"

Marcus grinned and shook his head.

For a moment, Hannah wasn't sure what he meant. "You're experienced with building. When you offered to help, I had no idea how handy you were."

Marcus lowered his gaze to the floor and didn't respond.

But Ben pressed for an explanation. Finally, Marcus satisfied the group. "My dad was an architect and a builder. I apprenticed at a very young age."

Hannah couldn't hold back a smile. Because little did

this group know that this strong man had another strong interest: quilting.

Back at the barn site, Marcus couldn't get Hannah off his mind as he emptied another bag of dry, gray cement powder into a wheelbarrow. He was fully aware of the strict rules within this hardworking yet gentle group of people called the Amish, and although everyone had welcomed him with what had seemed genuine enthusiasm, Marcus knew instinctively that he wasn't one of them. That he never would be. That he never could be.

And not because he didn't like or respect them; they had his full fascination and admiration. But from what he'd seen of their dedicated lifestyle, his life was much easier and simpler than theirs. He was sure he didn't have the strength that was needed to be Amish.

Yet, for some reason, Hannah Lapp had been on his mind ever since the moment he'd first talked to her. And to his surprise, he'd discovered that he liked to impress her. Satisfaction had filled him when she'd been excited about the horse and buggy he'd welded. And it had been obvious in her eyes that she'd greatly appreciated his interest in her quilt.

As he stirred the mix while adding water, he was vaguely aware of the different conversations floating through the air, about everything from this year's crops to what the weather would be like in the coming week. But Hannah consumed his thoughts. Why was he still thinking about her?

Hannah's bubbly personality and obvious interest in her shop and her work had immediately captured his interest. He knew very little about the Amish. And next to nothing, really, about Hannah. What he was sure of, though, was that many things he had done would be frowned on by her tightly knit community.

His new landlord, Ben, interrupted his thoughts when he strode over to the pile of two-by-fours that Marcus had piled neatly in front of the wheelbarrow. "Sure appreciate that you came today to pitch in. *Denki.*"

Marcus continued to work while he offered a nod. "Glad to do it, Ben." After a short hesitation while he added more water to his mix, he went on. "As far as renting to me . . ." To his dismay, salty moisture stung Marcus's eyes, and he blinked to rid them of the sting. "I guess you could say you were a win for me."

Ben nodded. "I've been looking for a renter. Your timing couldn't have been better. Two of our welders recently left. One went to another company; the other moved out of state. Having you will greatly lessen my workload."

While a loud saw cutting wood seared through the air, Marcus lifted the pitch of his voice a notch so Ben could hear him. "It's no coincidence. I'd say the Almighty God arranged the whole thing."

To Marcus's surprise, his words prompted a surprised expression on Ben's face. In fact, Marcus reasoned, approval also edged the lines around Hannah's brother's mouth. "You're a believer."

Surprise accompanied the statement. Marcus acknowledged that of course this kind man knew very little about him. Glad to have the opportunity to talk about his newfound relationship with God, Marcus replied, "About a month ago, I asked Jesus into my life."

Marcus was quick to note the sparkle of moisture on Ben's pupils. The picture of emotion in front of him reminded Marcus of morning dew on a leaf.

For long moments, Marcus looked at him, expecting a reply. Finally, Ben smiled a little and offered him an affectionate pat on his shoulder. "I couldn't be happier for you, my friend. It's funny, but when we first talked, my instincts told me that you were a Christian. Because of that, you're my brother in Christ."

The third week in July was starting, and business at Amish Edibles was picking back up. On her knees, Hannah continued to run her feather duster over empty shelves. She proceeded to wipe a regular rag sprayed with wood polish over the already dusted shelves.

As she did so, she breathed in the cleaning scent and smiled a little. *There's something so refreshing about the smell of wood soap. And I love to dust.*

Letting out a sigh, she stood. Breathing in, she contemplated the containers of raspberry and strawberry jelly that she'd pulled from their places. Plucking one jar at a time, she returned the jellies to clean, shiny spots.

She crossed her arms over her chest and counted her supply, figuring out how many jars she'd need to replenish. While she did so, the soft cinnamon scent from her burning homemade candle filled her nostrils. The comforting aroma prompted a smile.

I can't wait for Christmas. Maybe by then, I'll know who to give my quilt to. Now, though, I need to focus on restocking these shelves.

She collected her feather duster and dustrag and

made her way back to the wall that faced the garden. As she placed the cleaning supplies in her plastic carrier, she looked down at the large box of jelly her *daed* had carried in for her earlier that morning.

The box sported a solid line of tape that needed to be cut to get into the box. She kept scissors in a small sack a few feet away. Taking the plastic in her hands, she searched for her means of ripping open the container.

She frowned, looking a second time. The scissors weren't where they were supposed to be, so she glanced down and crossed her arms over her chest while she pressed her lips together thoughtfully.

As she did so, her peripheral vision allowed a bonus view of her small garden, and she knew what needed to be done after restocking the jelly. The weeds needed to be pulled.

A scratching at the garden window caught her attention, and she went to the back door to allow Scarlet inside. Immediately, the cat headed to the blanket in the corner.

The bell above the door startled Hannah, and she turned toward the sound before saying to Scarlet, "I'll feed you after I take care of this customer."

Marcus entered with a warm smile. "Morning, Hannah."

Running her hand over her apron to smooth out the wrinkles and get rid of the dust, she quickly stepped toward him, waving her hand in a happy greeting.

"Hello, Marcus. It's *gut* to see you." After a slight pause while he closed the door behind him, she arched a brow and edged her voice with curiosity. "Did you get much done on the barn?"

He nodded with satisfaction and made his way to the jelly shelf. "We're making headway."

She glanced at the empty shelves and joined him. "Oh . . . I'm sorry. I was just about to restock."

He let out a low whistle. "I see you've done a lot of business since I last came in."

"*Jah.*" She cleared a knot from her throat. "Mostly this morning. Business always picks up every year around this time."

"That's good to hear." He focused on the empty shelf. He offered her a faux look of disappointment. "But bad news for me." He offered a shrug. "Guess I'll have to leave empty-handed."

She shook her head and waved her hand in front of her. "That's not necessary." She turned and motioned to the large box against the back wall. "Daed brought more . . . unfortunately, I've misplaced my scissors."

His eyes lit up. "Then it looks like I stopped by at the right time." He reached into the back pocket of his jeans and pulled out a small pocketknife. "You need it opened?" He followed her gaze to the taped box.

She nodded.

"This one?" He knelt and pointed to the box she'd motioned to. Hannah eyed the others that lined the wall.

"*Jah.*"

He knelt and opened the cardboard box. With a smile, Hannah looked down at the new stock of raspberry jelly. "*Denki.*" After a short pause, she corrected, "Thank you."

He stood and grinned down at her. "I'm getting pretty savvy with your German words." He winked.

"Oh yeah?"

He offered a proud nod. "In fact, I have a confession to make."

She looked at him to continue.

"I took German in high school. Little did I know that I might actually use it someday."

"I'm sure you're aware that we might not necessarily be understood in Germany. I mean, our dialect is just for our particular area."

"That makes sense." After a short silence, he eyed the open box before directing his attention back to her face. "You want me to carry that over to the shelves for you?"

Before she could respond, he added with an amused curve of his lips, "Believe me, I have an ulterior motive. I'd hate to leave here without your famous raspberry jelly."

She beamed. "I'm so glad you like it."

"Like it?"

He bent down and lifted the box. While he transported it, she followed him. After he'd placed the heavy container between the empty shelves, he stood and answered, "If you want my honest opinion, there's not a strong-enough word to describe the taste. Ms. Lapp, I've eaten jelly my entire life. And yours . . ." He let out a low whistle. "It would win any contest in the country."

She laughed. Not really because of what he'd just told her, but because of the way his face had displayed such an exaggerated expression. The tone of his voice, too.

"And while I'm here . . ." He paused as he eyed the large number of stock. "Let me help you put these jars back."

She waved her hands in front of her. "Thanks, but you've done enough already. I appreciate your kind offer, though. Besides, I'm sure you've got other things to do besides help me in the shop."

He began walking toward the cash register and pulled his leather wallet from his pocket to pay. Hannah quickly stopped him with her voice before he'd removed the cash. "This one's on the house."

Not looking up, he continued to pull out some singles. "I insist. Your offer's certainly generous, but I'm sure your shop won't profit if you comp everyone who comes in."

She lowered her hand, accidentally brushing his fingers. Slightly embarrassed by the feeling of his warm skin under hers, she continued to insist that he not pay. "Of course I'm not in business to give things away, but this time it's for helping with my brother's barn raising. Besides, generosity is a *gut* thing, *jah*?"

She lifted a challenging brow and curved her lips upward another notch. "So you should accept my token of appreciation."

Finally, he offered a nod of acceptance. "Point taken. But all in all, I'm definitely getting the better end of the deal."

As they stood close to each other, Hannah's heart warmed. For long moments, neither said anything. But the lengthy silence was anything but uncomfortable. In fact, Hannah enjoyed every moment. She savored the sweet sensation.

As they chitchatted, Hannah tried to think of a reason

why the way Marcus made her feel was different from how she felt around the single Amish men she knew.

Why? What is it that's different this time? She lifted her chin a notch. He made her feel special. That's what it was. And her instincts told her that his words and actions were genuine. It was just how he was. Calm, easygoing, and . . . As hard as she tried, she wasn't able to come up with a word that truly justified it.

"It was really nice of you to help with Ben's barn."

For a moment, Marcus looked down at his brown leather boots before lifting his chin to look at her. "I intend to work 'til the finish. Because of Ben, I've got a place to live."

He grinned.

"What?"

"Oh, I was just thinking that the meal you helped to serve was worth every minute of work I put in."

They laughed.

Several heartbeats later, he went on with a slight curve of his lips. "And come to think of it . . . Ms. Lapp, you're the one who I owe for that delicious meal. You told me to reach out to Ben." He grinned. "Which means I owe you another favor."

Hannah shook her head and laughed. "I'm glad I could help. But our Lord and Savior wasn't about to let you down, Marcus Jackson. And I believe He'll continue to protect you and watch over you."

Moisture formed on his pupils. Her statement prompted a lengthy, thoughtful silence. Finally, when Marcus spoke, grateful emotion edged his voice. "It's a whole new world for me, Hannah. Right now, I have no idea what path my life's gonna take; I'm just happy He will guide me."

Hannah's voice softened. "I don't want to pry or anything, but what caused you to believe? I mean, you said that your relationship with Christ was new."

Marcus glanced out of the front window. When he started to explain, his voice quivered with emotion. "To make a long story short, a friend took me to church in the city." He seemed to clear an emotional knot from his throat. "I nearly didn't go. But I did to get out of . . ." He stopped, and Hannah wondered what he'd been about to say. "It's the best investment of my time I've ever made, Hannah," he finished.

The pitch of his voice softened so she could barely hear him. "Inside, I'm a different person. There I was, sitting in my pew when the minister said something I'll never forget."

Hannah didn't look away. In fact, she couldn't. Because his expression was so sincere. So genuine. "What did he say?"

Marcus paused while offering a slight lift of his chin. "That it doesn't matter who your parents are. It doesn't matter what you've done. That it's all about who you know."

She whispered, "Jesus."

He nodded. Then, he smiled and offered her a wink. "I would love to stay here all day and talk to you, but I'd better let you get back to work." He arched a mischievous brow. "And I'd better do the same or your brother will wonder what happened to me."

After they said goodbye, she watched the door close

behind him and listened to his car engine start. For long moments, Hannah stood, contemplating the conversation they'd just shared. And how she hadn't been able to contain her smile since the moment he'd stepped inside Amish Edibles.

Time to get back to work. First things first. And that meant organizing the new jelly containers to appear attractive and appealing to customers. As she approached one of the shelves, her gaze landed on a metal clip stuffed with money. She bent to pick up the clip as her pulse zoomed at a nervous pace at the sight of the initials *MJ* and the hundred-dollar bills. She'd never seen so many at one time. Even in the store's cash register, this many large bills was an anomaly.

Obviously, the engraved clip belonged to Marcus. It must have slipped out of his wallet when he pulled it from his pocket. She rushed to the door and stepped outside. She could still see his car in the distance on the blacktop. And she waved her hands to try to get his attention. But he was gone.

Chapter Four

At Cabot a couple of hours later, Marcus removed his protective goggles and gloves. As he ran his fingers through his hair, an unexpected surge of energy swept up his arms and landed comfortably in his shoulders.

He didn't doubt the source of the much-appreciated energy. It was Hannah. Each time he'd spoken to her, he'd felt renewed.

A quick glance at his silver Casio watch told him it was break time. He carefully moved his equipment and protective hood and returned them to their normal storage spots. He looked down at his work and smiled satisfaction at the corroded pipes he had fixed for an outside contractor.

He'd often been told that he was a perfectionist, but his father had always stressed doing one's best, whether it was a small job or a large one. That a person's work showed what he was like on the inside. Marcus had heeded his father's words. He naturally had a critical eye, but it was important to him to display his very best work.

Today, he was welding fittings into pipes. The processing piping would be used for transporting ground-up corn that would eventually be made into syrup.

The air conditioner kicked in, and he stepped forward to take advantage of the cold air coming from the ceiling as it hit his neck. As he enjoyed the welcome comfort of the coolness, he looked ahead of him at the tubes upon tubes that loomed throughout the large area of workspace. There was plenty to do; that was for sure.

Right now, he was responsible for angling the metal so it would bend where it was supposed to. He took in the flanges on the worktable that would be welded into the tubes. Air coming from the vents carried the unpleasant scent of epoxy, a thickening agent.

Finally, he let out a sigh. Time to step outside for a break. His coworkers had already started their ten minutes, and the vast area of the shop was devoid of people with the exception of himself.

He stepped to the small washroom, where he soaped his hands, rinsed them, and dried his palms on a paper towel, which he quickly discarded in the trash can.

As the sound of laughter floated in from the outside, he proceeded to step to the lounge to the employees' refrigerator. Marcus pulled open the door's silver handle, bent, and reached inside for a bottle of Arrowhead Water.

After closing the door, he unscrewed the top and took a couple of swigs. Afterward, he bent to pull his newest container of raspberry jelly from Amish Edibles. He proceeded to the pantry, where he opened the plastic container of homemade bread that Hannah had sent with him.

He spread peanut butter and jelly onto a delicious-smelling slice, pressed another piece on top, and took a bite. As he enjoyed the taste, he closed his eyes for a moment while he recalled the happy expression on Hannah's face as she'd attempted to convince him that she owed him the jelly and bread.

While he smiled, he placed the jar lid on the container and screwed it back into place. Same with the Jif lid. He left the room and stepped toward the exit that led to the parking lot, where he and his coworkers spent their breaks.

With his right hand, he held the sandwich. Automatically, he shoved his free hand into his deep jeans pocket as he made his way toward the door. Stopping, he narrowed his brows. His wallet wasn't thick. He pulled it from his pocket and opened it. His money clip and the cash inside it were gone.

Tapping the toe of his boot nervously against the floor, he pondered where his savings could be. Finally, he decided the clip must be in a different pocket. Impatiently, he switched the sandwich to his other hand and shoved his fingers into his front pocket. Then his back.

Finally, he put his lunch on a shelf on the side wall that led to the back. Using both hands, he felt around in all his pockets. Letting out a frustrated breath, he repeated the actions.

Where is it? He stiffened and pressed his lips into a straight line as he tried to recall when he'd last used it. The money was definitely important to him, being that it was all he had to live on until his first paycheck. But more important was the silver clip with his initials on it that held the bills in place.

The cash could be replaced. The clip couldn't, because it had been given to him on his tenth birthday by his dad. For a moment, Marcus thought his fast-paced heartbeat would jump right out of his black T-shirt.

Be calm. It must be in the car. Quick steps took him outside, where he clicked the lock of his Chevy. Inside, he checked under the seat. In front of it. Behind it. In the middle console. Inside the driver's door pocket.

A friendly pat on his shoulder made him look up.

"You lookin' for something?"

Marcus found himself face-to-face with Ben Lapp. The last thing he wanted right now was to have a conversation with his landlord about why on earth he'd had such a wad of money on him.

Marcus wasn't quite ready to share that he had left the Windy City because his brothers were in trouble with the law, that they'd tried to drag him into their trouble, and because of that, he'd fled with three months' salary in cash to start over. He wasn't ready to discuss it.

He noted the concern etched around Ben's mouth. Marcus needed to respond, so he tried his best. "I misplaced something. But it'll show up."

When Ben stared at him with an expression that was a combination of strong curiosity and uncertainty, Marcus let out a defeated sigh. He motioned to the nearby wooden bench. At the same time, they sat next to each other. And Marcus told Ben most everything.

Soon after Hannah's discovery, a handful of women stepped inside Amish Edibles. As their voices broke the silence, Hannah quickly slipped the wad of cash back into the money clip and stashed it behind *The Adventures of Sydney and Carson*, which she hid on the shelf near the cash register.

She had to hide it somewhere, and the voices coming into her shop told her that she didn't have long to decide where. Trying to stop her hands from shaking, she stepped forward and welcomed them. "Morning! Happy shopping! If I can be of help, please let me know."

Immediately, she recognized the customers. They belonged to her church, and their families had known each other for years. As Hannah watched them file in, the last one, Martha Wagler, closed the door behind her.

Hannah couldn't stop a smile from tugging at the corners of her lips. Martha was a widow who'd lost her husband years ago. Hannah was fully aware of the unkind joke that went around about her: that her husband had died from the tart taste of Martha's sugarless pies. Whoever had started the joke had been in the wrong. Plain and simple.

Still, Hannah was quick to recall the moment she'd once bitten into one of the pastries at a wedding and had quickly rushed to a washroom, where she'd spit out the bitter taste.

The mélange of voices drew her back to the present. There was the high pitch of the two Troyer sisters. There was also the fast-talking, newly married Mrs. Schultz. Leading the group was one of Hannah's teachers from over a decade before, Mrs. Graber.

Hannah had never known her first name; Hannah only knew her as Mrs. Graber. But thoughts of her quickly floated into Hannah's mind in a fond way. The old teacher was easily recognizable throughout the community for her twitching eyebrow. When Hannah had been one of her pupils, she'd routinely watched for Mrs. Graber's sign of disapproval, which was that twitching brow.

No doubt Hannah was fully aware that it had been a blessing from *Gott* that she hadn't been born with such a negative identification mark. Whenever Mrs. Graber had scolded a student, her brow would twitch, and the habit had made for numerous jokes.

Despite that, Hannah knew what was inside her former teacher. Although Mrs. Graber had always presented an unbending impression, Hannah knew that the woman who was quick to correct grammar slipups had an especially kind heart.

One particular event had carved a special place for Hannah's teacher in her own heart. Before Christmas break, Hannah had accidentally left a story she'd written for English class at home and, therefore, hadn't turned it in on time.

The moment Hannah had noticed the missing paper she'd spent days writing, she'd attempted a reasonable explanation. That day, when school ended, Hannah had stayed behind the other kids and approached Mrs. Graber with shaky hands.

Hannah would never forget the moment she'd explained what had happened. An apology had come out of her mouth, and to her amazement, Mrs. Graber had smiled a little and offered Hannah a soft, affectionate pat on her shoulder.

When she'd spoken, the expected cross tone had been accompanied with a much-needed and unexpected reassurance.

"Not to worry, Hannah," she'd spoken in a soft, forgiving voice. "You've never once been late with a paper, and surely everyone's allowed a mistake, *jah*?"

That very response still made Hannah's jaw drop in

surprise. In a nervous yet grateful tone, she'd replied, "*Denki*, Mrs. Graber."

The teacher had then offered another surprise when she'd winked at Hannah. "Besides, I'm sure your paper will be worth the wait." A grin had tugged those usually stern lips upward, and the words that had followed had stunned Hannah even more.

"I enjoy your stories." With the lift of a gray brow, amusement had edged her voice. "You've got quite an imagination, and your writing . . . for your young age, well, it's superb."

As Hannah glimpsed the stern demeanor of her former teacher in the midst of the group, Hannah's heart melted. Maemm had always stressed to her and her older brothers that a book could never be judged by its cover. Certainly with Mrs. Graber, that was the case.

Hannah focused on her customers as she watched them shop. Judging by their past buying history, they might very well clean out Hannah's new inventory.

Hannah's *maemm* had taught her that sometimes, customers liked to be left alone to look around, so today, Hannah heeded that advice and quietly stepped back to the register, trying to look busy. Inside, her heart raced. Because of her find. She knew that Marcus's initials were MJ, and he'd recently stood in the place where the money had been found, so she was confident the money clip belonged to him. She wondered what he was doing with so much cash. Why wasn't it in a bank? Or anywhere but with him?

As she contemplated her surprising discovery and how to reach Marcus after her shop closed, the conversation between the women floated over to her. The voices carried, so it was easy to overhear what they said.

"King's Bakery?" The last thing Hannah wanted to do was to eavesdrop . . . Maemm had scolded her more than once for being too interested in other people's business. Still, despite Hannah's awareness of her guilt, she strained to hear the rest of the conversation.

As she stood in the encircled area behind the cash register, she moved her pen on a pad of paper, trying to pretend interest in what was in front of her, but she wasn't even paying attention to what she scribbled.

She pressed her lips together, hoping the ladies would raise their voices a notch so she could overhear their entire conversation. The words "King's Bakery" had immediately piqued her interest.

For years, she'd attended church with the large King family. She'd also gone to school with over half their clan. And she adored the cinnamon rolls that had made the in-town, family-owned bakery famous. Her mouth watered at the thought of the delicious pastries.

Martha Wagler lifted an excited voice as she leaned closer to the others. From Hannah's peripheral vision, she could see the ladies' eyes grow wide from excitement and anxious expressions appear on their faces, waiting for the rest of the story to spill out.

"You heard me. They were robbed. After closing time."

She stopped to wag a finger. "I kid you not. John King himself said that it happened late last night or early this morning."

Another voice lowered. "Did he call the police?"

Martha chimed in with her typical negative tone.

"*Jah*, one of my nieces talked to Rebecca Conrad earlier this morning, and Rebecca said he filed a report, but the police and the King family have no idea who emptied their cash register.

"I wonder who it was? There aren't any new faces around . . ." She snapped her fingers. "Except the city guy who just moved into . . ."

She glanced at Hannah and stopped whatever she was about to say. Pretending disinterest when one of the ladies glanced her way, Hannah ordered the urgent, fast beat of her heart to slow for three reasons. The first was that this conversation wasn't meant for her ears. The second was that she wished she didn't possess such a curious streak. Especially when most things that strongly interested her were none of her business. And thirdly because she'd just found a wad of money that obviously belonged to her new friend, Marcus, and that her find, unfortunately, might be linked with the conversation taking place inside Amish Edibles.

Time after time, Maemm had scolded her for making things her business that weren't. She'd once said, "Hannah, *Gott* didn't bring you into this world to involve yourself in others' lives. I'm sure He would prefer you spent your time serving Him."

A strong wave of guilt swept over Hannah and she shrugged to rid herself of the uncomfortable, unwanted sensation. But an even stronger feeling filled her stomach until it ached.

Fear. Her role model had often reminded her that everyone deserves the benefit of the doubt. Hannah thought of Marcus, his kind demeanor, and his sudden emergence in her life.

While she continued to listen, she immediately connected the wad of money she'd found with the gossip she knew she should ignore. She tried common sense. *I've always been a* gut *judge of character, and I am sure that, even if I barely know Marcus Jackson, he did not steal from the bakery. But why was he carrying so much cash?*

She swallowed an emotional knot that blocked her throat. *If what I'm currently hearing is true, someone robbed King's Bakery. But the thief is not Marcus. But what will happen if people start thinking it's him? Just because he's new and because he's from Chicago.*

While the background voices continued in a softer, more difficult-to-hear tone, Hannah's mind kicked into high gear, like when she turned her battery fan to high and the blades picked up an immediate speed.

I've got to return this money. There must be a logical explanation for the large amount. At the same time, I feel a responsibility to ensure that Marcus is aware of the theft I've just learned about. Or, at least, the rumored theft. He's new in town. And people don't know him.

Even though the women seemed to be sure there had been a robbery, Hannah would withhold judgment until Maemm confirmed what Hannah had just heard.

While she thought through everything, she nervously strummed her short fingernails to a nervous beat against the wooden cabinet that housed the cash register.

She guessed that Marcus's city upbringing, and that the theft had occurred right after he'd landed here, might cause brows to immediately rise, and the last thing she wanted was for him to be wrongly accused of something he hadn't done.

Suddenly, the conversation shifted to family and the relatives who, according to what Hannah understood, Mrs. Graber would be having at her house. When her former teacher stepped toward her, Hannah attempted to hide any indication that she'd listened in on their conversation. She forced a smile and returned her notepad and pen to the shelf in front of her.

In her most helpful voice, she turned her attention to her former teacher. As the rest of the group split up to shop, Mrs. Graber smiled a little and met Hannah's curious gaze.

"It's *gut* to see you, Hannah."

Hannah offered a genuine smile. "*Gut* to see you, too, Mrs. Graber." After a short pause, Hannah put a palm on her hip. "How can I help you today?"

She expelled a sigh. "Relatives from Ohio are coming for the weekend, and I was wondering which of your edibles you'd recommend for breakfast?"

Relieved to break from the theft conversation and the wad of money Hannah had found, she pushed open the wooden bar that allowed her into the main area of the store. Behind her, it flipped closed.

With an inviting hand, Hannah motioned to her and proceeded to the aisle of delicious jellies. In a confidential tone, Hannah pulled down a jar and held it in front of the teacher.

"This is definitely my favorite."

The teacher lifted a doubtful brow while she eyed the shelf. "Usually I prefer strawberry."

Hannah offered a polite nod before meeting the woman's gaze. Hannah took in the gray brows and crow's feet underneath the hazy eyes. Serious lines accented the area around her mouth while thin gray hair was pulled back and tucked neatly under a white *kapp*.

Hannah wasn't surprised at the black dress that covered most of the woman's petite body. Hannah wondered why the teacher never wore navy. In all the years Mrs. Graber had stood before her students, Hannah had never seen her in anything but black.

Hannah realized that she'd just planted a strong seed of doubt in the woman's mind as to which jelly to purchase for her guests. So Hannah decided to make the customer's decision easier.

She edged her voice with complete understanding, exchanging the container for a strawberry jar and handed it to the woman she respected. "If you prefer strawberries, then definitely go with what you know you like."

The comment seemed to satisfy the teacher, and she nodded with appreciation. Hannah returned to the cash register, and her thoughts returned to the surprising conversation she'd just been privy to and the large wad of cash hidden close to where she stood.

After thinking things through, Hannah acknowledged that the combination of the robbery's timing and her finding the money prompted a lot of questions. So she definitely would return the money to Marcus. And not mention her find to anyone.

Chapter Five

A short time later, Marcus pulled into the parking area in front of Amish Edibles. Gravel crunched under his tires. The horse tied to the nearby post swished its tail before letting out a long-drawn-out whinny. Hannah's empty black buggy was behind him.

Turning off the engine, Marcus pressed his lips in a straight line, considering what he'd lost and contemplating that a shop in town had just been robbed. Before he'd left work, he'd heard about the robbery at King's Bakery. And here he was, about to ask Hannah if she'd found his cash.

Hannah was an innocent girl. At least, that's what he figured. From what he knew, she'd grown up in a God-fearing community. Now, he was going to have to explain to her why he'd been carrying so much money.

As he exited his car and stepped toward Amish Edibles, he could smell cinnamon wafting from the small building. He glimpsed Hannah on the other side of the front window and wondered how this unusual visit would go. Hannah didn't know much about him, and if she'd found his money clip, he was sure she had a lot of questions. And some suspicions, too.

Hannah ran a paper towel over the front window at Amish Edibles to clear the Windex she'd sprayed on the glass. As she wadded up the paper towel to throw it into the trash, a car pulled into the parking lot. The speed of her heart stepped up a beat. Because she quickly recognized the vehicle. It was a white Chevy. Marcus stepped out on the driver's side and strode to the entrance.

She wasn't sure why she jumped when the bell sounded, but she did. And moments later, she faced the new man in town, the person she already liked a lot but knew very little about.

"Good afternoon, Hannah."

"*Hallo*, Marcus."

As they stared at each other, she took in his strained expression and the tense set of his shoulders. And her heart melted.

He narrowed his brows. "Could we talk?"

She nodded. "Of course." After a lengthy pause, she went to the shelf next to the cash register and retrieved the money clip. Without saying anything, she returned to where he stood and handed him the green wad.

He slowly took the pile of bills from her and stuck it into his wallet. "There's so much I need to tell you, Hannah." After clearing the knot from his throat, he softened his pitch. "I know this looks bad. I heard about the robbery. If you think I stole the money, I understand."

The shop was so quiet, Hannah could hear the

clopping of Miracle's hooves outside. She returned his serious tone. "I don't believe you robbed King's Bakery, Marcus."

She lifted the palms of her hand to the ceiling. "But I hope they find out who did. Especially because you're new in town." After a brief pause, she softened her voice. "Nothing like this has ever happened here. And because you just got here and people don't know much about you . . . I don't want anyone to think you had something to do with it."

He closed his eyes, and when he opened his lids, salty moisture stung his pupils. She motioned to the two rocking chairs in her shop. He followed her to them and they sat.

Marcus cleared his throat and started. "Hannah, I don't know what to say." He lifted his palms to the ceiling and shook his head. "Your faith in me . . ." He lifted his shoulders a notch and took in a breath. "I told you that I came here to start a new life. A life for Christ."

She waited for him to continue.

"The night I invited Him into my life, I knew I had to get away from my environment. In particular, my three brothers. They very much wanted me to sell drugs. To steal."

She drew in a shocked breath while she drew her hands over her chest.

"And I was afraid that I'd eventually join them unless I left." He raised a defensive hand. "Even though I knew it was wrong. It's funny, but the night I was saved, I listened carefully to the pastor's words. He said that you become who your friends are. That's when I knew I needed a change."

For long moments, she absorbed what he'd just said. As she studied him, the green shade of his eyes deepened a notch. The hazy flecks shadowing the color did, too, reminding her of a summer storm cloud.

Lowering his voice, he kept his gaze on her face. "I tried to figure out where to go. I knew it had to be away from the city's chaos. I needed to be far from the temptations around me. A place where I could live a simple life and at the same time learn about Jesus and serve Him."

He lifted a set of defenseless palms in the air. "Even though I wasn't sure how."

As she watched him, she noted the shadow behind his eyes and how he took on an even sadder appearance than when she'd first met him. His voice quivered. He sat with his hands resting over his lap, leaning forward, as if deciding what he would say next. His fingers shook.

"First of all, Hannah, I got away from my three brothers. And I want to make sure you understand that I'm not like them."

She parted her lips, awaiting the rest of his story. "They're older than me . . . they used to be good people, I mean, when Mom and Dad were alive. But after my folks passed, my brothers took a bad road."

The admission nearly took Hannah's breath away.

"They've all been in jail at one time or another."

"Oh . . ." She drew her arms over her chest in disbelief and surprise.

"Hannah, I couldn't let them influence me." He shook his head. "I never broke the law, but I lived for me. Not for Christ. I want my brothers to know their Creator."

After an emotional clearing of his throat, he added,

"I want them to go to heaven." He looked straight ahead, as if he were living in the past. "After my parents died, Colby, the oldest, started drinking heavily. I did the same. My nights were spent at bars. My life was going south, and I knew it."

He expelled a sigh and sat up straighter. A small smile curved the corners of his lips upward. "Until I went to church with Matt, my friend. The night Jesus came into my life."

Hannah swallowed the knot that blocked her throat.

"A long time ago, my mom made me promise I'd follow my heart. I did. I decided to leave it all behind."

His amazing story prompted a sudden pain in her chest. She'd never dreamed that he'd been through so much. That his family was involved with the law.

"Anyhow, while I was deciding where to go, I pulled cash out of the bank and closed my account. I realized I might go some time without a permanent address to give my credit card company and a financial institution."

Locking her gaze with his, she said, "I understand all that. But you've got a home now. Why didn't you leave the money at your place?" She lifted her shoulders. "You surely didn't think anyone would steal it there. At least, I don't think they would."

He shrugged. "I know. I guess with starting my new job and adjusting to my new life, I just didn't think about it. I'm so used to being around my brothers, I felt safer having it on me, not in a place where it could be taken."

He pressed his palms against his thighs and straightened a bit, as if he'd made an important decision. "But I'm not sorry this happened, Hannah. And I hope you believe me when I tell you I had nothing to do with what happened at King's Bakery."

She parted her lips in surprise.

"My carelessness prompted this conversation. And after talking things out with you, I realize how very lucky I am to just be here with you. In this town, where I'm at ease. Where I can get my thoughts in order. Get my life straight."

She smiled a little. "I understand. Apparently, though, your cash wasn't safe in your pocket either."

He grinned. "You're right about that." After a slight pause, he lowered his voice to a more confidential tone. "By the way, thank you for returning it."

She lifted a challenging brow, and the corners of her mouth lifted in amusement. "How d'ya know it's all there?"

She took in his surprised expression and laughed, throwing her palms in the air. "I'm just kidding."

He joined her in laughter before his face took on a more serious expression. She immediately noted the shift in his mood.

"What's wrong?"

"It's the other thing I need to talk to you about, Hannah. The robbery at King's Bakery."

She continued looking at him to go on.

"Hearing about it brought back everything I wanted to forget. For the first time, I acknowledged how very serious my situation in Chicago was. How much my brothers need God."

A long silence ensued before he went on in a voice that was barely more than a whisper. "What's most important to me right now is keeping you safe. Until they catch whoever did this, how do I know they won't try to rob your shop next?"

That evening, Hannah helped her *maemm* serve their family at two large dining tables and one small card table. There were eighteen mouths to feed. Tonight, five of Hannah's brothers and their wives and children had joined them.

Hannah was carrying a chicken and noodle casserole to the largest table when one of her young nephews ran in front of her, chasing his brothers.

"Oh!" Hannah stopped, nearly dropping the dish.

"I'm sorry," the small voice apologized, catching a breath.

Immediately, two adults scolded the youngster. Hannah pressed her lips into a straight, thoughtful line. Most of the time her nieces and nephews were well-behaved, but of course, they weren't perfect. No one was, for that matter. Maemm had always told her that.

Seats at both tables began to fill while raised voices floated through the house. "Don't forget to wash your hands!"

Each one took a turn using the small hall bathroom, and as soon as everyone was seated, Daed's gruff, low voice asked his family to join him in prayer. Before bowing, Hannah took in all the dishes in the middle of the table.

Chicken and noodles. Hot yeast rolls. Corn on the

cob from one of Daed's gardens. Fried chicken. Fresh tomatoes. Mashed potatoes and gravy. Her mouth watered.

After the "Amen," conversations started. Hannah reached for the fried chicken, helped herself, and passed the dish to her right. Noah's voice was edged with interest as he turned to share the plate of sweet corn ears with Ben. "How's everything at Cabot, Ben?"

"Couldn't be better. I guess you could say that *Gott* blessed me in two ways. My workload got a little lighter, and my new coworker has paid me three months' rent, cash, up front."

Hannah pretended an interest in cutting a piece of fried chicken into small pieces as she contemplated Marcus, the cash she'd returned to him, and the serious conversation that had resulted between her and her new friend.

A different one between two of her sisters-in-laws, Miriam and Ruby, started up as Hannah buttered a warm yeast roll.

Ruby's tone was casual while she dished a helping of garden tomatoes onto her plate. Silverware clinked lightly against glass. "Can't believe someone broke into King's Bakery."

In response, Miriam looked up and took a drink of iced tea before returning her glass to the white napkin. "I know. It's all the whole town's talking about. I heard about it this morning when I went to mail bills at the post office."

Ruby raised a brow before meeting Miriam's gaze. "Any update?"

Miriam responded with a quick shrug. "I don't know.

But I did stop by to have coffee with Lydia King late this morning. When we sat down, she was all shaken up. I asked her what was wrong, and she told me. Said the whole family's trying to deal with what happened. That they'll be okay without the money. They're mainly relieved that no one was inside the bakery when it happened. And they're concerned about it happening again. Either at their shop or somewhere else in town."

"How much cash was missing?"

"Nine hundred and twenty-two dollars."

Hannah tried to pretend disinterest. In a calm voice, she asked between bites of a homemade yeast roll, "Do they have any idea who took it?"

By now, Ruby had ceased eating and was leaning forward to converse with Miriam across the table. "Not a clue. They took fingerprints from the doorknob; of course, unless the King clan wiped off the handle each time a person came in, every customer's prints are on it."

After a slight pause, Miriam added, "I heard some talk in town that it's highly coincidental that this happened right after your new renter . . ." She glanced at Ben. "Moved in. I mean, our town has never experienced anything like this before. Ever."

Daed's commanding voice claimed everyone's attention. "It's wrong to accuse a man just because he's new here. Let's just let the cops and investigators do their jobs. I'm sure, tonight, everyone in town's wondering the same things we are."

Maemm's calm, positive voice ended the conversation. "I'm sure the Kings are all grateful that no one was hurt."

"*Jah*," Daed agreed as he gave an agreeable nod.

He looked around the table before lifting his chin. "But until they catch who did it, we all need to be careful."

In Maemm's kitchen that evening, Hannah dried the last clean dish and placed it in the beautiful cherrywood cabinet, which had been made by William Conrad. After laying her damp towel over the water spigot, she made her way up the oak stairs to her room, where she stepped inside and quietly closed the door behind her. As she stepped to her desk, she could hear Maemm's flyswatter meet a wall.

Hannah stopped a moment and smiled. In front of her was most of what she owned. Her bed, with the beautiful quilt Maemm had made her years ago. Different shades of purple prompted a breath of awe and a pleasant childhood recollection. When Hannah was young, purple had been her favorite color. Now she preferred blue.

She lifted her gaze to the two pegs on the wall. A spare navy dress hung from one peg. The other held her nightgown. She looked down at her polished oak desk and chair that brother Elijah had made at their family furniture shop at the edge of town. She took in the slick, dark, glossy finish and ran her finger over the smooth top.

Her favorite part of the room was the large window overlooking the backyard, which seemed to go on a million miles before meeting their large red barn. Her heart warmed at the simple, homemade curtains that were pulled back and hooked to their pegs.

A yawn escaped Hannah's mouth as she bent to lift

her miniature hope chest and put it next to her on the handwoven rug at the side of her bed, where she took in Old Sam's beautiful etching of the Ten Commandments. Getting comfortable on her hips, she took her usual seat on the floor covering, reaching back behind her to pull *The Adventures of Sydney and Carson* from beneath her pillow.

She traced her finger over the Ten Commandments. As she did so, she contemplated Marcus's huge move from Chicago to Arthur, a place she was sure was the antithesis of the city. Not that she'd ever been to Chicago; she hadn't, but she'd read enough about it in library magazines.

She thought of the talk they'd had. Of the conversation she'd overheard from the women at Amish Edibles. She began to read another scene from *Sydney and Carson*. Her heart pounded as she imagined her and Marcus in the dangerous episode.

> *He had to get to Sydney. Had to get her out of the building. If he didn't do it fast, she'd be engulfed in the fire that was rapidly spreading.*
>
> *Carson kicked the door open. Inside, smoke was so thick he could barely see. He glimpsed Sydney, facedown, trapped by a wooden beam that covered her legs, and rushed to her.*
>
> *As he leaned over her, he could hear her soft groan of pain. With all the strength he could muster, he lifted one end of the beam. After he did so, she rolled onto her side.*
>
> *He put down the end, careful it was away from her, lifted her, and carried her out the door. The*

*moment they were outside, the front of the building
burst into huge flames. "My leg . . . I think it's
broken," she said in weak, drawn-out words.*

*"You'll be okay. Because I'm here. But we've
got to get far away, in case there's an explosion.
Keep your arms around my neck. And hold on
tight."*

Hannah caught an excited breath that escaped her
throat. She rested the paperback on the floor to her right
and rested her hands on her lap. Her pulse pumped to
a fast beat. *They're going to be okay. Sydney will live.
Because of Carson's bravery.*

As the scene filled her thoughts, she shook her head.
But a new idea struck her, and she quickly recalled Mrs.
Graber's words to her years before. "You've got quite an
imagination. I enjoy your stories."

Inspired by *The Adventures of Sydney and Carson* . . .
Inspired by Marcus and his bravery, which had led to his
change of landscape . . . Inspired by her unexpected
feelings for her new friend, she stood and made her way
to her small oak desk, grabbed her small notepad and
pen, and returned to her comfortable spot on the rug.

As her real-life story filled her thoughts, she settled
into a more comfortable position and started her own
book. *My very first story. By Hannah Lapp.*

At the top line, she narrowed her brows as the pleasant, relaxing scent of the cinnamon sachet she kept
between her pillows floated through her room. *What
should I call it?*

For several moments, she strummed the tip of her
finger against the paper. Then she put pen to paper. With

a smile, Hannah printed *The Adventures of Marcus and Hannah*. Bringing her knees closer to her chest so the notepad was easy to reach, she imagined being involved in an exciting adventure with her new *Englisch* friend. And began writing.

Hannah's feelings for Marcus were forbidden. He wasn't of the Plain Faith, and most likely never would be. But one day bonded them together, heart and soul, Amish and Englisch, *forever.*

It was Friday the thirteenth. Hannah wasn't superstitious, nor had she ever been. However, she knew of Englisch *friends who were. On that day, something in the quiet countryside of Arthur, Illinois, happened that was so unusual. So unexpected.*

It was a typical evening. It seemed to be, anyway. In the back room of Amish Edibles, Hannah tallied the week's profits. Outside, the sun was setting. Inside, she knew that the minutes of daylight were nearly at an end as the stray cat she'd taken in, Scarlet, quietly sat in the corner of the room.

Outside of the back window, she glimpsed a kaleidoscope of colors that reminded her of different beautiful paints dumped onto a single canvas. Letting out a sigh, she stacked the green bills from her cash register and began to fill out a deposit slip. Next, she laid the money in a neat pile and neatly slipped the bills into the bank envelope in front of her.

She looked forward to the evening. Marcus was

to come by any minute to pick up the lone jar of raspberry jelly she had saved just for him. She smiled a little at the thought of the Englischer. Marcus Jackson. *Honest, hardworking, and* Gott*fearing. He was everything she'd ever dreamed of in a man.*

Except for one thing. He wasn't Amish. She frowned. As she sealed the envelope and clipped the contents with a black binder, an unusual sound caught her attention, and she stopped. She stayed very still while she turned toward the source of the noise. She watched the back-door handle jiggle.

Hannah's eyes widened with fear. She swallowed a knot that blocked her throat. Her heart pounded at a dangerous pace prompted by fear. Because Amish Edibles was closed for the day.

Outside, the CLOSED sign was on the front entrance. The back door was locked. Besides, no one ever used it.

Not only that, but there was no reason to try to enter through that entrance. Unless someone wanted to get in unnoticed. Unless that person intended to steal from Amish Edibles. She pressed her lips into a straight line, immediately recalling her daed*'s recent warning to be careful. She didn't dare go to the small window to see who tried to get in. Even if she did, she probably wouldn't be able to get a look at the person since the window was several feet away from the door.*

She glanced at the clock and pulled in a hopeful breath. Because Marcus was due here. Maybe it would be better if he came late. Because his life could be in danger, like hers was. Still, she'd give anything to hear his car pull into the parking lot. To know he was here with her in her time of need.

She contemplated her situation and applied her God-given logic. Whoever tried to get in must know she was inside. Even if they hadn't peeked in the small window, Miracle was tied in front. And her buggy was next to him.

Those things alone indicated that someone was aware of her presence. As quietly as she could, Hannah grabbed the envelope and said a quick, urgent prayer before hurrying to the other side of the door that separated the back room from the main shop area.

Behind her, she quietly closed the door. She frowned, wishing she could lock it. But there was no lock. Because of that, she questioned why she'd even bothered to close it.

Money in hand, she rushed out into the main area, to the shop's phone. She started to ring the emergency number for help. But there was no dial tone.

She tried, over and over. The result was the same. But whoever was attempting to get in didn't give up. Even from where she was, it was hard to ignore the handle rattling, which was becoming louder. A chill swept her spine. Her heart pumped to a fast, fearful beat. She sensed urgency. As if someone would break the door down.

Hannah stopped and stretched her legs. As she laid her notepad and pen to her side, she relaxed her head against the quilt that fell over the sides of her bed. She considered the first part of her story and smiled with satisfaction.

A sense of excitement swept through her as she imagined being in a real robbery. Although that was the last thing she wanted.

She knew that of course. That was why fiction was so much fun to read. Because in your mind, you could be in danger, when in reality you were safe. She expelled a sigh and reasoned that reading about a break-in was definitely much better than actually witnessing a theft.

She interlaced her hands on her lap and straightened as she considered recent events. *There has never ever been a robbery in town. What if someone had been inside the bakery when it was broken in to? Would they have been hurt? Or worse?* She thought of the King clan and shook her head. *Thank* Gott *they're okay.*

She paused her thoughts a moment to enjoy the warm summer breeze coming in through the screens. The smells from the outdoors were a combination of freshly mowed grass and manure that had been used to fertilize the garden. Besides the nightly sounds coming from the cicadas, it was relatively quiet.

While Hannah considered the long, serious conversation she'd had with Marcus that very afternoon in Amish Edibles, she yearned to talk to someone about the robbery and the wad of money she'd found.

The yearning within her to talk about her feelings for the *Englischer* was so strong, she closed her eyes and clenched her palms together. After a moment, she opened her lids and relaxed her fingers.

But there was no one to share that information with.

Not without arousing suspicion about Marcus. Besides, she was all too aware of the negativity they'd both endure if anyone found out how she felt about the Chicago native. However, it wasn't really herself that she was concerned with; it was her family. The last thing they deserved was to suffer because she followed her heart.

She definitely didn't want to deal with disapproval, which was exactly what she'd be confronted with if she conveyed what was going on inside her.

She also felt the need to share her forbidden feelings about him with someone who could advise her on what to do. Someone who would listen without passing judgment. She couldn't think of anyone who qualified. No one alive anyway.

She contemplated one person who'd been known to offer expert advice. The best listener. *Old Sam.* She was fully aware of the positive influence he'd made in her life. He'd been old when she'd met him; still, the positive impact he'd made would stay with her forever. She pressed her lips together, wondering what he would think of everything that had happened so quickly.

As the calming scent from her homemade cinnamon candle swept pleasantly through her room, she whispered, "Old Sam, you were full of wisdom. What would you have thought if you'd found a wad of cash right after the bakery was robbed? What would you had made of all this?"

How could anyone plan how to react in such a situation? She recalled where Old Sam had gotten his advice and smiled a little. She pushed herself up from her position, stood, and stepped to the window, where she took in the full moon and the stars scattered throughout the sky.

As she put her faith in her Creator, she closed her eyes and whispered a simple prayer. "Dear Lord, please protect us. And I say a special prayer for Marcus, that You will bless him and help him start a new life here in Arthur. Amen."

Chapter Six

Inside his Chevy the following morning, Marcus rolled down the driver's side window and cruised the narrow, winding blacktop outside Arcola.

He had prayed for God to protect the town of Arthur. More importantly, he'd asked his Creator to keep Hannah safe.

He trusted his Lord and Savior. At the same time, disappointment welled inside him. Even though he'd left his roots with the good intention of beginning a Christian life, could he move forward without changing his brothers? *I can make my future what I want it to be, but I can't do anything about the past but learn from it.*

Before he attempted to change his brothers, he had to learn what God wanted from him. How He intended Marcus to serve. Yesterday, Marcus hadn't planned to reveal so much about his family to Hannah; not yet anyway. But the King's Bakery circumstances and his missing money had forced him to spill as much as he had needed so she'd understand why he'd kept so much cash on him.

He slapped his hand against the steering wheel in frustration and swallowed the uncomfortable knot that blocked his throat. *I like Hannah. A lot. Even though I hardly know her. I'd love to date her. Of course, I've no doubt that wouldn't be permissible because I'm not of the Plain Faith. I wish there wasn't so much in my life to straighten out.*

Something within him that was so strong pulled at his heartstrings whenever he thought of her. Even so, he acknowledged that his relationship with the beautiful Amish woman could never be more than friendship. From the moment he'd glimpsed her quilt, he'd experienced a strong bond with her. Somehow, her work had connected him to a life that had been filled with goodness and love. A life he yearned for.

He recalled the emotional moment he'd glimpsed her quilt. At that very moment, every worry and concern had evaporated, like steam from a teakettle. And amazingly, being with Hannah had somehow filled him with a sense of security. He wasn't sure why; he barely knew her. He reasoned it was because she represented safety and goodness, all that had been missing from his life for a long time.

She had returned his money as he'd spilled his sad story that very afternoon; he had taken in the surprised expression on her face, a combination of fear and disbelief. What he'd seen on her porcelain visage forced a pain in his stomach.

What he'd offered her was fear and disbelief. He let out a sigh of disappointment. On the contrary, what he yearned to give her was comfort and happiness. Stability. What had happened at King's Bakery had stirred up his worries again.

I pray the thief gets caught right away. But in the meantime, how can I ensure that Hannah's safe? That her family's protected?

As he strained to see around the tall stalks of corn when he turned, what he needed to do came to him. A sudden calmness enveloped him as he remembered the pastor's words the night Marcus had changed inside.

It doesn't matter who your parents are. It doesn't matter what you've done. It's who you know.

Faith took over. He was doing what his mom had always stressed. Following his heart. And Marcus prayed again for God to guide his life. Afterward, Marcus knew everything would be okay.

The following morning, Hannah made her way to town for groceries while Maemm ran Amish Edibles. She enjoyed the uneven clomp-clomping of hooves and the ups and downs of the buggy as it traversed the narrow blacktop. As she watched her horse, Miracle, swish his tail, she took a moment to say a quick prayer of thanks for her simple life and for *Gott* blessing her family. She even said a prayer of thanks for Miracle: that *Gott* had put the two of them together. And that Miracle knew he was loved.

As her body swayed on the blue, velvety cushion with the uneven movement of the buggy, she thought of another quick prayer. "And dear Lord, please heal and protect Marcus. And I pray that his brothers will find You. Amen."

Inside the local store, she beamed when a familiar

voice caught her attention. She turned to the sound of Mary Conrad.

"*Hallo!*"

With a quick wave of her hand, Mary stepped to the middle of the aisle where Hannah was selecting flour, and they hugged each other affectionately.

Afterward, Mary shoved her glasses up her nose and grinned. "It's so *gut* to see you!"

"You too! How's your flower garden?"

Hannah couldn't help but grin amusement while Mary went on and on about her favorite Chicago Peace rosebush, how it had nearly died and how she'd managed to bring its beauty back with her secret formula. Automatically, Hannah equated her friend's excitement about plants to her own excitement about the adventure series she read and now was secretly writing.

As they went from aisle to aisle, Mary brought up the robbery. As they conversed, Hannah couldn't help but think what she'd acknowledged before: how odd a break-in was in this extremely noneventful neck of the woods.

In line, Sarah, the Amish checkout clerk, jumped in on their conversation. In an excited and breathless voice, she said, "They stole money from the cash register!" She threw her hands in the air. "Can you imagine what could have happened if someone had been in the shop?"

Hannah closed her eyes for a moment to try to stay calm. Although she'd already heard what Sarah reinforced, the reality hit her with such a ferocity, her heart pumped to a fast, wild beat.

She drew her hands over her chest as she said a silent prayer that the thief would be caught. Soon. At the same time, her vivid imagination went to work on the story she was secretly writing.

Sarah continued to go on and on about the theft that had turned into the talk of the town until, finally, Mary cut in. "Still no word on who did it."

Suddenly, Hannah realized that the two were looking at her to say something. Automatically, she said the first thing that came to her mind. "I believe the police will catch whoever did it."

A combination of fear and excitement edged Sarah's voice. "*Jah*, but what if the thief robs again?"

The plausible question forced Hannah to swallow the knot that suddenly blocked her throat. "We don't have control over that, Sarah. All we can do is pray that won't happen. And to be cognizant of what's going on around us."

Outside, Hannah helped Mary load her paper bags of groceries into her buggy. Afterward, they stepped side by side to Hannah's buggy and repeated their actions, careful to make sure everything was tucked away so that nothing would fall out during the bumpy ride down the blacktop.

Hannah motioned to the velvet cushion on the front bench and motioned to her friend. "I've missed you! We used to chat all the time. Nowadays, we barely talk. How 'bout getting together like we used to?"

"Come over soon, and I'll show you my flower garden as we solve the world's problems!"

At lunch the following day, Marcus took a seat next to Ben on the rustic-looking wooden bench behind their work building. As the warm summer breeze gently lifted the short sleeve of Marcus's T-shirt from his skin, the ambience brought back a melancholy feeling in his chest.

Memories, good and bad, flooded him while he unfolded the crease in his lunch bag and continued to pull the cellophane-wrapped sandwich from the brown paper. He envisioned his parents together with him and his brothers in their backyard eating homemade ice cream.

Today, the twenty-fourth of July, would have been his father's fiftieth birthday. As cars, trucks, and horse and buggies traversed the blacktop that loomed in the distance, the old Chevrolet he had helped his dad refurbish for months zoomed into Marcus's head. He, his brothers, and his dad had taken a ride in the vehicle to celebrate his dad's birthday. Marcus could almost hear the words and expressions of appreciation as family members had enjoyed the homemade ice cream his parents routinely made for special occasions.

Marcus swallowed an emotional knot and tried to think of something else. Of course, his parents would always have his heart. But sadness overcame him at how disappointed they'd be at his brothers' behavior.

And he was sure his dad would expect Marcus to help get them back in line. Their love of cars had bonded him and his father closely together. Chevrolets, specifically; his dad had never driven anything else.

At the same time, Marcus and Ben ate. As Marcus bit into his peanut butter and jelly sandwich, he nodded satisfaction.

"I tell you, Ben, your sister's raspberry jelly is the absolute best." Turning to his coworker, he pointed to his lunch.

Ben smiled, bobbing his head back as he took a swig

of water. "Doesn't surprise me a bit. Hannah always was the family cook."

That statement prompted Marcus to lift a challenging brow. "Not your mom?"

Ben took in a breath, extending his arm and turning his hand in an undecided motion. Finally, he met Marcus's gaze while he swallowed. As he opened a potato chips bag, he pressed his lips together in a straight, thoughtful line before responding.

"Maemm's a great cook, no doubt about it. But ever since Hannah was a child, she somehow managed to take over in the kitchen." After a slight pause, he offered a nod. "Here's my best explanation: Maemm cooks to feed us. Hannah cooks because she loves doing it."

Marcus swallowed before commenting. "I get it."

Ben bit into his chicken salad sandwich. "For as long as I can remember, my sister always tried out new recipes from her friends. And oh . . ."

He stopped a moment to chew another bite. While they sat behind the welding shop, a large cumulus cloud blocked the bright July sun. In front of them, a horse pulled a buggy on the blacktop headed toward the town of Arthur.

"Hannah has a knack for making food taste *gut*. And I know for a fact that sometimes she doesn't even measure. She can throw a dish together in no time at all and make it taste delicious. It's a talent *Gott* blessed her with."

After swallowing a bit, he went on. "She's also *gut* at math."

"Really?"

Ben nodded. "She keeps the books at Lapp Furniture.

Somehow, she works at the shop, does chores, and manages to do the records at our family store."

For a moment, Marcus took in the surprising news while he enjoyed the caress of a warm breeze on his face. His eyes followed the buggy, wondering who was inside the jet-black carriage. Then, recalling the barn raising and the amount of work needed to finish the building, he finished his first sandwich, wadded up the cellophane, and returned it to the bag after pulling out the second sandwich. As he took a swig from his bottled water, he turned to Ben. "When d'you suppose we can have your barn finished?"

Hannah's brother scrunched his empty bag and hooped it into the nearby trash can. As the trash landed in the metal bin, he offered a slight shrug of his shoulders.

"Depends on the weather."

Marcus couldn't help but note how much Ben resembled his sister. Both had the same large, chestnut-colored eyes speckled with green flecks that danced whenever they spoke about something that enthused them.

Ben's new barn excited him. When he talked about it, enthusiasm edged his voice. Unconsciously, Marcus compared Ben to his sister and smiled a little. Numerous things enthused Hannah. Her quilt, raspberry jelly, and, although she hadn't yet explained it to him, whatever she was secretly reading.

After he'd glimpsed her returning a paperback to a spot next to the cash register, her eyes had been wide with excitement. He couldn't help but wonder what was on those pages.

Even Ben's wide smile reminded Marcus of the Amish Edibles lady. Despite the similarities, there were also huge differences between the siblings. Ben was tall, thin, and walked in a slow, lackadaisical stride, while Hannah's taller-than-average build was curvy.

She never did things in slow motion. Seemed like she was always in a rush. He loved watching her light into something, like whatever it was she was getting to might escape before she got there.

He tried to stymie the way the pulse on his wrist picked up to a fast speed. He pressed his lips together in a straight line while he acknowledged his forbidden interest in her.

She's Amish. I'm a believer now, but I'm certain there's absolutely no way I'm ever going to join her faith. Their rules are so strict. I can't imagine not being able to drive. It would be like breaking the bond between my dad and me.

I bet their thoughts are as pure as their actions. And here I am, thinking about how I'd like to take Ben's only sister for dinner just to spend time with her. I'd love to walk with her just to hold her hand. And kiss her good night at her front door.

Marcus silently ordered himself to stop thinking about the only young woman in the Lapp family. *If Ben knew what's going through my mind, he wouldn't be happy. Not at all.*

Automatically, Marcus considered the way his heart stepped up a notch at the mere thought of beautiful, kind Hannah. He couldn't stop the corners of his lips from curving upward as he came up with an accurate analogy. *If my pulse was the speed limit, I'd have a ticket before I even put the car in Drive.*

The next thing that entered his thoughts was the theft

at King's Bakery. Relieved that he'd switched mental gears, he started a conversation about the family that owned the bakery. "Any word yet on who stole money from King's shop?"

Ben's expression turned serious as he stood and shoved his hands into his pockets. He paced a few steps and came back to where Marcus sat. When he plopped back down on his spot, he leaned back and stretched his long legs.

A short silence lapsed before he gave a quick shake of his head and turned toward Marcus. "The last I'd heard, no. In fact, it's my understanding that the police don't even have a suspect."

Marcus decided to be totally open. "Ben, there's something I want to get straight with you."

Ben lifted a curious brow.

Marcus cleared a knot from his throat. "I'm grateful for all you've done for me. You've given me a place to stay. And talking to you; well, what can I say?" Before a response could be made, Marcus went on. "You're an answer to my prayers."

Marcus pressed his palms against the bench and the corners of his lips dropped a notch. "But I realize that to some folks around here, I'm different."

Ben frowned.

Marcus gave a slight lift of his shoulders. "You know what I'm saying."

Ben merely looked at him to continue.

"I'm from the city. And I realize that this theft occurred shortly after I came to town."

Ben narrowed his brows. "What are you getting at?"

Marcus let out a breath and locked gazes with the man he already considered a true friend. "Your friendship means everything to me. So does your trust. And I don't take it for granted."

Several heartbeats later, he went on with a half smile. "Ben, my life and all I've been through probably seems complex compared to the simple way you and your family live."

Ben sat up straight and leaned forward before he pulled his legs up to the bench and offered Marcus's thigh a friendly slap. "There's one thing I'm sure of."

"What's that?"

"That I consider you part of our family. And I'd sure like you to join us for dinner tomorrow."

Chapter Seven

That evening, Hannah knelt beside her bed, pressed her palms together, and whispered, "Dear Lord, thank You for Mary Conrad. If it be Your will, please have Wayne Miller ask her parents' permission to court her. And please continue to protect our town from danger. Amen."

She stood, stepped to her desk, and pulled her story in progress from the top right corner. As Hannah glanced around the four off-white walls, she smiled in satisfaction. She loved her room.

In here, she felt secure. This was her special place to think. And for some reason, whenever she sat on the hand-woven rug and leaned back against the side of her bed, nothing seemed impossible.

Resting against her soft purple quilt, she expelled a happy sigh and silently reread what she'd started. Satisfied with what she'd penned so far, she paused to consider what to write next. Turning toward a breeze from the open window, she looked out at the stars that twinkled in the distance. She strummed her fingers against her notepad, her short nails meeting the paper making a light, tapping sound.

After breathing in and staring at the blank pages in front of her, she narrowed her brows. *What should my characters do? I was trying to ring for help. There was no dial tone.*

She put ink to paper and brought her knees closer to her chest so she could more easily write.

> *Hannah glanced out the front as she tried the phone again, wishing she could run out of the shop to get someone's attention.*
>
> *But the only living creature around was Miracle. No neighbors within a couple of miles. Every time the horse glimpsed Hannah, he whinnied for attention.*
>
> *Hannah gritted her teeth. Because by the time she hitched the horse to the buggy, the thief would surely see and hear her. She'd never yearned for a car, but right now, she contemplated how convenient it would be for her to merely step inside, close the driver's door, and turn the key in the ignition.*
>
> *There were definite advantages to being* Englisch.

The following morning, the sun was starting to appear as Hannah stepped toward the chicken coop to gather the morning eggs. Basket in hand, she frowned. As an Amish girl, she'd done many chores during her twenty years. This was, without a doubt, her least favorite.

After she crossed this one off her list, there was certainly plenty more to do before she hitched Miracle to the buggy to head to Amish Edibles. Closing her eyes momentarily to enjoy the warm breeze against her lashes, she let out a sigh of satisfaction.

This morning, there was no time to waste if she was to leave the house by nine thirty and be at Amish Edibles at ten till ten to open up and light the scented candles that her customers appreciated while they shopped.

As she approached the coop, as usual, she could hear the clucking of chickens. Automatically, she frowned and prepared herself for collecting the dirty eggs. She could already smell the feather dust.

She hunched to avoid hitting her head on the ceiling and opened the door. As she stepped inside, she considered everything going on in her life. Marcus. The theft at King's Bakery. The story she'd commenced. The money she'd found in her shop and the conversation she'd had with Marcus about it.

She blew out a deep breath as she acknowledged the task she'd come here to perform. "May as well get this over with," she muttered, stepping inside. As usual, feathers filled the air. She took in the urgent flapping of wings.

"Don't worry, you guys," she said under her breath. "I'm not here to put you into a pot for chicken and dumplings. I'm just here for your eggs."

A loud squawk made her hit her head on the low ceiling. She dropped her basket and quickly bent to retrieve it. For a moment, she rubbed the sore spot. Then she began collecting the eggs. Most were still warm.

As she carefully placed the white and brown shells in her basket, she tried to ignore the filth. The smell that she'd tried unsuccessfully to get used to over the years. Every once in a while, the feather dust prompted a sneeze.

She practiced optimism, fully aware that life was filled with things she didn't like to do. On the upside, once the eggs were cleaned with a warm rag, they'd look more appetizing. Besides, they served a very important purpose. Because of these feathered creatures, she was able to bake delicious treats, like the sponge cakes and beautiful hot rolls that tasted best right out of the oven.

Outside of the coop, she stood up straight and breathed in the fresh air. For a quick moment, she placed the egg-filled basket on the ground while she brushed small feathers off her dress sleeves and work apron. Last, she gently dusted her *kapp*, bent for the basket handle, picked it up, and took the long dirt trail that led to the Lapps' side porch.

Outside, she breathed relief, straightening and closing the wooden door behind her and turning the wooden board to hold the entrance shut. She took in the sun that was beginning to appear and acknowledged that *Gott* had blessed her with another day. *Dear Lord, help me to use this day for You. Help me to serve You and only You.*

When she came to the side of the house, she opened the screen and stepped inside. The door sprang shut and made a quick, snapping noise. Inside the kitchen, she carefully removed the eggs from the basket, laid them out on a dish towel, and began gently cleaning each one with water and a warm rag. Miraculously, they cleaned up quickly.

As she removed the undesirables, she looked out of the window in front of her and smiled a little. She took in the barn in the distance. She could see the cattle in the fenced-in pasture.

Two goats played in the backyard. She frowned. *How did they get out of their pen?* They sometimes looked like fun-loving creatures, but they were mostly ornery.

While she finished the task at hand, she took in the vast area of jade-green grass.

For a moment, she stopped to appreciate the panorama in front of her. From where she stood, she had a full view of the dirt path that started at the side porch and wound its way all the way to the old barn that had been passed down from her grandparents on Maemm's side.

Four workhorses trotted in the nearby pasture. Milking cows grazed. Clumps of green leaves on the tall, old oak trees provided shade. A long rope dropped from a large limb of one of the trees. In the center of the backyard, her *daed*'s large garden looked like a plant oasis in a picture frame of black dirt.

From where she stood, Hannah glimpsed six red bell peppers ready to be picked. Cucumbers were more difficult to see amid the mélange of green vines that covered them. The same with the red tomatoes, most of which were enclosed snugly within leaves and vines.

Easy to detect were orange pumpkin blossoms that were fully opened. Hannah's mouth watered as she imagined dipping them in egg, then crushed cracker, and then transferring them to a skillet of hot oil until they were browned on both sides.

Hannah's favorite produce from Daed's garden were sweet cherry tomatoes. She also loved the peppers in the winter when they went into her homemade chili.

Suddenly, Hannah became aware of the morning catching up with her, rushed to dry the eggs, and carefully put each into a holder on the inside of the fridge so she could make her way to the garden to collect the ready-for-picking produce.

Before leaving the house, she rounded up the goats and put the hook over the fence to lock them back inside their pen. She took one last glance at the barn and hoped there'd be enough time to clean the animal stalls before she hitched her horse to the buggy for the three-mile ride to Amish Edibles.

Happiness warmed Hannah's heart until a smile pulled up the corners of her lips. She loved working at the store, and even the thought of the robbery at King's Bakery didn't deter her. The thief or thieves still hadn't been caught, and the police had no suspicions about who'd done it. But she wasn't afraid. Because Maemm had always taught her that something *gut* came from something bad. Like sponge cakes from dirty eggs. In this case, the robbery had propelled her vivid imagination into high gear. The past couple of days, Hannah had thought so much about what had happened at King's Bakery, and what could still happen.

The kind man who'd welded her horse and buggy back together floated into her thoughts. And all the while, she pictured herself and Marcus in the fiction she'd started. *But not all of it is fiction. It doesn't really matter, though. No one will ever read it but me.*

Between the robbery and her new friend, Hannah's imagination had been working overtime. Her heart pumped to an excited pace as she contemplated where she and Marcus were in her story. *I can't wait to continue my adventure story with Marcus.*

That evening, Hannah gave Ben's wife, Ruth, a tight hug as she stepped inside the house where Ruth and Ben now lived with their four children. Maemm and Daed followed her in the kitchen entrance.

Immediately, the homey ambience forced a sense of familiar comfort up Hannah's arms that landed in her shoulders. For a moment, she savored the wonderful sensation. The aroma of meats and sweets floated throughout the kitchen. Kids seemed to be everywhere.

Hannah's gaze immediately landed on the tiled countertop, where an array of desserts were displayed. Ruth was lifting a foil-covered baking dish out of the oven. As she peeled off part of the foil, the delicious smell of pork roast and cabbage escaped and blended in with the other smells.

At the same time, Hannah and Maemm offered to help. "What can we do?"

They were careful to stay out of Ruth's way as she carried the large dish to some pot holders that had been placed in a square on the countertop. The moment she set down the pot, Ruth turned to them and sighed a combination of relief and excitement.

"I'm so happy to have you for dinner at our new home!" She corrected, "At least, it's new to us!"

After a half smile and a brief wave, Daed made his way to the living room, where Ben and a couple of his brothers appeared engrossed in a farming magazine. Ruth raised the pitch of her voice a couple of notches to be heard over the men.

"I'll take you up on your offer, if you don't mind."

"Not at all. Point us in the direction you need us!"

Ruth pressed her finger to her lips before motioning outside. "Hannah, would you check on the boys?"

Hannah nodded toward the yard. "They're out back."

Ruth squinted, then voiced her concern. "I haven't heard them for a while, and I'm a little concerned. Would you find them and tell them it's time to come in and wash up for dinner?"

With a quick nod, Hannah stepped to the door and offered a definitive wave. "I'll go round 'em up!"

As Hannah stepped back to the door through which she'd just entered, Ruth put Maemm to work setting the tables in the neighboring room.

Outside, Hannah let go of the screen door, and it quickly sprang closed. Enjoying the smell of freshly mowed grass, she hollered, "Isaiah! David! Samuel! Mervin!"

She listened for a response, and when none came, she quickened her steps, making her way back to where Pebble Creek came into view. Although it was a distance away, Hannah was able to easily glimpse the well-known hill. She also took in the barn that was in its initial stages.

That most special hill, where Old Sam had asked for Esther's hand in marriage. That union had lasted nearly sixty years. For a moment, Hannah forgot her mission while she stood and gazed wistfully at the out-of-place hill in flat central Illinois. The very place where Levi Miller had asked Annie Mast to be his forever.

For long moments, Hannah allowed herself to imagine being a wife. A mother. She even dared to envision Marcus as an Amish man who came to her home to ask her parents' permission to court her. Better yet, she pictured the two of them at the top of the hill that overlooked Pebble Creek.

Her heart warmed at the idyllic thought. A dream that could and would never materialize. *But there's nothing wrong with imagining, I don't think.*

The sound of boyish laughter broke her reverie, and she turned toward it, which appeared to come from the small dwelling in the distance. The very place Marcus now rented. To her surprise, she glimpsed the boys on small bicycles as Marcus raced them by foot.

Hannah planted her palms on her hips and eyed the group. She wasn't sure why she was surprised by the scene. Of course, she'd known that her new friend lived here. But what stunned her was his fascinating interaction with the young boys.

As she continued to take in the fun-loving group, it appeared as though Marcus was one of them. So far, because of the tall, full oaks she stood behind, no one had seen her, and she was able to easily view them in full play. Stopped in her tracks, she looked on at the happy picture of Marcus racing the boys. The kids were on their wheels; he ran on foot.

What also surprised her was how fast he was. Hannah often babysat, so she knew firsthand the amount of energy required to keep up with boys her nephews' ages. And stamina.

For a blissful moment, the scene brought a smile to her lips, and she watched in amazement as Marcus raced the four youngsters down his lane, to and from his small rental. Back and forth. In fact, she reasoned that the picture presented such happiness, she felt guilty for breaking it up.

At the same time, she was fully aware of the amount of work her sister-in-law must have gone through to make such delicious-looking dishes. And she knew from experience that when Ruth said it was time to eat, she meant it! Now, not after the kids finished their game with Marcus. Hannah lifted her chin, squared her shoulders, cupped her hands on both sides of her mouth and hollered their names, one by one. When she managed to get their attention, she motioned toward Ben and Ruth's house and ordered the crew to come in and wash up.

At the sound of Hannah's command, all five stopped and looked at her. Then, they began peddling down the lone dirt path of the rental to where the path widened and continued to the main house. Marcus jogged in between the small bikes.

Hannah stood very still, watching the images come closer and especially taking note of the way the boys closely and so trustingly interacted with the Chicago native. When the five of them met Hannah, they were laughing and catching their breath. She couldn't help but join in the contagious laughter. Excited voices competed to be heard over one another until Marcus let out a low whistle.

At that, there was a welcome silence. Hannah felt a bit guilty, stopping their fun. But she had a job to do. Hoping they'd be able to transfer their excitement from their game to the dinner that was imminent, she lifted the pitch of her voice to her most enthusiastic tone.

"Time to eat, guys." Before the boys could get a word in, Hannah continued. "I'm sure you've worked up a big appetite. And your *maemm*'s a great cook."

The kids were usually obedient and well-mannered,

so the protests that followed surprised Hannah. David whined, "But we never get to play with Marcus."

Marcus looked down at the five-year-old and lifted a comforting brow as he lowered his voice to an understanding pitch. "Ah, but I think that if you do as Auntie Hannah says and go wash up for dinner, I might just get to sit by you." He eyed Hannah and winked. "That is, if Ruth doesn't mind."

There was a unanimous "*Gut!*" before the four jumped back on their bikes and peddled to the side door of Ben's home, which was a good distance away.

After their departure, Hannah looked up at Marcus and smiled with amusement. "The kids like you."

He offered her a wide smile. "If what you said is true, that Ruth's a great cook, we'd better take fast strides to follow them. I don't know 'bout you, but my lunch was a long time ago."

"Mine too." She paused. "You're joining us?"

"Yeah. Ben invited me. And knowing you Amish women are such good cooks, I wasn't about to decline the invitation."

With a wave of his hand, he motioned for her to go in front of him before finally joining her at her side. As the warm evening breeze fanned Hannah's lashes, they followed the path to the dinner smells that had floated out through the open windows.

They stepped quickly, and Hannah's heart pumped with excitement as she enjoyed her unexpected time with Marcus. As he talked, his voice bounced a bit with his strides. "Kids. They're really special. Being with them is a breath of fresh air."

He extended his hands in front of them as they

glanced at each other. "You surely remember what being young was like."

Hannah drew her palms to her heart as memories floated back to her. "*Jah*. There are so many *gut* memories. How 'bout you? What is your favorite childhood recollection?"

After a slight pause, his voice cracking with emotion, he said, "There are so many." He glanced at her; at the same time, she looked at him. "But if I had to choose, I'd say my favorite times were when my family got together with our relatives for holidays. My dad always made homemade ice cream. And Mom?"

She glanced at him to go on as they followed the curve in the blacktop.

"She made her famous Special K bars. Have you ever tasted one?"

"No, but now you've piqued my curiosity. What are they?"

"I'm not sure of the exact ingredients, but I remember they were made with cereal, white syrup, sugar, tons of peanut butter, and lots of Hershey's chocolate."

Hannah's heart warmed at the expression on his face and the soft tone of his voice. "Sounds delicious! You think there's any way you could find her recipe?" Before he could respond, she quickly added, "I'd love to make them."

"Oh . . ." He cupped his head with his palms and glanced up at the sky. "No promises, but once I'm more settled in here, I'll call my aunt to ask for the recipe."

"*Gut*." Several heartbeats later, she softened her tone. "I want to make sure you have those Special K bars again."

Surprise edged his voice. "Really?"

Hannah offered a shy "*jah*." She liked Marcus so much, she was a bit stunned that he seemed to be surprised that she wanted to make him what was obviously his favorite treat.

Ben's dwelling was closer now. "Hannah, if you could travel back in time, say . . . just for an hour or so, would you do it?"

The question prompted her to press her lips into a line as she contemplated the serious question. Finally, she nodded. "*Jah* . . . If I could choose the moment in time."

Together, they laughed before Marcus's tone became more somber. "I'd give anything to have any moment back with my parents. And I hope God tells me how to get my brothers to believe in Him."

After a long silence, their steps slowed as they approached the side entrance. From where they stood, the air smelled of a mélange of dishes. Hannah's mouth watered.

At the door, they stopped. As he pulled open the screen, he looked down at Hannah. When she met his gaze, the wistful expression in his eyes nearly stopped her breath. Finally, he responded in a soft voice. "Here we are."

Hannah's heart nearly stopped at the sincerity in his voice. In his eyes. She sensed that he needed something from her. A sense of reassurance, maybe.

She softened her voice with a combination of sympathy and reassurance. "Pray, Marcus. Eventually, you'll be with your parents again. In heaven. And as far as your brothers?" She expelled a sigh. "I'll pray for *Gott* to fill their hearts with His love." A thought struck her, and she immediately voiced it before giving it more serious attention. "Marcus, won't you come to church with us? I'd really like that."

Before he could answer, the door opened, and David and Samuel motioned the two of them in.

Right now, Hannah needed time to figure out why she sensed that they belonged together, when the truth was, the man from Chicago represented everything she could never, ever have.

Chapter Eight

Inside Ben and Ruth's home, Marcus breathed in all sorts of delicious foods. He offered a quick, friendly wave as he stepped into the roomy kitchen.

"This is one great-smelling house."

Ruth immediately laid her dish cloth on the countertop, left the stove, and made her way toward him, where she smiled up at him. "Marcus, we're so glad you could join us this evening."

Marcus already felt indebted to Ben's wife. Since Marcus moved into the house that belonged to the friendly couple, she'd made sure he was well taken care of. She'd brought plenty of homemade meals over to him. And the moment she'd learned that he'd come here with so little, she and Ben had provided him a bed frame from the family furniture store, a comfy mattress, and oh-so-soft bedding that she'd sewn herself.

Marcus stepped into the next room, where he greeted the men, who were discussing this year's crops. He'd already met them at the barn raising, of course. After he said a few words, the boys ran up to him, nearly knocking him over. Each vied for his attention.

Isaiah, the smallest of the four, pulled at his arm and begged, "Let's go back outside and play!"

David yanked on his free hand. "Can you race us again?"

The other two jumped up and down in anxious anticipation. Automatically, Marcus laughed as he gazed down at the small bodies of energy. "Dinner's ready. Besides, you've already washed up, right?"

There was a unanimous "*jah*."

Ben's low voice ordered the kids to calm down. As he pulled them away, he gave each a fatherly nudge in the direction of the kitchen. "Now, go offer to help your *maemm*."

Ruth's voice floated through the air in a tone that commanded everyone's attention. Marcus took in the two dining room tables that were neatly covered with sky-blue tablecloths in the room next to the kitchen. Beautiful oak chairs circled the tables, and there were napkins and silverware settings for twenty-two: Hannah's parents, Ben and Ruth, Marcus, Hannah, David, Isaiah, Samuel, and Mervin, and two of the other brothers, who all co-owned the family furniture store, their wives, and their children.

As everyone stepped toward the chairs, Marcus pulled out Hannah's mother's chair for her, and she offered him a half smile and a soft, grateful "*denki*." Hannah took her seat and pulled her chair closer to the table.

Ben looked around the room and told them all to bow their heads for the prayer. Marcus listened with great interest while Ben thanked God for so many things: the food, their family, their good health, the fresh produce. "And Lord, we thank You for bringing Marcus to us. Please bless him and lead him as he starts a life for You. Amen."

While Marcus watched Ruth begin sending the dishes around the table, Marcus considered the heartfelt prayer and swallowed an emotional knot. *Without a doubt, this is one special family. My brothers and sisters in Christ. God has already started my journey to live for Him by bringing me to them.*

In the middle of the meal, talk turned to the robbery and that the police had no leads. As Marcus bit into a piece of baked chicken, he listened to Ben, Ruth, and Ben's brothers talk about the family furniture store in town. Lapp Furniture was owned equally between all the brothers and, apparently, each filled his own role, even Ben, who worked outside the family business.

As Marcus took a drink of iced tea, Hannah's mother turned her attention to him and spoke in a polite tone. "I hear that you and Hannah met your first day here."

Marcus smiled appreciatively at Hannah, who sat across from him and offered a quick nod. "When I saw the store sign, my mouth watered," he joked. "Amish Edibles. Just by those two words, I guessed I could buy jelly for my lunch sandwiches."

Laughter filled the room as Marcus continued. "And once inside, not only did I get raspberry spread, but also the most delicious wheat bread I've ever tasted."

Hannah chimed in. "I recommended the raspberry jelly over the strawberry. And that very morning, I'd just loaded the shelves with fresh-baked bread."

"What did you think of our little shop?" Mrs. Lapp

asked while reaching for homemade preserves and a hot roll.

Marcus scooped up a bite of sweet corn before answering. "It's absolutely charming," Marcus responded with an appreciative smile.

Hannah got in on the conversation. "Maemm, you remember that broken metal horse and buggy?"

After Mrs. Lapp offered a quick nod, Hannah went on. "Marcus took it home and welded it back together. Now it's on display in front of the cash register. It's as *gut* as new."

"That's wonderful." Mrs. Lapp directed her appreciative voice to Marcus.

He swallowed a bite and added, "It was an easy fix. Every now and then, my welding skills come in handy." He winked at Hannah, who was loading her plate with a second helping of chicken and dumplings.

Marcus took in the gentleness of the conversation between the family members, noting that there was not an unkind word. The boys were quiet and polite. And afterward, they dutifully took their empty plates to the kitchen sink. Automatically, Marcus carried his own, with Hannah behind him.

He lowered his voice so only Hannah could hear. "How 'bout we surprise Ruth and do the dishes?"

Hannah beamed. "What a nice idea, Marcus." She looked up at him and smiled, causing his heart to skip a beat. He couldn't look away from the light-green flecks on her irises. This evening, he had taken ample opportunity to better study her because she had sat opposite him.

The dinner had provided him a chance to see how the

beautiful woman who had unconditionally befriended him blended in with her family. Hannah seemed to do it all: run a shop, cook, quilt, and . . . He couldn't stop a grin of amusement from pulling up the corners of his lips. *And read adventure stories.* Of course, she'd never told him so, but more than once, he'd glimpsed *The Adventures of Sydney and Carson* sticking out of the shelf next to the cash register. Not only that, but he'd glimpsed her looking inside the cover when he'd been checking out her edibles.

He turned his attention to the sink. Automatically, Hannah stepped in front of him and began filling a tub of water, which she positioned in the left sink. Marcus reasoned that it was most likely a rinse container.

"I know we don't have to, but we *want* to."

When Ruth joined them, she nudged Marcus's shoulder. "Please. Allow me. I didn't invite you over to work, you know."

Marcus didn't budge. "You did all the cooking. I just wouldn't feel right having you do the dishes, too." He smiled a little. "Please allow us. We're willing and able," he added with a wink.

He darted a glance at Hannah. "Besides, I have an ulterior motive."

"*Jah?*"

"This will give me a chance to learn a little more about your community." After a slight pause, he added gently, "That is, if you wouldn't mind filling me in."

She nodded. "All right."

As Ruth stepped away, two familiar voices chimed in behind him. "But you said we could play after dinner."

Another little voice piped in, "*Jah,* I thought you were going to race us."

An idea came to Marcus and he bent so he was at eye level with Isaiah, David, Samuel, and Mervin. He looked from one to another as he spoke in a low, firm voice. "Tell you what, guys, I have an idea."

In silence, four sets of eager, curious eyes looked at him to go on.

"If all of us pitch in with the clean-up, I imagine we can have the job done lickety-split."

"Lickety-split?" Samuel's voice repeated. Laughter followed.

Marcus nodded. "That means in no time at all. And if my sunset estimate is close to what I guess it to be, there should be enough time left for me to outrun you guys on your bikes."

The four jumped up and down in excitement. "We get to race him!"

Marcus found it hard to hide his amusement at the four. He winked at Hannah. *Was I ever this young?*

Several heartbeats later, he still hadn't received a commitment from his young audience, so he lifted a challenging brow as he looked down at them. "Deal?"

Four heads bopped up and down before there was a unanimous, "Deal."

Marcus quickly acknowledged that working with his new friends would definitely require strategy and instruction. He looked at the obvious source of those two. "Hannah, would you mind assigning these young men jobs?"

He didn't miss her expression, a combination of amusement and satisfaction. She turned to all four and spoke in a faux serious tone. "Samuel, here; please take this cloth and wipe the crumbs off the table." After handing him the wet material, she quickly added, "And make sure the crumbs end up in the cloth and not on the floor."

With one quick, but careful motion, he grabbed the towel and disappeared.

Next, she tapped the toe of her shoe to a quick beat while she switched her attention to the second in line. "Mervin, I know you're a hard worker, but my question is, are you *gut* at taking garbage out?"

He offered a quick nod and started pulling the black plastic liner out of its holder.

She stepped over to him and showed him how to tie the bag at the top. "You think you can do that with the other two bags?" She waved a hand.

He gave a quick nod before she turned to the two boys who stood in front of her with eager expressions on their faces.

Hannah put her finger to her lips and called them by name. "David and Isaiah?"

Marcus nearly burst out in laughter at the wide eyes and overeager expressions of the remaining two.

"I'm leaving the most difficult job for you." She opened a couple of drawers. Removing two dry, folded towels, she unfolded them and handed one to each.

She told each child to stand to her left, and Marcus noted that somehow, she'd already managed to fill the left sink with water. She focused on Marcus next. "Okay, we can get this done, like you called it, lickety-split, if you scrub the pans down while the boys and I do the silverware."

For a moment, Marcus wondered if he'd exaggerated when he'd said they could get the work done "lickety-split." He took in the numerous pots and pans, plates and silverware, and acknowledged that this dinner wasn't just his parents and two brothers. There had been two tables of people. And a card table, too.

But the idea had been his, so he pretended confidence in what he'd so naively started. He offered a quick nod. "Sounds like a plan."

Then, as everyone moved in the directions of their tasks, he remembered something and lifted a palm in the air. "Whoa . . ."

The cleanup team stopped and looked at him in surprise. "What?"

"I forgot something. Because we're doing this as a team, shouldn't we put all our hands together and say, 'Let's go?'"

Marcus wasn't sure if these youngsters had participated in sports; still, they appeared excited about the concept of being part of a team, and without wasting a moment, they followed his lead and extended their arms so that their hands touched in the middle. "Okay . . . on the count of three, let's say, 'Let's go!'"

After a slight pause while all the hands went together, Marcus said, "One, two, three . . . Let's go!"

The pep talk prompted a storm of excitement while everyone got busy. Marcus was amazed with the way the young boys seemed accustomed to pitching in. Of course, he'd already learned that most of the Amish rose before the sun came up and completed an impressive list of chores.

Hannah's voice broke the silence. "So, you want to hear a bit about this community?"

As she handed him a scrub pad, he started with the hot bread pan and nodded. "If you don't mind sharing what's going on."

Hannah gave a smile, then began. "I guess I should start by telling you about some of our friends and the businesses they run. You probably have heard by now that we Amish are pretty handy with wood. As you're aware, nine of my ten brothers run Lapp Furniture."

"Right."

Light scrubbing sounds filled the air as she went on. "It's funny; you'd think there wouldn't be enough work for everyone, but amazingly, there is."

She smiled at Marcus while silverware clinked on the opposite side of the sink. "People from all over the state order custom-made furniture, and even with the other businesses in town, there's, fortunately, not a shortage of work."

"How did they learn that particular skill?"

"From an early age, Daed and my uncles taught them."

Marcus looked over at her. "They must have been good teachers."

"Then, of course, Ben works for Cabot with you. And fortunately, with the abundance of field pipes, welders are usually in high demand around here."

After handing more silverware to the young boys, Marcus rinsed his bread pan and laid it on the dry towels Hannah had set out on the countertop next to him. He proceeded with a large baking pot.

As they worked, he was so close to Hannah, he could smell the peach fragrance of her hair. Being next to her offered him an odd sense of security. He wasn't sure why; he reasoned that it was because she represented everything he considered safe and good.

"It may come as a surprise, but Arthur really has a lot of interesting history."

Marcus suddenly became aware that Ruth and Hannah's mother were only a few steps behind them. From the dining room table in the neighboring room, Ruth's voice floated through the kitchen. "Tell him about Old Sam."

Marcus stopped a grin of amusement that tried to lift the corners of his lips. He was fully aware of the two extra sets of ears who obviously intently listened to what was being said.

Hannah gave a regretful shake of her head as a splash of water landed on her hand. "Oh Marcus, I wish you could have met Old Sam."

Marcus caught the emotional expression on her face from his peripheral vision. "That name seems to come up often. Why is he such an important figure around here?"

"Was." Hannah's voice hitched. Hannah spoke in a soft voice. "Old Sam was a farmer who lived only a few miles away. But there's so much to say about him, I guess I should start with the hope chests he made."

"Did he work for your family furniture company?"

She shook her head as she scrubbed some silverware, rinsed it, and passed it on to the two eager boys to her left.

"No. Old Sam Beachy is somewhat of a legend. To start with, he was known for the hope chests he made. I mean, he wasn't famous for the actual chests, you see, but for the lids."

"No kidding?"

"*Jah*. He had a *Gott*-given, artistic ability to carve designs into the wood. Designs that looked real." A second later, she added, "Someday, I want to show you the hope chest he made for me. He personalized each lid. On mine, he etched the Ten Commandments."

"He's the man who owned Pebble Creek, right?"

"That's him." She paused for a moment to motion the two boys toward the silverware drawer. "He lived in an old house around here with many acres. And I'm sure you've noticed the hill?"

He nodded.

"As you're probably aware, Illinois is predominantly flat. And Pebble Creek . . ." A laugh of awe escaped her throat. "It's as if *Gott* pulled a hill from somewhere else in the United States and put it right here in this town."

Marcus smiled. "I did notice it seemed out of place. But beautiful."

"Uh-huh. And there's a creek that beautifully winds its way through the property. Actually, the whole place was coined Pebble Creek by Annie and Levi Miller when they were young."

"I've heard those names, too."

"Oh, those two are something else! They go to our church, of course, and have quite an interesting story."

Marcus glanced at the remainder of the pots and pans and grinned down at her. "I'm not going anywhere."

"They used to throw pebbles into the creek to see who could make the larger splash. That's when they were kids. I wasn't here then, but I've heard from many people that the two had an unbreakable bond. They shared dreams. Levi protected her. But anyway, something bad happened."

Marcus tried to imagine what it could have been. "Let me guess. One of them moved?"

Hannah gave a slight lift of her shoulders before answering. "You could say that."

"What happened?"

"Levi's father was shunned by our church, and his father took them away to another town in Illinois. Sadly, Levi didn't have a chance to tell Annie he was leaving. I mean, because of the shunning, the Millers left and completely deserted the Amish faith. They became *Englisch*."

Marcus was so intrigued, he quickly motioned Hannah to go on with her story.

"Annie was devastated. I guess Levi was, too. They'd been separated for life, or so it had seemed. And, of course, starting with the move, Levi completely changed his life. They didn't even live around other Amish. Then, about ten years later, Levi came back to town for his cousin's wedding. He came alone; I guess his *daed* was pretty bitter about the shunning, and—"

"This shunning . . . so the community really asked Levi's family to leave Arthur?" Marcus asked.

Hannah stopped for a moment to glance at him. "Let me clarify something. They didn't ask him to leave; they shunned him."

"That doesn't sound good."

"It's not. And it doesn't happen often, but no one made him leave. In fact, others have been shunned, but chose to stay here. But apparently, leaving was something Levi's father felt he had to do."

"Let me guess now. Levi came back for the wedding and he ran into Annie."

"*Jah*. They had a long heart-to-heart. At first, Levi had only planned to stay for a few days, but something happened . . . that's a story for another time. He and Annie knew that their hearts belonged to each other, but she couldn't become *Englisch*, and Levi told her he could never be Amish again after what had happened."

Marcus lifted a brow. "That's understandable. I don't see a happy ending coming here."

Hannah smiled up at him. "*Gott* works miracles, and I won't take the time now to explain how it all happened, but what counts is that the two ended up marrying. Oh . . . Old Sam even played a role in them getting back together."

"He did, huh?" As she nodded, he added, "I guess that shouldn't surprise me."

"You'll probably meet Annie and Levi. He builds houses, just as his *daed* did, and Annie Miller, well, she's kinda famous for making the best sponge cakes around."

"Are we almost done?"

Samuel's small, whiny voice pulled them from their conversation. Hannah glanced at the few pots and pans remaining to be washed and released the children from their cleaning duties.

As Marcus heard Ruth telling the boys they could go outside if they stayed on the dirt trail, Hannah continued talking. As the door slammed shut, Marcus couldn't help but grin as he glimpsed the four getting back on their bikes and making their way up the long dirt drive that ended at the house he was renting.

Hannah glanced up at Marcus and arched a brow. "Unless you want to stay here all night, let's just do one more story. And then you can keep your promise to the boys." The expression on her face warmed, and again, to Marcus's dismay, his heart fluttered.

"Rebecca and William Conrad run Conrad Cabinets. They're an amazing couple, Marcus. They, too, have an interesting story about how they stayed together."

"I've heard of them." He grinned when he looked down at her.

Hannah emptied the container of water and wiped down the sink with a clean dish towel while she talked. At the same time, Marcus dried the last baking casserole.

"Growing up, William Conrad and Rebecca Sommer were always close." She paused to shove a loose strand of hair under her *kapp*. "He carried her schoolbooks for her and things like that. He was protective of her, the same way Levi looked out for Annie when they were young. Anyway, when they got older, they planned to marry."

Marcus gave an understanding nod while he wiped down his part of the sink. He followed by doing the same with the countertop next to him.

"But something kind of unusual happened. Actually, it was way out of the ordinary."

He looked at her and arched a brow while he continued running the clean dishcloth over the granite countertop. "To make a long story short, William's *maemm* passed on to heaven when William was young. But . . ."

She stopped to rinse off her rag. "You would think that his *daed* would have raised him. But unfortunately, that wasn't the case."

Marcus frowned. He'd had such a close relationship with his own father, he couldn't imagine a dad leaving his own flesh and blood. He lifted his chin a notch and firmed his voice. "I hope he had a good reason not to raise his own son."

"Well, not in my view. Ya see, he fell in love with someone outside of the faith and eventually married her. Of course, Daniel . . . that's William's *daed* . . . he left William here in town to be raised by his aunt."

Marcus stopped and wrung his rag over the sink while he contemplated the severity of what Hannah was saying. He didn't know William or Daniel, but he did know that time between parents and their children was precious and not to be taken for granted. As he recalled his own mom and dad, he bit his lip and realized that Hannah was waiting for him to say something.

"I can't imagine, Hannah."

Behind them, Hannah's mother expressed disapproval. "Me neither, Marcus, but people do bad things sometimes. Especially when romantic love's involved. There were plenty of single Amish women; I can't imagine why he had to go outside of the church."

Marcus considered the comment. What had been said was reinforcement that he could never court and marry Hannah. At the same time, he tried to stop the amused curve of his mouth. By now, he knew that Hannah's mother and her sister-in-law were very interested in others' lives.

Hannah cleared her throat. "The story gets even more interesting. You see, Daniel had a heart attack and needed help running his cabinet business in Indiana."

"Let me guess what comes next . . ."

"Okay."

"He went to help his father and decided he wanted to move closer to him."

"Yes, and he fell in love with how his *daed* lived; you know, the television, air conditioning, and things that we Amish do without. Oh, by the way, I left out the part where Rebecca went with him, which in itself caused a lot of stir. Anyway, to make a longer story short, Rebecca thought she was going to lose William, but in the end, they married, and fortunately, William stayed Amish."

Marcus let out a low whistle. "You Amish folk lead interesting lives," he joked. But he knew inside that he meant it. And by looking at the simple, hardworking men and women in the community, it was difficult to imagine anything like what Hannah had explained.

"I'm glad things worked out," he said as she pressed her palms against her hips and smiled at him. Suddenly, he remembered his promise to the boys. He turned and stepped toward the door. "Now, I've got a commitment to keep."

He winked at Hannah before turning to Ruth and Mrs. Lapp. "Ruth, your dinner was delicious . . ." He smiled a little. "I can't even begin to thank you for your hospitality. And everything you've done for me since I came to town."

Ruth joined him at the door. "It's my pleasure, Marcus." She motioned outside. "Four little boys are waiting for you."

The kids peddled their bikes up to where Marcus stood.

Isaiah's young voice challenged Marcus. "You said you'd race us."

Marcus rubbed his palms together as if deciding whether to accept the invitation. Finally, he put his hands on his hips and looked at the eager group. "I did, didn't I? Okay, where do we start and where's the finish line?"

David got off his small bike and made an imaginary line with his shoe near the side porch. "From here . . ."

Mervin chimed in. "Okay, from here to the barn."

Marcus nodded in agreement. The barn was in between Ben and Ruth's home and the one-room rental where he lived.

"Sounds like a plan." As the boys walked their bikes to the imaginary line, Marcus narrowed his brows. "Okay, I'm going to say, 'on your mark, get set, go!'"

Hannah's enthusiastic voice chimed in as she stepped outside. "I'll do it."

Marcus smiled at her as the side door slammed shut. "Deal."

Hannah waved her hand. "Okay, Marcus, step in line with the boys."

Obediently, he made his way in between Isaiah and David.

To make the race seem as important as he could, he knelt and bent his knee, as he'd learned to do when he'd been in track and field at school.

"Okay, on your mark, get set, go!"

Marcus took off running while the boys on both sides of him stood up on their bikes and peddled. He knew his boots were a disadvantage and wished he was wearing tennis shoes; still, the point was to let the boys win anyway. They were so sincere, so earnest, so young.

At the finish line, Mervin shouted, "I won! I won!"

Marcus crossed the line after the boys and congratulated each one for a great race. Hannah began making her way to where they stood. Isaiah turned his bike in the other direction and shouted, "One more time! Now we have to go back!"

"Okay, let's find our positions."

Moving out of their way, Hannah said, "Okay, last race of the day. And the winners get the sponge cakes that are being made."

"Okay. On your mark, get set, go!"

As Marcus and the four made their way to the imaginary finish line, Hannah hollered, "Go, Isaiah! Go, David! Go Mervin! Go, Samuel! Go, Marcus!"

At the line, Marcus threw up his hands in defeat as Samuel screamed victory.

As the boys put away their bikes for the night, Hannah smiled up at Marcus while they stepped through the side door. "I just learned a lot about you."

He arched a brow and looked down at her. "Oh? What?"

She grinned up at him. "Three things. That you're great with kids."

"And?"

She laughed. "That I'll never race you." After a slight pause, she added, "I think you must have been a runner at some time in your life."

"Track and field. Junior high and high school. What's the third thing you learned about me, Miss Lapp?"

"That someday, you'll make a great *daed*."

Chapter Nine

That evening, Hannah smiled as she relaxed on her bedroom rug with her back against her soft mattress. She contemplated the evening and how she felt because of it.

I feel gut. *Inspired. I've met someone I love being with.* She expelled a satisfied sigh as she pulled up her knees and put her notepad on her lap. *But I know I can't share my life with Marcus. He's* Englisch.

She frowned, then decided to distract herself with the story she was writing. *However, in my imagination, we can be together. And in the story I'm dreaming up.*

As she settled into a comfortable position, she glanced down at the notepad on her lap. The warm breeze came in through her window screen, filling the room with the aroma of freshly cut grass. She breathed in and closed her eyes for a moment to savor the sweet smell. When she opened her lids, she quickly went over recent events.

Especially the time she'd spent with Marcus and how he and her nephews had appeared to be one happy family. *If my life were one of my stories, one day Marcus and I would be married.*

Hannah sighed and shook her head as she began to accept her reality. She glanced back down at the lined pages, her attention on what had already happened. *My life can be with Marcus in my fiction.* Her heart began picking up speed to an exciting pace.

As a bright moonbeam soared into her room via her large window, she put pen to paper. To both sides of her, lanterns helped to provide enough light to write by. Ideas sparked in her mind, and she began to fill the first page with ink.

> *Hannah waited. Still no dial tone. Frustrated, she tried again. And again. The phone was dead. Common sense told her that there wasn't time to hitch Miracle to the buggy and get away. She also was fully aware that she couldn't run fast enough to make it to the closest house, which was about two miles away. Maybe she could hide in the nearby cornfield.*
>
> *As she heard the loud noise in back, her instincts told her that whoever had tried to get inside had broken down the door. She looked around for something to use to protect herself. As her gaze locked on the Halon fire extinguisher attached by brackets to the wall, an idea struck her, and she went for it.*
>
> *Her fingers shook as she unlatched two metal brackets and removed the small red extinguisher. In the background, she could hear cabinets opening. Things being thrust against the walls.*
>
> *Extinguisher in hand, she glanced at the seal. She proceeded to twist it off. She'd never used anything like this, but logic told her that all she needed*

*to do to protect herself was to press on the silver
lever and aim at the person's face. If need be, she'd
use it.*

"What would Sydney and Carson do? Would Sydney
think of something better?"

Hannah focused as hard as she could on an answer.
Really, she couldn't know that, as much as she wanted
to. Because she was without her partner.

She continued writing.

*At that very moment, she heard a different
noise. It was the crunching sound of gravel underneath car tires. Her heart pounded to the fierce
beat of survival as she rushed to the front, where
Marcus was pulling into the parking lot of Amish
Edibles. They could use his phone to call for help.*

*Still gripping the Halon extinguisher, she rushed
to him. But while she did so, an armed man wearing a mask ran out the front door.*

*Marcus and Hannah stood absolutely still as he
pointed the gun at Marcus and then at Hannah.
"Don't move or I'll shoot."*

A light knock on the door startled her, and Hannah
straightened and looked toward the sound. Maemm
smiled a little. "May I come in?"

"Sure."

Maemm's gaze landed on Hannah's notepad, and
before she jumped to any conclusions, Hannah explained. "Just doing some writing."

Her mother nodded and came to sit on the edge of
the bed. Hannah wasn't about to tell her what she was

writing. With a slow motion, she closed her pad, set it on the floor, and joined her *maemm* on the quilt.

"Is everything okay?"

Maemm offered an indecisive shrug that indicated something was up. "There's just something I want you to be aware of."

Hannah narrowed her brows and frowned.

"It's about Marcus."

Hannah listened.

"He seems to be a fine young man, but since King's Bakery was robbed, there's been some speculation that Marcus might have been involved. In fact, I heard talk this afternoon in the grocery store."

Frowning, Hannah leaned closer toward her mother. "*Jah?*"

Maemm nodded. "From some of our church friends who were waiting in line. Of course, it's only chitchat. Still, I'm aware that you and Ben's renter have an odd sort of friendship. I just want you to be careful, Hannah. We don't really know him that well."

Hannah stood and looked down at her mother with narrowed eyes. "I can't believe we're even having this conversation. Marcus had absolutely nothing to do with that robbery. And to be honest, I'm surprised at you for even thinking he could be."

Maemm pressed her lips together in silence.

"You and Daed always taught me to give others the benefit of the doubt, didn't you?"

Before Hannah's role model could respond, Hannah went on. Frustration edged her voice. "I know the theft happened right after Marcus came to town, and that's unfortunate. Because Marcus is one of the nicest people

I've ever met. He's trying to start a life for *Gott*. The last thing he'd do is go out and rob a store."

Her *maemm* raised a surprised brow.

"I'm sure Ben would agree."

"Hannah, just be wary . . ."

"I don't need to be wary. Not of Marcus anyway. I'm ashamed of whoever started this gossip. Because that's what it is."

Her mother waved a defensive hand. "I'm sorry, but I thought you needed to know."

"You surely don't think Marcus robbed King's Bakery, do you?"

Finally, Maemm shook her head.

"Marcus had absolutely nothing to do with that robbery." An idea struck her, and she put her hands on her hips. *But how can I prove it?*

The following afternoon, inside Amish Edibles, Marcus met Hannah at the cash register. As he paid for two containers of raspberry jelly, he broached going to church with her family.

She responded with a quick nod, despite the brief conversation she'd endured with her *maemm*. "I think it's *gut*."

As he handed her some bills, he took in her small work area. Again, he glimpsed *The Adventures of Sydney and Carson* sticking out from a shelf near the cash register. Amusement curved his mouth as he answered her question. "I've been giving it a lot of thought."

His gaze stayed on the book.

She looked at him and narrowed her brows. "What?"

He pointed. "Sorry. I just happened to notice. You like adventure stories?"

Her cheeks turned rosy red, and she lowered her gaze.

He softened the pitch of his voice. "It's okay. I just couldn't help but wonder . . ."

She lifted her chin, glanced at the book, and pulled it from the shelf. "Marcus, I just love these adventure books. And please, don't say anything to my brother."

Marcus gave a quick, firm shake of his head. "No worries, Miss Hannah. You've got my word." He paused for a moment before his lips widened into a wide smile. "So, our Hannah's an adventurous woman."

Color returned to her cheeks.

He realized she was extremely embarrassed. In fact, the more he thought about it, the more he acknowledged that Hannah was a far cry from the typical Amish woman, or at least what he knew so far about Amish women. He wanted to reassure her that what she was doing was okay.

"Hannah, there's nothing to be embarrassed about."

Her voice took on a defensive tone. "Who said I was embarrassed?"

He grinned. "The color in your cheeks."

Several heartbeats later, she laughed. He joined her in the laughter.

The pitch of her voice softened. "I just love these." She pointed to the book she was holding.

He took in the bold print. "*The Adventures of Sydney and Carson*."

Without hesitation, she offered an eager nod. "This is just between us . . ."

"Of course."

"Sometimes, Marcus, my life seems . . ."

The pensive look in her eyes told him she was trying for the right word. He thought a moment, then offered, "Mundane?"

She nodded. "I guess you could call it that." The blades of the large battery fan behind them continued to whirl in a continuous motion. The pleasant aroma of cinnamon filled the air. The view outside the front window revealed Hannah's horse, her black buggy, and his Chevy. Fields of corn and soybeans loomed in the distance.

Hannah's pitch took on a more defensive tone as she organized some homemade hot pads into two neat piles. She followed the act by straightening them.

Then she faced him. "Don't get me wrong, Marcus. I'm not complaining. In fact . . ." She offered a gentle lift of her palms. "That's the last thing I'm doing. When I think of my life, I'm sure that I must be the luckiest woman in the world to have been born into so much love."

Her statement warmed his heart, and he was certain that she must be right.

"To you . . . to anyone, really, my life must look aw-fully simple, but all in all, *Gott* has provided me with the things that are most important."

She lifted her hands in front of her and began count-ing with her fingers. "Food on the table. This wonderful store. A Christian family."

After a pause, she continued while enthusiasm lifted the pitch of her voice. "And now, I've met you." She squared her shoulders in confidence. "And that surely must be the ribbon on the package."

He grinned at her analogy.

"I'm blessed with so much, it's a bit overwhelming. What else could I ask for?"

He looked at her to answer her own question. When she didn't, he did it for her. "Good question. What more *could* you possibly want?"

She looked away for a moment, as if considering what to say next. When she finally continued, she looked at Marcus and narrowed her brows. At that particular moment, her face took on the most vulnerable expression.

The sincerity and innocence that filled her eyes and the flush of soft pink that filled her cheeks prompted his heart to speed up its pace to a beat that was a combination of excitement and tenderness. A breath caught in his throat. He couldn't find his voice. All he could think of was how intrigued he was with Hannah Lapp. *What's wrong with me?*

She let out a small sigh. "I guess that, really, there's nothing more for me to yearn for."

Her sentence took an uncertain dip, and he narrowed his brows. "But do you feel something's missing?"

She looked around; he wasn't sure why, no one was there but them. A few seconds later, she waved a dismissive hand. "Marcus, there is something I would like. Something I don't have."

"What is it?"

She pulled in a deep breath and let it out. "If I spill this, you'll be the only one I've told." Before continuing, she waved a dismissive hand. "Just listen to me talk about myself. I feel guilty for even telling you this. Even more so for wanting something I don't even need. I mean, I have everything that's important."

The more she tried to avoid answering his question, the more curious he became about this Amish woman and what she did not have that she obviously yearned for. Something she must feel guilty about. Otherwise, she wouldn't have such difficulty confessing whatever it was.

She motioned to the shelf that held the containers of jelly. At the same time, they stepped to the next row and Hannah began evening the jelly into straight rows.

A long silence ensued before she finally offered him a wide smile. As he watched her slender fingers, he couldn't help but notice what beautiful skin she had. The color reminded him of his mother's porcelain china set. He wondered if her hands were as soft as they looked.

"Sometimes, I would love to hike."

He considered what she'd just said and finally lifted his shoulders into a shrug. "And what's stopping you?"

Her eyes widened. "Nothing, really. I love climbing Pebble Creek, but there are two things missing when I do it."

With growing interest, he waited for her to go on as he pretended an interest in some wooden, hand-carved buggies in front of him.

"I dream of hiking with my husband, a little one on my back, and a whole line of toddlers behind us."

He laughed. She joined him.

"I guess it sounds kind of funny when I say it out loud." She lifted her hands in a helpless gesture. "But that's it, Marcus. That's what I dream of. Nature hiking with my family."

The pitch of his voice lowered into an understanding softness. "Hannah, that's the sweetest thing I've ever heard."

"It is?"

He nodded. "But when you think about it, there's not much, really, stopping you from having your dream. All you've got to do is find a husband. One who likes to hike," he added with an amused chuckle.

"*Jah* . . ." She lowered her voice to a more inquisitive tone. He wondered what was coming next. "Marcus, do you mind me asking you something?"

Wondering what her question would be, he offered a quick shake of his head. "Of course not. Go ahead."

She pressed her lips into a line before meeting his gaze with a serious expression. "I certainly don't have any type of degree in human nature, but I know we are who *Gott* created us to be. And I've always been taught that wanting to be someone else is an insult to *Gott*. But Marcus, do you think there's anything wrong with imagining yourself in a life that's so very different from your own?"

The question didn't take much thought. Several heartbeats later, he offered a decisive shake of his head. "Not at all. I think . . ." He tapped the toe of his boot against the floor and narrowed his brows, trying for the best explanation he could to help Hannah. "Speaking from my own heart, I believe that imagination is an asset, not a liability."

She lifted an uncertain brow.

While he decided his explanation, a fly buzzed in

front of her face, and she swatted it away. She followed the motion by running her palms over her apron to rid it of a small crease.

"Imagination: It's just another unique trait God blessed you with."

That statement seemed to please her. Her eyes lit up.

"Come to think of it, your imagination is kind of a creative thing, don't you think?"

"I'm not sure."

He nodded. "I believe it is." He pressed his lips together a moment while he considered his train of thought. "Having an imagination is like being an artist. Or a writer. In fact, when you get right down to it, imagination comes in handy for a lot of things. Even cooking."

He pointed to the shelves that surrounded them. "Just look at these shelves."

She glanced around the shop before her gaze landed on his face.

He continued, "Almost all your knickknacks were made with imagination."

She nodded in agreement. "What you say certainly makes sense. In fact, I've never thought of it that way. That's an astute observation."

"It's part of you, whether you like it or not. It's something God stuffed into your DNA, Hannah. And being that you were born with that unique trait, I'm not sure you could get rid of it, even if you tried."

"I like the way you reason things out, Marcus. I'm really glad you offered your thoughts." She sighed. "For years, I've been ashamed of my active imagination. Even tried to hide my adventure books. But now, after talking to you, I'm starting to see the upside of it."

"You're welcome." He lifted his chin a notch. "The more I think about it, I guess you could equate your imagination to my interest in cars."

She lifted a brow in interest.

"In no way am I an expert in God's reasoning for creating us the way He did . . ." He wagged a hand and chuckled. "But I think the interests God blessed us with are sort of like the color of our hair and our eyes."

She put a hand on her hip as she waited for him to go on.

He shrugged. "They're God-given, so I think it would be safe to say that an imagination is truly a blessing. And there must have been a reason He incorporated that in your unique self, Hannah."

As they faced each other, the clomp-clomping of hooves could be heard. At the same time, they glanced at the front window to see a horse and buggy traveling the blacktop in front of the shop.

When the Amish mode of transportation faded into the distance, Marcus smiled a little at Hannah.

"You, Hannah Lapp, are very different on the inside from the way you look on the outside."

She lifted an amused brow. "I guess this long dress and *kapp* make me look pretty quiet, huh?"

He thought a moment. "There's nothing wrong with that. At the same time, everyone's got something they like to do. A sport. A hobby."

"I guess you can say reading adventure stories are my sport, then."

He contemplated her response. As he did, unexpected questions sprang into his mind, and an even stronger curiosity about this Amish woman filled his head until he had to have answers.

"Hannah, your love of reading intrigues me."

"Don't you enjoy reading?"

"I do. But not like you do, I don't think. I go for car magazines. Mechanic stuff." Suddenly, he realized that he'd lost track of the time, and he glanced at his watch. He straightened and nodded toward the door. "I should get going."

Hannah followed him as they moved closer to the entrance. He turned the knob and glanced back at Hannah. "I've about used up my break." He winked. "Now, it's back to work." He stepped away before turning to her.

"There's something . . ."

She narrowed her brows. "What?"

He shrugged. "I just remembered something I wanted to mention."

"What?" she asked.

"It's about going to church with you. Let's make sure we're on the same page."

His comment prompted Hannah to frown. "What?"

"My past . . . I mean, I'm new at being a Christian. And to be honest, Hannah, I feel like I don't quite measure up to your family."

Surprise flickered in her eyes. "Marcus, church people are simply that."

He cocked his head.

She nodded. "People who go to church." She lifted her palms to the ceiling. "That's all we are. And believe me, nobody at church is perfect. In fact, Maemm used to say that church is a place for sinners."

He considered her reasoning.

"Marcus, that's why we go. Of course, we go to worship. But we also are there to repent. As a new believer, you might think that everyone in church is pure." She offered a disappointed shrug. "We're not."

"I've never really thought of it like that."

"Still, I would never want you to be uncomfortable. I'd hope that wouldn't be the case. Even though you're not Amish."

He looked at her to go on.

"You don't have to be Amish to worship *Gott*, Marcus."

She stopped. He studied her. The expression on her face was uncertain. It was as if she might go back on what she'd said. But she didn't. And finally, she smiled a little.

"You're *gut* for me, Marcus."

"In what way?"

"You make me think about things. Before, I'd never really given much thought to the way others worship. But just now, I realized that we can't all worship the same. What I am sure of is that Scripture speaks the truth. In the Book of John, you'll find a verse that says whoever believes will have eternal life. And with all the people in the world, being raised by different mothers and fathers who've had different life experiences, there's no way everyone could ever worship in the very same way. In fact, that would be impossible."

Marcus parted his lips in surprise and contemplated what he'd just heard.

She softened her pitch. "The point of going to church

is to worship and to glorify *Gott*. At least, that's the way it should be."

Marcus nodded in agreement.

"And I don't think there's anyone who doesn't want to be forgiven of their sins. I suppose that there's this big misconception by many."

He lifted a brow.

"That churchgoers are without sin. But Marcus, they're not."

"I like the way you see things, Hannah. You've just convinced me to come. That is, if it's okay with your parents. I would like their approval. And I also want to make sure folks know I'm there because of Ben's invite, not yours."

After clearing his throat, he went on. "I mean, I know how strict your faith is about dating and things like that. I guess what I'm saying is that I want to make sure gossip doesn't start about the two of us. Because I'm there with your family."

She looked at him with an expression that was an odd mixture of anticipation and uncertainty.

"Both you and Ben have invited me, and I'm grateful. At the same time, I want to make sure that it's obvious I'm there with your brother."

Outside, Miracle let out a loud whinny. Automatically, Hannah glanced toward the sound.

"It might sound like a ridiculous request, but you've got an impeccable reputation to protect. And I can only imagine what people would say if they thought we were together. An innocent Amish woman and an *Englischer* from the city," he added.

She considered his wisdom and realized that he did

make a *gut* point. She could imagine the talk that would start if her congregation got wind that she'd invited him to church. And that talk would most likely turn into gossip. Sad, but true. Even more disappointing was that Marcus was being mentioned as a possible suspect in the robbery.

Hannah carefully weighed the advantages of having Marcus at church against the disadvantages. Her opinion automatically left her lips. "I know how easily talk could start about us. At the same time, I'm sure *Gott* wants you at our church."

Hannah wanted so desperately to warn Marcus of the gossip that was brewing. But what purpose would it serve? He had enough on his plate right now, and the last thing she wanted was for him to know how cruel and irresponsible people could be. And she definitely wouldn't mention that she was trying to think of a way to catch the thief.

They studied each other for several moments before Marcus furthered the conversation. "I really like you, Hannah." A long silence ensued, until he finally added another sentence. "I guess what I'm afraid of more than anything is that people will be able to read my thoughts."

The following day, Marcus contemplated his conversation with Hannah while he helped Ben carry a long pipe for water irrigation into the welding room. The more he thought about her dream of hiking with her husband and children, the more he wondered who she'd marry. He found himself imagining a life with Hannah.

He smiled a little before looking around and returning to reality.

A strange sense of déjà vu hit him. He swallowed an emotional knot. Everything around him looked pretty much like where he'd worked in Chicago. As a mixture of noises filled the air, he took in the particulars. To his right was a bench grinder to sharpen tools. To his left was a hand grinder to bevel edges. His former company even had the same off-white paint on the walls.

Ben's voice pulled him from his reverie. "Hey, I have something to share with you. Something that'll make you smile."

Glancing at him, Marcus was careful to balance his part of the pipe before setting it down. "One, two, three." At the same time, they laid their ends on the cement floor.

"It was nice having you at dinner last night. Apparently, you made quite an impression on my boys. After you left, you're all they talked about."

An amused smile tugged the corners of Marcus's lips up as he recalled racing the energized youngsters who were so full of life. And happiness. For a moment, Marcus recalled his own childhood and knew that his joyful life had quickly evaporated with the loss of his parents. The moment he'd learned of his parents' auto accident, his life had gone south.

Marcus rubbed his hands together and eyed Ben. Then he realized that Ben was awaiting a response. A laugh escaped Marcus's throat. "Ya know, that's the most fun I've had in years. And I owe it all to you. And your kids, in particular. They're fantastic."

"*Denki*, Marcus."

Memories of being with the large family, with all the casserole dishes in the middle of the table, brought on a warmth inside him. "In fact, everyone at your house was so down-to-earth and so kind. And the dinner . . ." Marcus let out a low whistle. "I've never had anything like it. And if I understand correctly, everything, even the butter, was homemade."

"You've got that right." Ben gave a firm shake of his head before he grinned. "It could be I'm partial, but Amish women are great cooks."

"I won't argue that one."

As Marcus stepped to his work spot to light his torch, he grabbed his protective goggles. Before he put them on, Ben came over to where he was and lowered the pitch of his voice to a concerned tone. "I hope everything at the house is okay."

Automatically, Marcus offered a quick nod while he moved the beam so it would have direct sunlight from the side window. He let out a satisfied breath and assured Ben he had everything he needed. "Hey, and thanks again for the bed frame and mattress. And especially Ruth's meals."

An amused grin curved Ben's lips a little. "We were concerned about how little you brought with you. I'm not one to probe, but Ruth and I do care about you. My wife's got this protective nature. And she wants to make sure you're okay."

While Marcus considered his friend's statement, he reassured him that everything was fine. And because of all the Lapp family had done for him, he figured Ben deserved a brief explanation.

"My life in Chicago . . ." He gave a sad shake of his

head and looked down at his boots. "Like I told you, it was bad. I don't want you to worry about me or anything, but after I lost my parents to a car accident some years ago, everything changed with a snap of the fingers, that's for sure."

"I'm sorry. Losing two parents at once . . ." Ben's smile sank, and so did his shoulders. "That's a tough one."

"Yeah. But my three brothers took it worse than I did. I guess you could say they went off the deep end. Started doing drugs, and selling them. I'm ashamed to admit that they even landed themselves in jail."

Ben's jaw dropped. Several moments later, he edged his voice with sympathy. "I'm praying for them every night, Marcus."

Marcus lifted his shoulder a confident notch. "God led me here." After a brief silence, Marcus softened his voice to an emotional pitch. "And I already feel like He's putting me on the right path. By my meeting your family." After he cleared his throat, he softened his voice. "There's something I promised my mom. A long time ago."

Ben arched a curious brow.

"To follow my heart. And I guess you could say that my heart brought me here."

Ben's eyes sparkled with moisture. Marcus was quick to catch the emotion that edged his voice when he spoke. "*Gott* works in amazing ways. Now I not only consider you a brother, but you're a brother in Christ, and know that I'll do everything within my power to help you grow in the Christian faith."

"I appreciate that, Ben. I want to learn everything there is to know about the Bible and, eventually, get involved in some way to help young people find Jesus, just like I did."

"The Amish, well, we're a bit different from you *Englisch* folk." He winked. "But one thing's for sure: We try to follow the Bible and Scripture. And I sure am glad you're coming to church with us on Sunday."

Marcus offered a quick nod. "I'm looking forward to it."

Ben's eyes lightened, as if an idea had struck him. "Me too." Several heartbeats later, he softened the pitch of his voice. "Would you like to ride in the buggy with us?" Before Marcus could respond, Ben cut in. "I know the boys would love it."

Marcus smiled and offered a definitive nod. After Ben placed a friendly pat on his shoulder and walked away, Marcus pulled his welding goggles over his head. His thoughts about the boys drew a smile, but when he thought about being in church with Hannah, his heart warmed. As an image of Hannah came to mind, he envisioned her hiking up Pebble Creek with a baby clutched to her chest. The sleeves of Hannah's blue dress were rolled up to her forearms. Loose hairs had escaped her *kapp*. A string of toddlers followed her. Some were skipping. A small boy, barefoot and wearing suspenders, stopped to pick a wildflower along the way. And a little girl ran up to walk between Hannah and the man who walked beside her.

A knot stuck in his throat. Because that man was him.

Sunday morning, Marcus sat on the bench of Ben's buggy with Isaiah and Mervin on the left and David on the right. As their horse swished its tail, Marcus took in the uneven clomp-clomping sound.

Ruth and Samuel were in front with Ben. Marcus couldn't stop thinking with an amused smile that, apparently, there wasn't a law against having seven in a buggy. They were all bunched together. And warmth filled his heart.

As Marcus contemplated what he was about to do—attend an Amish church service—he straightened, suddenly acknowledging that he was nervous. "Ben, will we sit together?"

He nodded. "Basically, the women all sit in one half of the room, and the men sit in the other. We take communion twice a year." After a slight pause, he added, "Oh, and the sermon will be in German."

"Okay. Thanks for the heads-up. I'll try to understand as much as I can. My high-school German sure is coming in handy these days. I look forward to meeting Annie and Levi Miller, and Rebecca and William Conrad." He let out a small sigh of relief.

What is there to fear, really? I want so very much to learn about the One who created me and gave me breath, and this is as good a place to learn as any. Of course, my German is far from proficient. Dear Lord, please help me to relax and enjoy this time of worship with others who want to serve You. Amen.

I will get to see Hannah. That particular thought made the speed of the pulse on his wrist pick up to a quick pace. *I know I must be careful to hide my strong feelings for her. I'm sure rumors could spread like wildfire about me and the beautiful, kind Hannah.*

He decided to relax and make conversation. Before

he could get a word in, two little voices piped up, "Marcus, are you going to eat lunch with us?"

Marcus couldn't stop the grin that tugged the corners of his lips upward. He glanced at the boys, who were dressed to perfection, from their crisp white shirts and suspenders to their shiny shoes. He couldn't help but note the difference from the boys who rode their bikes with such vigor. "That's the plan."

"*Gut!*"

When Isaiah became restless and kicked the back of the front bench, he got a quick, stern scolding from his dad. Immediately, the youngster sat back quietly.

"So church is at the Yoders' house today?" Marcus inquired as the sun brightened a notch. In the distance, the landscape looked the same as when they'd started their morning ride a short time ago.

On both fields, tall corn and soybeans loomed, with an occasional white, two-story house stuck in somewhere. Marcus spotted another horse-pulled buggy on a different blacktop.

Ben offered a quick nod as he veered his horse and carriage to the side of the road to allow an oncoming car to get by. As Marcus bounced in his seat, he couldn't help but compare the narrow blacktop that was raised in the middle to Chicago's six-lane I-94. Also, this seemed to be a relaxed ride. Buggy drivers didn't try to pass other buggies the way cars did on the freeway. And there wasn't loud music blaring.

Sadness swept through him as he thought of his brothers. He was most certain they wouldn't be inside a church today. What were they doing? He squeezed his eyes closed and said a silent prayer. *Dear Lord,*

*please take charge of their lives and lead them to follow
You. Amen.*

Ben's calm, low voice brought Marcus back to what
he was doing. Rather, what he was about to do. He
clutched the Bible on his lap. "Almost there. And
Marcus, I want you to know how glad I am that you're
with us."

"Me too," chimed in small voices.

As the warm summer air floated through the buggy,
Marcus smiled a little. Because worshipping with this
family was a true blessing from God. His heart warmed
at the thought of the boys. Of Ben and Ruth. And he
swallowed an emotional knot. Because he realized that
he truly considered them family.

That evening, in her bedroom, Hannah closed the
door behind her and reflected on the day. Most especially, she thought back on how she'd felt having Marcus
at church. As the moonbeam floated in through the
window and the warm breeze came in with the smell of
the outdoors, Hannah retrieved her notepad and pen, sat
down on her floor rug, and rested her back against her
soft quilt.

She expelled a small sigh as a myriad of thoughts
floated through her head until she finally closed her
eyes and took a deep breath to relax. Marcus being at
church had felt right. He seemed to fit in. Despite
Hannah's sentiments, though, she'd taken note of how a
small group of women had frowned at him.

Of course, Hannah had not been surprised at the stir
of conversation prompted by an *Englischer* from the
city joining their congregation of two hundred and some

people. Hannah wondered how many of her church
friends actually thought Marcus had played a role in
robbing King's Bakery. She was glad she didn't know,
because she would be extremely disappointed in them.

She narrowed her brows pensively and looked down
at where she'd stopped in her own fiction. *Where did I
leave off in* The Adventures of Hannah and Marcus*?*
She strummed her fingers against the paper and finally
gave a slight nod of her head. *It's where the thief points
a gun at Marcus and then at her. Hannah's still holding
the extinguisher.*

The rest of the story began to take root in her mind,
and Hannah put pen to paper.

> *The gun was pointed directly at Marcus. The tip
> almost touched his nose. Hannah drew in a breath
> as her heart pumped a million miles a minute. The
> Halon extinguisher slipped from her hands. But
> Gott sent a blessing. Miracle let out a loud whinny
> that broke the dead silence.*
>
> *At that very unexpected moment, the man hold-
> ing the gun glanced in the direction of the sound.
> The second he did so, Marcus lunged toward the
> intruder, and, with one swift motion, shoved him to
> the ground. He proceeded to kick the gun out of
> his hands.*
>
> *Immediately, Hannah rushed for the weapon
> and kicked it farther away from the intruder. As
> she did so, her entire body shook.*
>
> *When she turned around, she saw that the thief
> was pinned facedown under Marcus. The two were
> engaged in what appeared to be a wrestling match.*
>
> *Hannah had an idea.*

As she rushed to the men, she pulled a piece of strong twine from her pocket. It was from a box she'd opened earlier. Remembering a scene from Sydney and Carson, *she quickly created a handcuff knot with two loops. She slipped the two loops around the intruder's ankles as Marcus held him down. She pulled the loops tight, but not so tight that it would cut off his circulation.*

No doubt this would keep him from moving. Marcus rolled the intruder onto his back and had the thief's hands.

"I've got more string! I'll tie his hands."

Marcus held the man's hands, palms facing out, while Hannah did another handcuff knot around the man's wrists. And prayed that Gott *would send help right away.*

Chapter Ten

Marcus's heart was leading him in a straight path to Hannah Lapp. But the more definitive his dream became, the more impossible reaching it seemed. Midday the following Saturday, Marcus sat at his small kitchen table eating a chicken salad sandwich. The longer he lived in this house, the more he appreciated Ruth's cooking.

Today's barn raising had been canceled due to the forecast for rain. As he chewed a bite, Marcus closed his eyes in delight and swallowed.

It didn't take him long to devour the remainder of the salad on his plate and push his paper dining wear to the side. In its place he opened up his new automobile magazine. It had come in the mail that morning, and he couldn't wait to look through it.

A warm, comfortable breeze came in through his opened window screens. Every once in a while, thunder rumbled in the distance. Rain was in the forecast, but not until later. Today, he just wanted to enjoy his free time. To appreciate that God had given him life.

It was nice to have a moment to absorb everything that had happened since his move from Chicago. He attempted to make sense of his feelings for Hannah and apply good logic to why he should immediately erase her from his mind.

There was no doubt he was falling in love with her. The longer he convinced himself that he wanted to spend the rest of his life with her, the more difficult it would be in the long run to give her up.

He emptied the remaining contents of the plastic bottle down his throat, returned the bottle to the spot in front of him, leaned back in his chair, and extended his legs.

He bent to grab the new magazine, removed the rubber band around it, and turned the pages to the newest Chevy SUV model. As he stared at the shiny black vehicle, he vividly recalled the last time he and his dad had taken their family car for a cruise on I-94.

Salty tears stung Marcus's eyes. But he didn't blink. Instead, he took the sting and prayed with his eyes open. "Dear Heavenly Father, please forgive my parents of their sins and bless them with eternal life in heaven. Please ease my pain because I miss them so much, it hurts. Amen."

As he stared at the vintage Chevy, he smiled a little. He vividly recalled his last ride with his dad. The smile on his father's face imprinted its mark in Marcus's thoughts as the warm summer breeze had floated in from all four open car windows.

The image seemed so real. Marcus bit his lower lip. Since his parents passed, a part of him had been missing. To his astonishment, this was the first time he had acknowledged it. He wanted his good life back. Yearned for it so much, he could almost feel it.

Follow your heart. He'd given his mother his word he'd carry out her advice. Of course, when he'd promised, he'd been young. At the time, he hadn't the faintest clue what a complicated request he'd committed to. Still, he'd given her his word. And a promise was a promise.

Following his heart was proving to be the most difficult task he'd ever undertaken. Because when he'd so casually committed, he'd had no idea that he would fall in love with an Amish woman. That a life with her would involve giving up what had bonded him and his father together. Their love for Chevrolets. Working on them. Talking about them. Driving them.

How could I ever give that up? It would be like emptying my dad from my life. He gave a frustrated shake of his head. Afterward, he considered his mother and Hannah. And how they were similar in personality. *Would Mom approve of Hannah?*

He nodded. The answer came easily. And Marcus had no doubt she would love Hannah's quilt. The raspberry jelly she made at home and sold in Amish Edibles. Even her love of adventure stories. Marcus grinned at a memory of his mom with a paperback in her hands.

Each night in the Jackson home, while his dad had watched the evening news, the mother of four had held a mystery in her hands. The memory of his mom's love of reading reminded him of Hannah.

Yes, Hannah would definitely have fit right in with his family. In many ways, she was so like his mom. However, that her faith didn't approve of driving made her much, much different. Amazingly, living without electricity was much easier than he'd imagined. In fact,

Marcus hadn't really given up that much since moving into Ben's rental.

He still had night lighting, thanks to the gas line that ran along the kitchen ceiling. He didn't have a washer and dryer; still, he could, if he wanted. The Amish didn't use electricity; however, they compensated in other ways that were compatible with their *Ordnung*.

The sound of laughter prompted him to stand and step to the window. Outside, in the distance, the four Lapp boys raced their bikes up and down the long drive that connected his house to theirs.

Watching them tugged at his heartstrings until a knot blocked his throat. He swallowed to rid himself of the discomfort. He wasn't sure why his reaction was an odd combination of happiness and sadness. He finally reasoned that the happiness was because they reminded him of when he and his brothers had been young with two living parents.

And sadness because that carefree life was gone. Now a sense of urgency filled him because he feared for his brothers' life paths . . . not only here on earth, but also in eternity. Did they even believe in God?

The last thing he wanted to do was to judge others; however, their actions caused him to think that they probably didn't. Yes, Isaiah, David, Samuel, and Mervin reminded him of a time in his past that had been nothing less than blissful.

Be optimistic. He lifted his chin a notch. He was thankful that he'd been proactive in his move to live for God. He expelled a sigh that was a combination of satisfaction and relief. *At the same time, I feel stuck. How can I feel stuck if I'm relieved I'm where I am?*

Which direction do I head to serve my Creator? There are numerous churches, many of which have much more lenient rules. My family used to attend a Methodist church. But obviously, what my brothers and I learned there didn't stick. Follow your heart.

A chill ran up his spine, and he shook his shoulders to ease the uncomfortable sensation. His mother's advice was beginning to drive him crazy. Had she known, at the time, that her words would be so difficult to carry out?

He cleared a knot from his throat before praying in a soft, urgent voice: "I believe that You've given me Hannah and her family to ease my pain. And Lord, You know I love her. And I love everything the Amish stand for. But even if I joined their church, deep down inside, I don't know if I could ever be the man Hannah deserves. At the same time, Father in heaven, you know it's important to me to keep my commitment to my mother."

He hesitated, contemplating his promise to her. Then he continued in a hoarse tone, finally squeezing his lids closed with a sense of desperation. "You know I can't alter how I've lived the past two and a half decades, and You are aware of how difficult it would be for me to give up driving my Chevrolet, the very thing that emotionally connects me to my dad. Even changing the oil makes me feel close to him. And I don't know if I could ever give that up. So, I'm asking You to please let me know Your will. And I pray that You will save my brothers and that we'll all spend eternity with You. Amen."

I'm here on this earth to serve God. I'm not here for me. I am trying to move on with my life. But the two roads from which I can choose lead to two totally different worlds. One has Hannah; one doesn't.

Unfortunately, Marcus hadn't been privy to Old Sam's wisdom, but something Hannah had mentioned gave him a silent nudge. She'd said that whenever Old Sam had been unsure about what to do, he'd gone to the Bible.

Narrowing his brows thoughtfully, Marcus stepped toward his only piece of living room furniture, a small oak stand, and stared at the leather cover in front of him. The Holy Bible.

His instincts told him that every answer he needed was in these pages with bold print. *But this book has many, many pages.* He stopped to put his logic to work. *How will I even begin to find what I'm looking for?*

She needed to be here. She just did. That afternoon, as her mother ran the shop, Hannah took in the wonder of Pebble Creek. At home, her yeast bread was rising. Emotion tugged at her heart while she contemplated every feeling whirling inside her. The thief who'd robbed King's Bakery still hadn't been caught.

While Hannah thought long and hard about the theft, uncertainty swept through her chest until it ached. She'd allowed the police time to do their jobs. But so far, nothing.

So it was *gut* to be alone to sort things out. To Hannah, this place was sacred. Longingly, she fixed her gaze at the top of the hill, where Annie and Levi Miller had placed their sitting stones years ago, and where Old Sam had asked his wife of nearly sixty years, Esther, to spend the rest of their lives together.

Nothing bad has ever happened here. At least, not

that I'm aware of. On the contrary, great memories were made at Pebble Creek. Will Gott *bless me with something so precious that I will one day call Pebble Creek my special place?*

Today, Ben had canceled the barn raising. Apparently, they were ready to lay cement, which would have to wait until after the rain that was predicted. So Hannah had time to reflect. And that was exactly what she intended to do.

Because so much had happened since Marcus Jackson had stepped into Amish Edibles and purchased her raspberry jelly, she wasn't sure what to think any more. She'd allowed her heart to go where she'd never imagined. And now she acknowledged that they were emotions without direction.

As large, white, fluffy clouds moved across the sky, Hannah looked up at the top and smiled a little. She put her hands on her hips and pressed her lips together thoughtfully. *I need to sort out my feelings for Marcus.*

At that, she started her way up. She hadn't seen Marcus since Sunday, but she'd thought about him all week. About them. About the sense of familiarity and satisfaction that had filled her while she'd been at church with him.

She'd barely said two words to him, and he'd spoken very little to her. However, she was fully aware that he'd been trying to protect her, and for that, she loved him even more. But she needed to protect him. From unfounded speculation that he'd robbed King's Bakery.

And that was why she'd decided to take this walk up Pebble Creek. To make clearer her feelings for Marcus and where to go with them. And to decide the best way to catch the person who'd robbed King's Bakery so people would stop thinking Marcus had done it.

A fly buzzed close to her ear, and she swatted it away. *Wonder if* Maemm *could get this one.* She stopped for a moment, contemplating her parents. She loved her *maemm* with all her heart. But she'd never been able to please her. At least, that's what Hannah believed.

But her *daed* . . . Hannah drew her arms across her chest and pulled in an emotional breath. Her *daed* loved her unconditionally. Always had.

The sound of light footsteps made her turn. Startled, her jaw dropped. "Marcus, *gut* afternoon."

"Hello, Hannah. I didn't expect to see you here."

She hesitated, considering his statement. "Same here." After a lengthy silence, she decided to go for complete honesty. "I have a lot on my mind. Pebble Creek is where Old Sam found answers. Levi and Annie, too. So, I figured . . ."

"You might find answers here, too."

She nodded. At the same time, they started walking. Thunder crackled. "Rain's coming."

Hannah nodded. "*Jah.*" She pointed to the sky. "Not till later today, though."

She considered the way he seemed more pensive than usual. His set jaw. "Marcus?"

He looked at her.

"Is something wrong?"

After a slight hesitation, he asked, "Hannah, do you ever get the feeling that you're supposed to do something, but you don't know what it is?"

She laughed. Because that mimicked her sentiment. "That's how I feel right now."

"Me too."

Hannah decided on brutal honesty and tried for the best words to speak what was on her mind. "Marcus, I've been praying for us."

He glanced down at her and narrowed his brows as they stepped up the hill.

"I have strong feelings for you, and, well . . ."

She paused for a moment. "Ever since we met, I've been thinking about you."

Sincerity filled his voice. "Me too, Hannah. You're on my mind all the time. I told you about the promise I made to my mom."

"To follow your heart."

"It was really important to her because she'd married my dad when they were young, despite her parents' disapproval. Apparently, they'd wanted her to wed someone who provided a better living for their daughter. And at the time they married, my dad was working on the roads for the state of Illinois."

Hannah contemplated his words.

"It was one night before bedtime. I promised my mom I'd follow my heart." He offered a slight shrug of his shoulders. "At the time, I had no idea what I was committing to. To be honest, Hannah, with you, it's not simple."

Immediately, she understood. Because she felt the same way. "I know, Marcus. I mean, you're a Christian. I'm a Christian. But our lives . . ." She offered an uncertain shrug as she lowered her voice. "I realize that it would be hard for you to live the way I do. You surely plan on going back to the city, don't you?"

A long silence ensued before he finally responded. "I don't know."

His response stopped her. In fact, what he'd replied gave her hope that he might stay and join her faith.

"Hannah, I love it here."

For long moments, she took in the deep green of his eyes and the flecks that hovered in the background. She'd never felt like this about a man. Even so, she was fully aware that she and Marcus Jackson were still worlds apart.

Finally, they continued up the hill in a silence that was a strange combination of comfort and uneasiness.

Hannah's *maemm* had always told her not to be so straightforward. But Hannah's nature wasn't to be shy. And today, she was true to herself. "Marcus, do you suppose you could join our church?"

Before he responded, she took a small breath and went on in her most logical tone. "When you were at church with us last Sunday?" She shrugged and darted him a half smile that was edged with a pinch of hopefulness. "It just seemed so right."

She hoped he'd agree. But Hannah was fully aware that she couldn't make him want to be who she wanted him to be. Still, she waited for some sign of agreement. Moments later, he stopped and looked down at her.

As she gazed up at him, she knew that true love was rare. And at that very moment, she knew, without a doubt, that they had it. She felt it throughout her entire body; the realization was so strong, it was a part of her. It didn't matter that neither had confessed that love. Still, he was *Englisch*. And she was Amish.

And the difference between the two was much more

involved than merely liking different flavors of ice cream. But there was another thing Marcus wasn't aware of. And that was talk of his possible involvement in the robbery. Something she was determined to end.

"Hannah, I have this emotional connection to my dad. It's Chevrolets. Ya see, when he was alive, cars were our common interest. The bond that made us close. We even put a new engine in an old Camaro together. And to give that up . . ."

Sadly, she understood where he was coming from. "Marcus, I wouldn't ever want you to make a decision that your heart couldn't go along with. I guess, well, it would be like me joining a faith that didn't allow me to read adventure books."

He laughed.

She joined in the laughter. "We're so serious today."

"I know. Do you think God will find a way for us to be together?"

She shrugged. "I don't know. Because I only see two options. That you become Amish. Or that I be *Englisch*. And I think that if either of us changed, we'd be giving up a huge part of ourselves."

"You think Old Sam would've had a solution?"

The question prompted the corners of her lips to curve upward. "*Jah*. I do. He got answers from reading the Bible. Marcus, tonight, before you go to bed, would you ask *Gott* if there's a way for us to be together?" Before he could say yes or no, she added, "And I'll do the same."

He lifted his palms to the sky with a helpless expression. "Maybe God led me here to talk to you."

His sincerity warmed her heart. For some reason,

she was sure that what he'd just said was true. Looking around, she stopped and smiled at him before her gaze wandered up the top of the hill.

"History was made up there," she said in a soft voice.

He smiled a little. "Then we'd better venture up there to experience it."

The idea made Hannah sigh with relief.

He motioned in the direction of the hill. "After you." He hesitated. "But what if the rain starts early?"

She shrugged. "We'll be okay."

Hannah stepped ahead of him before he joined her.

"It's beautiful here. Even with the sun behind the clouds."

She glanced up at him. To her surprise, there was an expression on his face that she'd never seen before. Light lines edged the corners of his eyes. His jaw was set. She changed her focus to the ground, careful not to lose her footing on the unlevel terrain.

In silence, they walked for some time, occasionally glancing down at the sprawling stream. Hannah began to relax. She pointed. "I've told you a little bit about Pebble Creek."

He gently bumped into her as he changed his path to avoid a stone. "Sorry."

"It's fine." A mélange of stories about what had happened on this very hill floated through Hannah's mind until she parted her lips in awe.

"So Old Sam owned Pebble Creek, and now that he's gone, it belongs to his great-niece. Is that true?"

Automatically, she nodded. "*Jah*. It's such a long story; in fact, Pebble Creek is really a number of stories. And at the end, they all spell true love."

"We talked a little about Old Sam when we washed the dishes after we ate dinner at Ben's. I'd like to hear more."

"I never knew his wife, Esther. I've heard a lot about her."

"Oh?"

"Old Sam Beachy was something of a legend. He lived to be just over a hundred."

The pitch of Marcus's voice lifted in surprise. "You don't say."

"Uh-huh."

Hannah paused for a moment as she stopped to tuck a hair back under her *kapp*. Next to her, Marcus stopped, too. While she shoved the strand under the covering, she heard Marcus expel a satisfied breath.

She looked up at him and smiled a little. "It's breath-taking, isn't it?"

He nodded as they stepped upward. "It is. And now you've got me hooked on Old Sam and Esther Beachy. I can't wait to hear what happened to them."

"I'll tell you," Hannah said as she swung her hands back and forth to pick up speed as the hill steepened. "Esther went to the Lord years ago, but Old Sam talked about her all the time. Especially while he made hope chests."

"I did hear something about that."

"*Jah.* Years ago, when he lost Esther, Annie, Rachel, and Rebecca tried everything they could to make sure he was okay. And because of that, he loved the three like they were his own."

"What did they do to help him?"

"Rebecca Sommer; now it's Rebecca Conrad . . ."

"Yes, I met her at church. Lovely lady."

"She took him fresh flowers. Annie Mast, now she's Annie Miller, baked him sponge cakes, because Esther wasn't around to do it. And Rachel, she married Doc Zimmerman; he's the vet everyone around here relies on . . . she listened to his horse-and-buggy stories."

Marcus chuckled. "Sounds like Old Sam was a lucky man."

Hannah grinned at the thought of the three trying to take care of him. "I think so. Anyway, those three supposedly were recipients of the most beautiful hope chests Sam ever made."

"I believe you. But what is it that made his hope chests special?"

"It wasn't the actual chests; it was the lids. I think I told you, Old Sam was extremely talented at etching designs into the wood. His carvings actually looked real."

"Interesting."

"And he designed lids for people all over the United States. Personalized lids; for example, Annie's had a sponge cake recipe. Rebecca's was a bouquet and Rachel's was a horse and buggy."

Marcus stopped for a moment. Hannah did, too, and she put her hands on her hips while she caught her breath.

"Marcus, the top of this hill was a very special place for Old Sam. The story goes that he'd made Esther a very special gift to celebrate their sixtieth wedding anniversary."

"What a blessing, Hannah."

"Well, unfortunately, Esther passed before that day. But Old Sam wanted to make the occasion really special, so he hid her gift." Hannah swallowed an emotional knot. "At the top of Pebble Creek."

In silence, the two stood next to each other while the sun smiled down on them. Hannah closed her eyes for a moment to enjoy the warmth. As she pondered Old Sam putting so much love into a present for his beloved wife, a tear of joy started down her cheek, but she caught it with her hand.

Marcus spoke in a softened voice. "I can already feel the special ambience of this place."

She turned to him. "*Jah?*"

"Uh-huh. Hannah, this is a very special day for both of us. In fact, already I have so much appreciation for Pebble Creek and what it meant to Old Sam. I've no doubt he was a good mentor."

The observation took Hannah by surprise, and she stopped to look at him. "That's interesting."

"What?"

"I've heard Old Sam referred to as many wonderful things, but it's the first time I've ever heard the word 'mentor' associated with him. But you're right. He mentored Annie, Rebecca, and Rachel . . ." She threw her hands in the air as a honeybee buzzed close to them. "And so many more people."

In silence, they continued stepping up the hill. For a moment, Hannah stopped to catch her breath. Automatically, she turned to look down at where they'd started. Marcus did the same.

He let out a low whistle. "Now that's something ya don't see in the city."

Hannah laughed. "I don't imagine you would." A few

moments later, she softened her pitch to a more serious tone. "You really love it here, don't you?"

An odd combination of happiness and sadness filled his eyes. She understood why he'd be happy. At Pebble Creek, who wouldn't? She didn't want to pry, but suddenly, she guessed that the sadness in his expression must have to do with why he'd ventured here for a walk. After all, Pebble Creek wasn't exactly in his backyard.

As they stood in a comfortable silence, he glanced down at her.

A long silence ensued while she studied Marcus. The lines around his mouth finally relaxed, and he smiled a little. "You're good for me, Hannah."

She tried to understand why.

He went on to explain, "You're the epitome of what a Christian should be." He lifted his palms to the sky and gave a defeated shake of his head. "We have to forgive, don't we?"

She nodded.

"I guess that being a Christian is so new to me, I'm slowly realizing exactly what it means to follow Christ. And now I clearly see that it's not always going to be easy to do that."

"I know people in our church who struggle to forgive. Marcus, pray for help. Sometimes we just can't do what's expected of us on our own. But that's what faith and prayer are all about."

At the same time, they began taking slow steps up the hill again. Hannah decided to share some of Old Sam with Marcus. She spoke softly as she looked up at the top of the hill.

"Marcus, *Gott* makes all things possible. That's what

Old Sam always said. And even after he lost his four sons and his wife, he never complained."

Catching her breath, she held up the bottom of her dress to avoid tripping in a place where the earth dipped. In the process, she bumped into Marcus.

"Sorry about that."

"You're fine. But please . . . go on. Tell me more about Old Sam."

"He loved animals, Marcus."

"Yeah?"

"Uh-huh. I'm told he always had at least one horse. As well as a dog, squirrels, and basically any furry creature who needed him. And he spoiled them rotten."

Marcus laughed. "I like him already. And I've never even met him." After a thoughtful silence, he lifted the pitch of his voice to a more optimistic one. "I wish I could meet Old Sam, Hannah. It sounds like he had a lot of wisdom."

"*Jah*, he did. In fact, word has it that when Annie Mast was about to lose Levi Miller, she went to Old Sam for advice. He gave it. She followed it. And in the end, the two married."

Hannah would give anything to ask Old Sam what to do. Because she couldn't picture Marcus giving up the life he'd always had, including a car and a cell phone, to join the Amish faith. And she knew that in her heart, she could never be anything but who she was.

Hannah Lapp, an Amish country girl, wanted more than anything to marry within her church, and although Marcus was a true believer, trying to follow the path Christ had paved for him, she couldn't imagine any life other than what she had. Growing old within the Amish church with all the families she'd known forever.

They continued walking. Hannah sensed that something serious was on Marcus's mind. She was dying to know what it was; maybe she could help. At the same time, she didn't want to pry.

Maemm had once told her that loving someone meant being there for them, even with no words said. And oftentimes, Hannah had been told, it was best not to ask. When the loved one was ready to talk, they would come to you.

Marcus lightened the pitch of his voice to a more upbeat tone. "You think Sam's anniversary gift for Esther is still buried at the top of this hill?"

Hannah's heart warmed as she recalled the beautiful story. She couldn't wait to share it with Marcus.

"You want to hear what happened?" Before he could answer, she went on. "It's pretty amazing."

At the same time, they stopped. Hannah put her hands on her hips. "We're almost there."

"And I can't wait to hear it!" Curiosity edged his voice.

They resumed their pace. "I don't know every single detail, but the story goes that dear Old Sam loved Esther so very much, he decided to give her something very unique and special for their sixtieth wedding anniversary."

Marcus whistled. "Six decades of marriage." His body touched Hannah's as he stepped around a bump in the ground. As he got back into step at her side, she immediately missed the comforting feel of his nearness.

She was fully aware of the strict rules of her church, which wouldn't permit her to even hold hands with a single man, let alone someone who wasn't of their faith; yet, his gentle touch sent a comfortable, it-will-be-okay sensation up her arms that landed in her shoulders. She didn't shrug to rid herself of the welcome sensation. On the contrary, she wanted to savor it for as long as she could. His presence alone reminded her of a protective shield. She trusted him.

"You were saying?"

She thought for a moment to choose her words. "Old Sam . . . he did something so romantic for their sixtieth, like I said." She turned to him and lifted a hand to the sky. "I just want to remind you that, unfortunately, Esther went to the Lord before that day."

"So, of course, she never opened the present."

Hannah shook her head. "No. But he made something . . . actually, you would expect it to be a hope chest, but it wasn't."

"What was it?"

"I'm not exactly sure, but anyway, here's what I've heard. Old Sam, you see, never did anything that wasn't extraordinary. So he decided to bury his gift for her."

Marcus glanced at her to go on.

"You won't believe this, but he hid her special gift at the very top of this hill. And . . ." Excitement made Hannah's words come out faster and faster as the story came from her. "He even left clues to where it was."

"So . . . let me get this straight. If Esther passed away before their anniversary, the gift remains hidden?"

"For a long time, it did. But something else that's kind of miraculous happened."

Marcus laughed. "This is quite a story, Hannah. You're sure you're not making this up?"

Before she could respond, he grinned. "Just kidding. But who'd have imagined something like this could have happened here . . ." He extended his arms in front of him. "In this small, country community."

A big smile lifted the corners of her lips as she agreed with him. "Old Sam left a will." She cleared a knot from her throat. "Long story short, his great-niece found his hidden note to Esther and became so engrossed in finding the gift he'd made, she found it." Hannah pointed to the top. "Right up here."

"I wonder what it would be like, finding someone you loved so very much that you'd spend nearly sixty years with them."

Hannah's breath caught. For some reason, she'd been so engrossed in her story, the observation Marcus had just made took her by surprise. Because it was something she'd never really thought of.

"Don't you wonder, too?"

Hannah softened her voice. "It would be a miracle." She contemplated everlasting love and a breathless sigh escaped her throat. "But *Gott*'s all about love. And I guess it shouldn't be a surprise that He would bless two of his best followers with so many years together."

At the top, they stopped. Together, they looked down at two sitting stones.

Hannah motioned to him and carefully hiked up the bottom of her dress as she sat down on one. Marcus sat down next to her on the other.

As they looked down at the beautiful creek that wound its way through the area, Marcus spoke in a low voice. "I've never seen anything like this."

"Me neither, Marcus." After a slight pause, she eyed

him with a lifted brow. "I've been doing a lot of thinking about the theft."

"Do the police have any leads?"

Hannah shook her head. "Not that I'm aware of." With a soft, concerned tone, she added, "Marcus, I'm really concerned that whoever robbed King's Bakery hasn't been caught. We don't know who it was, or if they plan to rob again. I've been thinking that I need to take things into my own hands. I think it's time I try to catch whoever it is."

Marcus held up a hand to stop her. "Whoa, Miss Hannah."

After a pause, he went on in the most logical tone he could. "I know you're a smart woman and that you make your own decisions. And I have no doubt that you're probably savvy enough to catch whoever broke into the bakery. But I don't want you trying to do something so dangerous. Please, Hannah. Let the police do their job."

She studied him for a moment, then smiled in agreement. "I will, Marcus." Her cheeks flushed, and she lowered her gaze to the floor before lifting her chin to look at him. "I like it that you're protective."

He turned to her, and emotion filled his voice as he looked at her. "Thank you, Hannah. That's a load off my mind."

They sat in silence while the warm breeze fanned the backs of their necks. The landscape beneath them was like a beautiful picture, with the creek winding its way through the countryside.

"There's something about this very spot . . ." He motioned to the stones. "That's making me feel something I've never experienced before in my life."

Hannah's heart thumped in anticipation as she waited for him to go on. She yearned to share everything with him. Every secret. Every fear. Every dream.

But despite their growing bond, there was a stronger barrier that would prevent her from ever being his life's partner. He wasn't of the Amish faith. And the way she lived and worshipped her Lord and Savior were two things she'd never, ever give up.

But maybe *Gott* wanted her to be with Marcus . . . even if she had to part from her faith. After all, believing was what Christianity was all about. So, was she being selfish? Should she consider breaking from the only way of life she knew to have true love?

While they sat at the top of Pebble Creek, an ache filled Marcus's chest. Why were his heartstrings pulling so hard? He narrowed his brows as he tried to reason things out. The ache was a combination of pain and of joy.

All that he'd learned about the Arthur community raced through his mind. He thought of Old Sam's gift to Esther. Her death before he could let her find it. Of Hannah assuring him that she'd leave finding the King's Bakery thief to the police. And finally, the sweet story Hannah had shared with him. Of what she yearned for.

He contemplated her dream to hike with her husband and children. The image was as vivid to him now as when she had first shared her dream of hiking with little ones following her up the very hill they'd just climbed.

Before hearing her words, Marcus hadn't thought much about a family of his own. He was just starting a new life, away from the trouble that so tempted his brothers. But now, his heart ached to be the man who hiked with Hannah and the children. To be the man bringing up the rear as Hannah's family made their way up Pebble Creek. Despite not being Amish, despite feeling he could never be devout enough to marry Hannah, he could clearly see himself with the group. At that very moment, nothing made sense to him. Nothing except the fact that he wanted nothing more in the world than to marry Amish woman Hannah Lapp.

Chapter Eleven

Why did Lapp Furniture seem so quiet? July was over. To Hannah, it seemed as though she had just been at this very chair, in this small office, doing the June tallies. For the past several years, Hannah had been the designated bookkeeper.

She'd spent many afternoons and evenings in this small room, but until this particular evening, she'd never paid attention to the defining silence. Usually, she could hear branches of the large oaks surrounding the store as the wind shoved them against the building.

Or, other times, she'd caught traffic noises from cars traveling the main road to the side of the shop. Last winter, when she'd done the books in this very room, there had been a stray cat outside the door, purring to get in. Of course, she'd let the furry creature inside and had even allowed it to cuddle up inside her winter coat. She'd even found a home for the creature at Mary Conrad's house. Hannah fell in love with every animal she met; she'd offered her home to plenty of strays, but when she'd taken that particular feline home, Maemm had told Hannah to find the little guy a different dwelling.

Hannah smiled a little at the happy memory of the

stray inside her coat and let out a sigh as she finished adding the column of July expenses. She stopped for a moment, shoved back her chair on the wooden floor, and stretched her legs.

Tonight, there was much to think about. Marcus, in particular. How to clear the doubts in people's minds that he'd been involved in the robbery at King's Bakery. And what to do about her forbidden feelings for him.

Since their conversation at the top of the hill, when she'd learned he was truly a protector, he'd been on her mind more than ever. And she was fully aware of the serious feelings she had for him. Love. That's what she felt. And she was sure it had nothing to do with whether or not he was Amish. If only she could reason with her heart.

For the short time she'd known Marcus, she'd learned a lot about him. That was how it seemed anyway. The family dinner and washing dishes with the boys had quickly stepped up her awareness of the *Englischer.*

For instance, he was fit. She was sure she wouldn't be able to run back and forth on the long drive, racing the boys on their bicycles. Secondly, he was extremely kind to children. To her nephews in particular.

Hannah had spent enough time with children to know that instinctively, they knew when they were cared about. And her nephews definitely felt Marcus's love for them. He'd been interested in them. Talked to them. Played with them.

Thinking about him prompted her to strum her fingers against the wooden desk where she was working. She let out a frustrated sigh. Unfortunately, thinking about Marcus made it difficult for her to focus on her math.

She looked around. There wasn't a window in this particular room; still, for some reason, she'd always enjoyed the time she spent alone here. She looked around at the cluttered shelves and workspace.

She'd brought *The Adventures of Sydney and Carson* with her. It was during this time that she allowed her imagination to work overtime. When she read, she was able to put herself in another world. And reading inspired her. Maybe a little too much, because she'd shared with Marcus the idea of catching the thief. While the thought was brief, and she likely wouldn't have acted on it, it was comforting to know that Marcus cared about her safety enough to dissuade her. So she'd leave trying to catch the King's Bakery thief to the police.

As she looked down at the numbers, she thought of how she'd been raised to spend every moment working and serving, because work and worship made you grow as a person. That's probably why Maemm disapproved of her adventure books.

Now, their house was filled with grandchildren and her brothers and their wives. Sometimes, she felt a bit guilty about needing her own space. Despite longing for alone time, she dreamed of the day when she'd have her own children running around barefoot. Surely she'd better enjoy her stories now, because once she became a *maemm*, there wouldn't be a moment to spare for anything that didn't contribute to her family.

As she started to add the last column, she sat very still and wondered if she'd really have a home full of children one day. If she'd be able to keep her family fed. Even though Hannah liked to cook, she was fully aware of the amount of work it took to feed a family.

She eyed *The Adventures of Sydney and Carson*, to the right of her papers. Even if she didn't have time to read, just having the book in front of her drew up the corners of her lips in a smile.

Her attention shifted to the four corners that encompassed her small workspace, and she automatically compared it to her office in the back of Amish Edibles. Similarly, a large battery clock hung on the wall in front of her there. The long, black, second hand crept continuously around the numbers. Two wooden rocking chairs from Conrad Cabinets sat on each side of the oak work chaise.

As she breathed in the aroma of wood polish and leather, she acknowledged that she preferred Amish Edibles' pleasant scents of cinnamon and flowers from the sachets made by Mary Conrad and her mother. In fact, when customers entered Amish Edibles, many immediately commented that the shop smelled like fresh flowers.

A quick glance at the clock told Hannah it was time to get back to work. While she resumed adding with her hand calculator, the wind suddenly began shoving large branches against the building. The squeaking noise of limbs rubbing against metal siding made chills run up her arms.

As she focused on the numbers in front of her, the impact of branches hitting the building increased. Letting out a yawn, a new sound made her straighten up. Her heart pounded to a combination of fear and urgency as Hannah looked for the source of the noise.

To her dismay, the knob on the door jiggled. She parted her lips in surprise. *Did I imagine that?* She swallowed and carefully eyed the knob, which moved again.

Someone's trying to get in. Just like in the story I'm writing. If it was one of my brothers, they'd knock and holler my name. Hannah stood, immediately recalling the theft at King's Bakery. *And the thief was never caught.* Suddenly, the work in front of her lost its sense of urgency. *It's unlikely that Marcus will show up to make a storylike ending. It's just me. What should I do?*

She recalled her own fiction and realized there wasn't an extinguisher close by. Hannah's quick thinking kicked in, though, and she stood. Trying not to make a sound, she reached underneath her work area for the key that locked the door that led out into the main area of the store.

Quickly, she rushed to the other side of the door, closed it as quietly as she could, inserted the key, and turned it to lock the door. Unlike the back office at Amish Edibles, this one had a lock.

If the thief or thieves broke in, which she considered a likely possibility, picking another lock to get into the furniture area would buy her more time to get help. As she checked to make sure the bolt was locked, she could hear someone making a more serious effort to pick the lock on the door outside.

Her heart pumped to an urgent beat. Shoving the key into her apron pocket, she rushed to the only phone in the store. It was to the right of the cash register. Her fingers shook.

Her entire body trembled as she dialed the police. Her heart pounded so loud, she was sure whoever was trying to break in could hear it. Her lungs pumped for air as the phone rang.

Once. Twice. Three times. She pressed her lips together in a tight line and she nervously tapped the toe of her shoe against the wood floor. Hannah's breath caught in her throat. She tried to stay calm as she waited. Finally, on the fourth ring, a woman answered.

Speaking as quietly as she could, Hannah quickly spilled out her name, her situation and location. To her relief, the woman's voice was firm and confident as she told Hannah what needed to be done.

"Is there anyone else in the store?"

"No."

"Is there a room close by that you can lock yourself into?"

Hannah's glance landed on the bathroom that was several feet away.

In relief, she automatically gave a quick nod of her head. She wasn't sure why. No one could see her. "*Jah.* The bathroom is close. I can lock myself inside."

Hannah stiffened and turned toward the main entrance at the front of the store. It was tempting to run outside, and she mentioned it.

"It's safer for you to be locked up inside a room. There might be an accomplice outside. If you ran outside, you might be in more danger than you already are."

"Okay."

She was quick to catch the decisive tone in the woman's voice. "Go lock yourself in the bathroom. And take your cell phone with you so we can stay in touch."

Hannah frowned. "I can't. I'm on a landline."

"It's okay. Just get yourself locked in there. The police are on their way. Don't leave the room until they come to get you. Now, go."

Hannah returned the phone to its cradle, rushed to the small bathroom not far away, and opened the door . . .

As she did so, she spotted an extinguisher attached to a bracket on the wall. Automatically, she released it from its metal holder, grabbed the red bottle, stepped inside the bathroom, and locked the door.

After doing so, she expelled a sigh of relief. But really, what was there to be relieved about? Nothing. Other than that she was locked in a small room, which meant she was safe for the moment.

How long will it take the police to get here? Does the thief know I'm in here? What would Sydney do that I'm not doing? And what would this extinguisher do to a thief? It must have some strong chemical in it to put out an electrical fire.

She contemplated the office and mentally sorted through the facts. *I left the light on. My books were opened. And my horse is tied outside next to my buggy. But they're in a general area, which won't give away that I'm in here.*

When I was in the office, I wasn't making any noise, so it's very possible the intruder doesn't know I'm here. The books could have been left open at any time. But the light is on. Of course, it could have been left on overnight. What else can I do to protect myself? What would Sydney do?

Immediately, Hannah acknowledged what was most important, something she'd forgotten. Quickly, she squeezed her eyes closed, pressed her palms together, and whispered, "Dear Lord, please protect me and please keep the police safe. I pray that whoever's trying to rob our store will be safe, too, and that You will come into that person's heart and fill it with Your love. Amen."

Finally, true relief swept up Hannah's back. She'd

spoken to her Lord and Savior. He watched out for her. He would protect her and everyone involved.

She didn't have a watch and had no idea how much time had passed since she'd called for help. *Now, all I can do is wait this out and continue to pray.*

She got up from the toilet lid, knelt, pressed her palms tightly together, squeezed her eyes closed, and prayed over and over for her safety and the protection of the police. Again, she prayed for *Gott* to come into the heart of the person who was trying to steal from the store. *Of course, this thief might not be the same one who robbed King's Bakery, but logic tells me that the intruder is the same.*

She breathed in a deep breath and expelled it before opening her lids and resuming her place on the toilet lid. Her Heavenly Father was with her. That was the best she could do in the situation she was in. And He'd always been there for her. Still, she gripped the Halon extinguisher until her knuckles turned white.

She couldn't hear anything. Using common sense, she attempted to figure out what was happening in the office. *Maybe the thief has already left. The safe is empty because the money has been taken to the bank. There's probably not much cash in the register out front because most customers use credit cards.*

The thief will surely get out of the building as quickly as possible. But I hope he sticks around long enough for the police to catch him, so our town doesn't have to worry about another robbery. And so everyone will know that Marcus is innocent.

On the closed toilet lid, she leaned forward and tapped the toe of her sturdy black shoe against the wood floor.

She clenched her hands in front of her and bit her lip. Suddenly, the story she'd started to write about her and Marcus swept into her thoughts.

As she considered playing sleuth, an amused smile tugged at the corners of her lips. When she'd written the words, she'd never dreamed she ever would be in real danger.

Suddenly, a commotion made her stand up. Her heart pounded against her chest as loud voices could be heard. Hollering, back and forth. And then a gunshot.

Marcus, Ben, and their crew were working overtime at Cabot to finish a big job. The ringing of the phone in the chemical shop wasn't unusual. However, Ben's tone as he spoke lent a reason for concern.

A combination of curiosity and uncertainty stopped Marcus from what he was doing. Immediately, he put down his torch, removed his hood, and quickly stepped to the area near the entrance where Ben talked into the desk phone.

Marcus knew not to interrupt. And he also was fully aware that it was wrong to eavesdrop. This time, however, he did so anyway. Because Ben had mentioned Hannah. And she was definitely his business.

As Marcus stood near Hannah's brother, he took in Ben's tone, and that his brows came together in deep concern. It wasn't hard to figure it out: Hannah was in trouble.

As Ben continued his conversation, Marcus regarded him with concern. The longer the conversation went on, the stronger and faster Marcus's heart pumped with fear.

Finally, Ben returned the phone to its cradle. His low voice cracked with emotion and concern. "Marcus, the family furniture store is being robbed. Hannah's inside, doing the books."

Trying to maintain his composure, Marcus contemplated the words that had come out of Hannah's brother's mouth. Before he could respond, Ben swallowed and motioned toward the wall on the side of the parking lot.

"Would you give me a lift to the shop?"

Swallowing, Marcus offered a quick, firm nod as he dug in his pocket for his car key. "Let's go."

Inside his Chevy, Marcus's breath caught in his throat. Absorbing Ben's words, he gripped the steering wheel so tightly, his knuckles ached. As he pulled out of the parking lot, loose gravel crunched under his tires. White dust clouded the air behind the vehicle as they left the shop.

Looking straight ahead, Marcus didn't bother to return the waves of two other welders who had listened in on the phone conversation. As he tried to stay calm, Marcus contemplated Hannah's situation. As he bit his bottom lip, he regretted his inability to make sure she was safe. Helplessness filled his chest.

What would I do without her? Is Hannah too brave for the thief? Will she try to outsmart him? Marcus pressed his lips together in a straight line, recalling her keen interest in adventures. And his brows narrowed in a worry slant. *Lord, please protect her.*

Automatically, he recalled Jesus and how He'd been crucified, suffered, and had risen from the dead, despite the cruel people who'd given all they had to get rid of Him. A sudden relief swept through his body, and he turned to the man next to him. As he took in Ben, the seriousness of the situation prompted Marcus to step on the accelerator.

"Whoa, friend. We want to get there in one piece."

Marcus let his foot up and allowed the car to slow. "Sorry about that. I just don't know what I'd do if something happened to your sister."

From his side vision, Marcus was quick to note the lines of surprise that deepened around Ben's eyes. Perhaps Marcus had better kept that remark to himself. At any rate, it was too late to recall it. Besides, compared to the danger Hannah was in, what did it really matter?

"Ben?"

"Yeah?"

"God hears our prayers wherever we are. And right now, your sister needs Him to protect her. I'd feel a whole lot better if we sent an urgent request for help to our Heavenly Father. Would you pray for both of us while I get us to Lapp Furniture?"

Without giving a yes or no, Ben lowered the pitch of his voice so that his tone was barely more than a serious whisper. As he immediately began to speak to God with his head bowed, Marcus glanced at him and expelled a sigh that was a combination of relief and urgency.

"Dear *Gott*, please keep Hannah safe." A deep intake of breath followed before he continued in an emotional voice. "Only You know the danger she's in and how to get her out of it. I know You have control over everything that happens here on earth. So please let her be all right."

After a slight pause, his voice cracked with emotion. "Lord, please keep our Hannah safe." After a slight hesitation, he followed with what seemed to be a second realization. "And please be with the police as they rescue her. Amen."

After the prayer, he expelled a deep breath. But he didn't relax in his seat. To his astonishment, Marcus could sense even more tension than before as Ben pressed his palms against his thighs and leaned forward, as if doing so would get them there faster.

To Marcus's surprise, his tight grip on the steering column only became tighter. *Prayers work. Have faith.* He gripped the wheel harder as the startling circumstances began to sink in.

As he absorbed reality, his chest tightened. He tried to stay calm. He found it hard to believe that what had started as a good day had turned into a nightmare. As he sat very still with his seat belt fastened, he pressed his lips together in a tight, determined line.

On both sides of him, tall stalks of corn hovered. For miles and miles, the same panorama ensued. And despite the urgent prayer Ben had sent to their Creator, a sense of helplessness swept up Marcus's back, leaving a muscle spasm at the back of his neck.

Lord, please give me faith. I know You are testing my strength, and I'm letting You down.

"Ben, my entire life, I've felt the need to be in control. Especially when my parents passed in an accident, I yearned with everything I had to make things okay. But I realize that most everything's out of my control."

"You've got that right."

"It's all about faith, isn't it?"

"Marcus, we can't control everything around us. That's impossible. But we can react. And we need to get to Hannah."

Marcus tapped the brakes to avoid a large pothole. As he did so, the tires briefly spun over loose gravel on the side, and Marcus focused on keeping the car on the blacktop.

A second later, he was back in the middle of the narrow road, and from his peripheral vision, he glimpsed Ben wiping his forehead. "Things could get worse, you know."

Marcus nodded. "Yeah, sorry about that. I'll slow it down."

Ben stretched his legs and laid his palms on his thighs. "You know what?"

In silence, Marcus offered a quick glance at Hannah's brother before returning his attention to the road.

"It doesn't matter if we get there in ten minutes. Or in fifteen, Marcus. You know that, right?"

Marcus didn't have an answer. "What do you mean?"

"We can't save her because we're not there. We just have to pray and hope for the best."

A stronger sense of realization hit Marcus until he finally relaxed his grip on the wheel and rested the back of his head against the cloth headrest. "You're right, Ben. At this point, there's nothing we can do but keep praying. All I can say is, I hope the police have the person who broke in. And I hope they got there in time."

Ben lowered the pitch of his voice to barely more than a whisper and a huge sense of urgency edged his tone as he begged the Lord to take the situation into His hands. "Amen."

Then he angled his left leg toward the driver's seat. "Marcus, you know what you said about liking to be in control?" Marcus nodded. "Just know that you're not failing at all. In fact, this could be a blessing."

Marcus immediately lifted a challenging brow, all the while keeping his eyes on the road. "You've got me there."

"What I mean is, maybe Christ presented this situation to us to build our faith and our trust in Him. Maybe we both needed a wake-up call, and this is it."

Marcus's jaw dropped in surprise as he absorbed the words coming from a devout Amish man. But the more he contemplated Ben's wisdom, the more what he'd said made sense.

"God must have really been looking out for me when He sent me to you and Hannah." He bit his lip with emotion before going on to explain, "I couldn't agree with you more. In fact, I'm convinced that you're right. God is bringing me closer to Him and teaching me to trust Him."

Ben smiled a little as he turned toward Marcus. "It works both ways, you know."

"What?"

"I believe *Gott* sent you to us, Marcus. And He's given me responsibility to help you along the way. There's a Scripture I want to share with you."

He turned his attention back to the blacktop in front of him and relaxed his voice. "It's from Joshua. It says something to the affect that *Gott* commands us to be strong and courageous, not to be afraid or discouraged, for the Lord our *Gott* will be with us, wherever we go. We'll get through this, Marcus, my brother in Christ."

Marcus glimpsed the amused way in which Ben's lips curved. "And something tells me that you want my sister safe as much as I do." He cleared his throat. "You're in love with Hannah."

Ben was absolutely right. But Marcus didn't respond. In fact, the comment surprised him. He thought about the woman who sold him raspberry jelly 24-7. But the last thing he wanted was for anyone else to be aware of his strong feelings for the beautiful Amish girl. Especially someone within their close-knit family.

He didn't want Hannah in trouble with her people. And public awareness of his love for her would only hurt him in the end. Because he was sure he didn't have the toughness to become Amish.

And if he did, could he carry that faith through for years and years to come? If he joined the Amish church, it wasn't a temporary thing. A trial run. It was a lifetime commitment. And that's what it would take to marry Hannah Lapp.

A sad, guilty lump formed in his throat. He tried to swallow. He couldn't. *Faith. Have faith.*

As long as my Lord and Savior has control of Hannah's life, she'll be okay. Then why does my gut feel like it's been struck with something heavy? He strummed his pointer finger against the wheel to a nervous, uncertain beat.

In front of him, he barely noticed the soybean and cornfields on both sides of the road. Automatically, he pulled over to allow another vehicle to come the opposite way. The narrow road was barely wide enough for two cars to pass. Right now, the warm air coming in through the open windows didn't even provide him comfort.

Next to him, in the passenger bucket seat, Ben didn't say a word as they cruised the county road leading to Lapp Furniture, on the outskirts of Arthur. As Marcus eyed his coworker, he acknowledged that his friend had most likely never been faced with a situation like the current one.

In fact, Marcus's understanding was that theft and crime had never played a role in the area in which they lived. That was, until King's Bakery was robbed. It seemed to be public knowledge that many in the area didn't even bother to lock their doors at night. Of course, the burglary at King's Bakery had most likely changed that.

Marcus glanced over at Ben, who sat up straight in his seat. Hannah's brother clutched both of his hands in his lap. From Marcus's peripheral view, he glimpsed the worry lines that etched his friend's mouth.

Finally, Ben broke the silence. "She's okay, Marcus. And soon, we'll see so with our own eyes."

The softly spoken words offered Marcus just enough comfort for him to smile a little. Thoughtful seconds later, he responded with a nod. "I know. I'll just feel better when we see for ourselves."

Marcus pulled his Ray Bans from the console and slid them over his nose. As he took in the country in front of him, he couldn't help but admire the beauty of the fields of soybeans and corn. When he'd lived in

Chicago, he'd never really paid attention to other parts of the state.

"We're almost there." An odd combination of excitement and dread edged Ben's voice as he turned a bit to Marcus. "Maemm always tells us to use logic when something's bothering us."

The statement prompted Marcus to nod his approval. As he did so, he slowed his car to make room on the narrow blacktop for another oncoming car. As the two vehicles met, loose gravel crunched under the tires as Marcus moved off the road.

Afterward, he stepped on the accelerator, and his heart pumped with a sense of relief as the furniture store came into view. "That's good advice."

Ben cleared a knot from his throat and relaxed his palms on his thighs. "Well, let's go with what we know. The store was robbed. And the police were called. Hannah was alone inside the shop."

"Do we know who called the police?"

Ben offered a shrug of his shoulders. "No. But it could've been Hannah . . . that is, if she used the phone at the cash register."

A long silence ensued while Marcus tried to picture Hannah rushing to a phone and calling for help. A grin tugged at the corners of his lips.

Irritation edged Ben's voice. "What on earth are you smiling about?"

Marcus realized that his expression might seem insensitive, but in fact, recalling Hannah's interest in playing sleuth couldn't stop him from nearly laughing.

"It's something I remembered."

Ben glanced at him to go on.

"I'm not sure how much you know about your sister's interests, but she's tied up in this adventure book series."

"That's what Maemm said."

Marcus offered a quick nod. "By no means am I making light of the seriousness of her predicament, but trust me . . . If there's anyone who can outsmart a burglar, it's your sister. I had told her I'd keep that information confidential, but I mentioned it because I thought it would help both of us to ease some of the tension."

The statement didn't alter the concerned expression on Ben's face. Afterward, the two sat in complete silence. The only sound was the smoothness of rubber meeting blacktop. And Marcus arched a doubtful brow as reality sank in.

It doesn't matter how clever Hannah is. She doesn't own a weapon. He swallowed an emotional knot as he wondered if the police had caught whoever had broken in to Lapp Furniture. Most likely, whatever had been done was done. And unlike any story Hannah read for enjoyment, this ending wasn't decided by a writer. The denouement could be good. Or bad.

Chapter Twelve

Inside the small bathroom at Lapp Furniture, Hannah continued to grip the Halon extinguisher. If the thief tried to break the door down, she'd spray him in the face.

She automatically recalled a Scripture from the book of John. *I have told you these things, so that in Me you may have peace. In this world you will have trouble. But take heart! I have overcome the world.*

"Thank you for helping me to remember that. Amen."

As Hannah swallowed an emotional knot, automatically, the brief conversation she'd had with the woman on the phone came to mind. *Do not leave the bathroom until the police come to get you.*

Hannah had lost track of time; she didn't know if five or thirty minutes had passed. She stood and went to touch the door handle and stopped.

She said not to leave this room until the police come. Hannah stood very, very still as the sound of footsteps approached her.

She put her ear to the door, struggling to hear anything she could. As she listened, she made out two different voices that appeared to be coming her way.

Her heart picked up speed to an even more eager,

anxious pace. Her fingers began to move the lock. *No. I have to be sure it's the police. But how will I know who's on the other side?*

A strong voice sounded, and there were two knocks on the door. "Hannah Lapp? You're safe, and you can come out now. It's Officer Barrington. I'm happy to tell you that we've taken the thief into custody. He's handcuffed and en route to the station. He confessed to robbing King's Bakery."

As Hannah acknowledged that only the police would know her by name, a different voice came through what Hannah was sure was a radio. That was enough evidence for her that the police were indeed there.

Expelling a breath, her fingers shook as she unlocked the door and stepped out. She didn't let go of the Halon extinguisher. Suddenly, as she faced two uniformed officers, reality sank in, and tears of joy and relief dampened her eyes. She blinked to rid them of the sting. She didn't know what had happened, but whatever it was, it was over. *Thank You, Gott!*

Without thinking about what she was doing, she put down the fire extinguisher, grabbed the closest officer, and hugged him as tightly as she could. He was a tall, large man, so her arms didn't quite make it all the way around his waist.

The embrace didn't last long. The officer took her at arm's length and spoke in a deep, strong voice. "This was a scenario that could easily have gone awry. But we've got him, Hannah. And it was largely because of your phone call." After a quick pause, he added, "That and the advice the 9-1-1 operator gave you."

He gave a quick shake of his head and whistled.

"God must surely have been watching over you, because the guy in custody was armed."

Hannah drew in a deep breath.

Another officer lifted a brow. "Of course, it looks like you were armed, too. But a fire extinguisher can't match a gun. If you hadn't gotten yourself in that bathroom . . ." He motioned to the opened door. "And locked the door that leads out into the store's main area, we might not've been able to make it here to take him down before he got to you."

Suddenly, Hannah remembered the gunshot.

Her eyes widened with fear as she met Officer Barrington's gaze. "But the gunshot . . ."

The police gave a firm nod. "What you heard was his gun. And Officer Williams, here . . ." He nodded with great appreciation to the uniformed officer standing next to him. "It just so happened that my friend, here, uh, used his martial arts skills to kick it out of his hand. That's when it went off. Thankfully, no one got hurt."

Williams grinned. "Except the wall in the office. It's gonna need some fixin'."

As Hannah took in what she'd just learned, two familiar voices made her turn to the front, where Ben and Marcus rushed inside.

"Hannah!" The two men shouted. Hannah was quick to notice the obvious relief that edged both voices.

"Ben! Marcus!"

The following evening, Hannah was mentally sifting through everything that had happened at the family furniture store and thanking *Gott* that she was here, in her home, pulling a fresh wheat loaf from the oven. As she breathed in the delicious-smelling aroma of yeast bread, Maemm's voice made her turn.

"Hannah . . ." After placing the hot tin on two cloth pads, Hannah turned. To her astonishment, Maemm's eyes were moist. The wetness sparkled on her pupils like dew on a morning pumpkin blossom.

When she continued, her voice cracked with emotion before she cleared her throat and squared her shoulders. It was obvious to Hannah that Maemm was trying her best to appear strong after surviving a sensitive situation that had tested them all. Hannah quickly acknowledged that her role model's behavior was much different from her normal, composed, stern self.

As Maemm came closer, a set of arms reached for Hannah's shoulders. With great tenderness, Hannah enjoyed the comfort of her mother's gentle, loving touch. She closed her eyes a moment to enjoy the welcome sensation that was a wonderful combination of love and reassurance.

"This is the first time we've been alone since . . ." She stopped for a moment, appearing to maintain her strength and composure. "I guess you could say that I never, ever imagined that something like that could happen."

Hannah shook her head in dismay. "Me neither, Maemm."

"I'm grateful for this time alone to tell you how happy and relieved I am for everything you did to help the police catch the member of our community who tried to rob us."

For a moment, Hannah stood very still as she took in

the significance of her mother's statement. The member of our community. *Surely it wasn't someone who knows us . . . please, Lord.*

Hannah tried to find her voice, afraid to ask Maemm who had thrown their lives upside down. She stood with her mouth open, waiting for her mother to explain what she'd just said.

Maemm had never openly given away her sentiments. Instead, she usually displayed a tough façade. Un-emotional. But this evening, Hannah recognized that she regarded a very different woman. A mother who was obviously trying to engage in a very serious conver-sation with her daughter.

"Maemm, do we know who tried to rob us?"

A slow nod followed. "Not well, but it's Nate Jen-kins . . ."

Hannah pressed her lips together thoughtfully.

"He works part-time in the delivery department at our furniture store."

Hannah took a quick intake of breath. Her heart sank at the thought of someone trying to rob her family; what made it worse was that, apparently, this was a man who'd been on the family's payroll.

"I can't believe it."

"Neither could we, Hannah."

Hannah's mind went to work as she tried to put to-gether more of the pieces in her mental puzzle. "That would mean that he was aware of our safe and where it was."

Maemm nodded. "Not only that, but he didn't know anyone was inside." After a short pause, Maemm lifted her shoulders. "Think about it. It's rare that you're there doing the books. Your horse and buggy were at a place where others were parked. And I'm sure he thought he'd have free rein of the store."

After expelling a sigh, Maemm lifted her palms to the ceiling in a helpless gesture. "Honey, he was armed. And if he'd broken in before you got out of that room . . ."

Maemm started to cry.

Hannah took her mother in her arms and hugged her with everything she had. Because it only made her more fully aware how very close she'd come to facing much more danger than she'd actually confronted.

As they embraced, Hannah closed her eyes in new-found joy. She'd always loved Maemm, but now she fully realized how much her mother loved her. And Hannah would never forget this precious moment in which she had bonded with the woman who'd given birth to her and raised her with ten brothers.

"I love you, Maemm. So much."

"I love you, too, Hannah." After a short intake of breath, she smiled a little. "I'm so glad you're okay."

Hannah made sure the baking pan was on the hot pads she'd placed on the countertop before she embraced her *maemm* again. Hannah couldn't help the joyful tears that slid down her cheeks.

A long, emotional connection took place before Maemm finally broke the embrace and caught a tear with her hand. Then, she seemed to reclaim her composure and lifted her chin a notch.

"You had us so worried." Maemm motioned to the kitchen table, and Hannah took the seat opposite her role model.

"It's over. The thief is caught."

Maemm nodded agreement. "And to think it was a man right here in town." She offered a sad shake of her head. "Someone no one suspected."

"And now, everyone will know that Marcus is innocent." Hannah lifted a defensive hand. "But we've got to feel sorry for someone who becomes so desperate for money, they rob to get it."

A long, tense silence ensued, while Hannah wondered what would become of the middle-aged man she'd seen on occasion, Nate Jenkins. His wife had been through a number of health crises, and earlier this summer, he had been let go from his full-time job in Decatur for missing too much work.

"I feel sorry for him."

The expression on Maemm's face changed to that of shock. "Hannah, if he'd relied on *Gott* to help his family instead of turning to breaking the law . . ."

Hannah lowered her eyes and gave a sad shake of her head. "That's why he needs *Gott*'s help. We've got to pray for him, Maemm. Right now, he needs *Gott*'s love. He needs to know that he has a Lord and Savior who's looking over him."

The corners of her mother's lips curved into an amused grin. "Hannah, you always have been the most forgiving girl I've ever known. How'd I become so fortunate as to have you for my daughter?"

Hannah drew her arms over her heart as she tried to absorb her *maemm*'s obvious love for her, and that she was actually expressing it. Hannah didn't know what to say. Then something occurred to her, and she raised an inquisitive brow. "I wonder what Old Sam would've done if he'd been in my shoes."

Several heartbeats later, Maemm lowered her gaze to her shoes. When she lifted her chin, warmth and tenderness filled her eyes.

"What?"

"I know what he would've told all of us, Hannah. How could I forget?"

Hannah parted her lips in anticipation, waiting to hear what she was sure would put things into perspective.

"Dear Old Sam. He knew every Proverb. And I'd heard him talk enough about forgiveness at church, I'm ashamed of myself for not having stopped to think about how he'd have handled this situation."

After taking in a breath, Hannah's mother went on. "I can't remember exactly how he said it, but it went something like this: Love's power to forgive is stronger than hate's power to get even."

"I guess I'm the way I am because of you and Daed. You raised me in the church. Always taught me to forgive. To give others a chance."

"Because Jesus died on the cross so we could all be forgiven and have eternal life." Her mother's voice hitched. Then she swallowed and looked away before returning her gaze to Hannah. "Sometimes, I forget what *Gott* wants us to do. To love everyone as our neighbor and to forgive, lest we will be judged, too." She frowned before expelling a breath. "Hannah, you're exactly right." A wide smile lifted the corners of her lips. "We've got to forgive Nate. And help him with his debt."

Hannah agreed. "Most of all, we've got to lead him to *Gott*. When that happens, everything else will work out."

The following day, Marcus prayed the moment he awoke. As soon as he said amen, he strode to his small bedroom window, which offered a partial view of Pebble Creek. For some reason, he felt the need to spend time there. His schedule had changed, and now he had Mondays off.

The attempted theft at Lapp Furniture two days before had presented him with emotions he hadn't known he had. When he recalled the sickening, helpless feeling that had filled his chest as he and Ben had made their way toward the store, a chill swept up his spine, and he shivered.

Even the beautiful hill that stood out in predominantly flat Illinois didn't calm him when he recalled the moment he'd learned about the danger Hannah was in.

But God had been with Hannah. *And she's okay.* He swallowed an uncomfortable knot that blocked his throat. Even though things had worked out, he still needed to apply reason to the uncertainty that had kept him up most of the night.

A redbird perched on the sill in front of him. In the distance, he could see that no one was outside at Ben's home. The kids were at school, Ben was at work, and Ruth was most likely inside cooking.

Narrowing his brows, slow, thoughtful steps took him to the back door, where he stepped outside. As he took in the warm breeze and the beautiful, old oak trees, he fully appreciated the full view of the hill where significant things had occurred over the years. At least, that was what Hannah had told him. But bits and pieces he'd heard at work and in town backed up what she'd conveyed.

I'll figure out what I'm feeling. I need to be patient. He stretched his arms and stepped back inside to make a quick cup of coffee before he started his walk. Caffeine helped to facilitate clear thinking.

Of course, his dwelling wasn't wired for electricity, so he did what he'd gotten used to: He boiled water in a saucepan on the gas burner and then poured it into the coffee filter he held over a wide mug that said *Chicago* on it.

A few minutes later, he sat outside on the patio chair and took in the vast area of soybeans, corn, and alfalfa. As he sipped black coffee, he closed his eyes and said another prayer of thanks that Hannah was okay.

Again, as he realized that with any slight change, things could have taken her from him, he squeezed his eyes closed a moment to reflect on the positive. When he opened his lids, he got up from his chair, returned the mug to the kitchen table, and went back outside.

As he glimpsed workhorses pulling someone through a field in the distance, he smiled a little. And something big hit him. *Two days ago, I prayed to my Lord and Savior in desperation. It's the first time I've asked God for something with such urgency and need. And my prayer was answered.*

What had happened had awakened him to the huge impact God now played in his life. *How did I ever get through the day without God? How did I survive the deaths of my parents without faith and belief?*

So many thoughts flitted through his mind, he drew in a deep breath and expelled it. *One thing at a time.* Without thinking, he started in the direction of the hill. As he breathed in the combination of earthy scents from the nearby fields, the significance of knowing God hit him with such force that the miracle of it all nearly took his breath away.

He looked up at the clouds. The sun hid underneath one that reminded him of the mashed potatoes his mother used to make. He swallowed an emotional knot. *Are my parents in heaven?*

Marcus pressed his lips together in a thoughtful line and continued toward the hill, which was some distance away. Slow, thoughtful strides brought him to Pebble Creek as if the coveted place was a magnet pulling him in its direction.

As the sun continued to rise higher in the sky, the hill drew closer. Marcus took in the ambience, and a peaceful sensation filled his entire body. *Everything around me is a gift from God Almighty. The fields. The sun and the clouds. The breeze.*

The smell of a freshly mowed ditch floated through his nostrils, and he breathed it in with great appreciation. *These gifts cannot be created by man. These are signs that the Creator of the Universe included in His plan when He created the earth.*

How can people not believe in God? How did I go for so many years without a personal relationship with the One who created me? God put me here with a purpose. What is it?

* * *

That evening, as the sun created beautiful colors in the west, Marcus ate a sandwich at his small kitchen table. As he chewed a bite of ham salad, he looked around his house. The robbery at Lapp Furniture wouldn't leave his thoughts. He'd never, ever forget the happiness he'd experienced when he'd seen Hannah, safe and sound, with his own eyes. Now, he felt even more determined to make the big decision that faced him. The very choice he thought about all day and at night.

He paced the living room, contemplating what the room would look like with a sofa and chair set from Lapp Furniture, before stopping in front of the window.

While he'd been at Lapp Furniture, he'd glimpsed beautiful polished woods. Hand-carved, intricate details. A particular dark oak table had grabbed his attention as he'd waited while Hannah had assisted the police with their report.

What am I going to do? Should I stay here? Should I move back to the city and try to rescue my brothers? That question prompted a frown. At that moment, he acknowledged that the city no longer appealed to him. At all.

He ticked off reasons on his fingers. *Number one, I prefer the countryside. There's something about fresh air and openness that appeals to me. I like the quiet. It allows me to appreciate the sounds of nature.*

Number two, I have no desire to sit in traffic every night on my way home from work.

Number three, here in Arthur, people are hardworking. Honest. He smiled a little. *Except for the thief who robbed King's Bakery and Lapp Furniture.*

Number four, what would I do without Hannah's raspberry jelly?

And number five—He expelled a deep, serious sigh. *What would I do without Hannah? I truly love her.*

After he'd downed the remainder of his sandwich, he shoved the wrapping to the side and reached for the Holy Bible that Ben and Ruth had given him. He opened it to a passage from Matthew that he'd found while deciding whether to stay here and ask for Hannah's hand in marriage. He reread the verse from chapter six that had sparked serious thought:

Do not lay for yourselves treasures on earth, when moth and rust destroy and where thieves break in and steal, but lay up for yourselves treasures in heaven, where neither moth nor rust destroy and where thieves don't break in and steal. For where your treasure is, there your heart is also.

Bible in hand, he stepped to the living room couch, where he stood very still, contemplating the passage. *This countryside is beautiful.*

Corn and soybean fields. Country houses. His heart warmed while he contemplated his decision to come here. *I never dreamed that I'd fall in love with a place that offered so little.*

He pressed his lips together and arched a brow. But did Arthur really offer very little? Or did it offer a lot? As he sat back in his chair, he stared at God's Holy Word and tried for an answer.

Compared to Chicago, there were very few restaurants. No retail stores. But really, what did the city offer him? He ticked off the first things that came to his mind.

Restaurants, gas stations . . . He stopped the moment he realized the difference.

The city provided plenty of food to eat. The countryside offered him food for his soul. His breath hitched at that very serious acknowledgment. The Lapp family offered him more opportunity to grow spiritually than anyone in the city.

Not only that, but he'd changed. To his astonishment, he didn't miss drinking a beer with coworkers in the evenings.

And he hadn't missed the episodes of *NCIS*. That thought prompted a smile. Instead, he'd learned to appreciate the night sounds. The way the moonbeams made their way into his bedroom.

He could attend church in the city, if he wanted. There were all denominations, and he could take his pick. But strangely and amazingly, his heart had taken root in this little town in the middle of nowhere.

In particular, in Amish Edibles, where he'd met Hannah. He could move away, if he wanted, but would he be as happy anywhere else as he was here?

Automatically, he thought seriously of committing to Hannah and relinquishing his car. To have one, he needed to give up the other.

As he contemplated his destiny, his gaze drifted to the Bible that was opened and bookmarked to Matthew 6:19–21. In silence, he scanned the verse again. And his attention stayed on the very last part. *For where your treasure is, there your heart is also.*

What exactly does that mean? He ran his hand over his jaw. His thoughts returned to his father. To their car talk. To his goal of owning his very first Chevrolet. To him and his dad taking their very first ride in it.

If I no longer drove a Chevrolet, would that break my connection to my father? After serious thought, he shook his head. No. *My connection to my dad goes way deeper than our love for cars.*

For a surprising moment, he imagined helping Hannah to step up and get into a black buggy, closing the door, and sitting next to her as their Standardbred clomp-clomped down the country blacktop.

A smile tugged up the corners of his lips. He imagined helping her to load their kitchen shelves with groceries. He could almost smell her homemade grain bread in the kitchen oven.

While questions flitted within him, he closed his eyes for a moment and mentally ordered himself to stay calm. So much had happened in such a short amount of time, uncontrollable emotions flitted through his heart until his chest ached. But the ache wasn't painful, really.

It was more of a feeling similar to what he'd experienced when his parents had surprised him with a new bicycle on his tenth birthday, or something like that. A sense of urgency prompted him to stand and pace. He made his way outside to the backyard, where he took in the distant view of Pebble Creek. Sounds of cicadas and crickets accompanied the night breeze.

He let out a low whistle as an excited shiver coursed through him. Then he lifted his chin and stepped to the nearest oak tree, where he pulled a green leaf and ran his finger over the veins.

Only God can create this. God must have made Old Sam to be His messenger. Old Sam sounds sort of like a disciple. But I don't know much about the Bible. There is so much to learn. But I've got time. Time to learn and time to serve.

Everything that had happened since he'd planted himself in Arthur started to sort itself out in his mind, and his shoulders relaxed. He dropped the leaf and fixed his gaze on Pebble Creek. The setting sun cast a shadow on the hill that held so much sentiment.

Hannah instantly became my best friend, and now, I'm sure I'm in love with her. I almost lost her. I realize how much she means to me, and I'm so grateful she's alive. Amish folks don't marry outside of their faith. And I'm far from Amish. I don't know all their rules, but from watching these conservative, faithful people, I'm sure there are many things in my past that would immediately disqualify me from becoming one of them. I've sworn. I've been to bars. I've even taken for granted the life God has given me. That's all changing. But I've sinned, and I can't erase things I've done, even if I found nothing wrong with them when I committed them. They're on my life's résumé.

Amish in this part of the United States don't even use computers or cell phones. I don't know how they survive on so little. I wish Hannah lived with more reasonable rules.

Amusement pulled up the corners of his lips. *No, I don't. I love her just the way she is.*

Suddenly, Marcus pressed his lips together as he recalled why he'd come here in the first place. *I want to follow Christ. In order to do that, I need to find out what the Bible says. God has a plan for me. And I won't know what it is unless I understand what He does and doesn't want me to do.*

As he expelled a breath of full realization, he turned and made his way to the front of his house. To the paved sidewalk that led from his place to the Lapp home.

This is my new life, and I'm grateful. Dear God, please tell me how to live. I want to live for You, but how do You want me to do it?

When he spotted a figure coming his way, he immediately stood and waved a friendly hand. "Ben!"

"Marcus!"

When they met in between the two homes, they shook hands. "Watcha up to tonight?"

Marcus lifted his palms to the sky and offered a half smile. "Just doing some reflecting. Trying to figure things out."

To his surprise, the corners of Ben's lips curved into an amused smile. "It doesn't have anything to do with Hannah, now, does it?"

For a moment, Marcus looked away in embarrassment. The last thing he wanted was for his friend and coworker to know how strongly he felt about Ben's sister, who was out-of-bounds for the Chicago native.

Ben gave him a friendly nudge on the shoulder. "Wanna talk about it?"

Before Marcus could reply, Ben motioned to the path leading to his home and lifted his chin a notch. "I thought you might wanna come for dinner. There's plenty of time to talk." He gave a nod at the remainder of path to where he, Ruth, and their four boys lived.

Finally, Marcus agreed. "Ah, why not?"

As they began their walk, Marcus acknowledged how nice it was not to have to worry about locking up. And even though Marcus preferred to keep his feelings for

Hannah to himself, it was obvious Ben had figured them out. Perhaps he could shed light on what to do.

"I still can't believe what happened at your family's furniture store," Marcus started.

"It is remarkable, but *Gott* watched over us. Over Hannah, in particular."

Marcus didn't respond.

Ben lowered the pitch of his voice. "You're in love with her, aren't you?"

When Marcus tried to ignore the question, Ben went on. "You know what Old Sam used to say, buddy?"

"What?"

"That every miracle Jesus does starts with a problem."

The words prompted the corners of Marcus's lips to curve upward. "I wish Old Sam were here right now. Maybe he could tell me what to do."

Marcus offered Ben an expression three parts annoyance and one part seriousness. "Isn't it obvious?"

When Ben remained silent, Marcus went on. "I love your sister, but I'm not good enough to marry her." When Ben glanced at him with a lifted brow, Marcus went on. "Your family . . . the people in your church . . . you've all lived such Godly lives. And my life résumé's far from pristine. Hannah doesn't deserve someone like me."

"My friend, let me tell you something." After a short pause, he continued. "There's no such thing as a back-seat Christian. Marcus, everyone sins. And I admire you for being open. This is just my opinion, but it's the people who think they've got a straight line to *Gott* we should be wary of. I believe that *Gott* likes us to humble ourselves before him. And you, my friend, are doing just that. The moment you accepted our Lord as your Savior, you were saved from everything you've ever done."

Marcus's head began to spring a dull ache. He frowned. The Scripture from the book of Matthew floated through his thoughts. So did life without Hannah. So did forfeiting driving his Chevy.

Then another piece of a sermon swept into his head. But instead of making the picture more complicated, it made it clearer. *It doesn't matter who your parents are. It doesn't matter what you've done. It's who you know.* And then his mother's words made the finale. *Follow your heart.*

"Marcus, love is a blessing. And it's something you can't decide. It just is. So instead of worrying what to do, be grateful that you have something. The Apostle Paul said, 'And the greatest of these is love.'"

"But what about becoming Amish? I don't know if I can do it, Ben."

To Marcus's surprise, the man next to him laughed. "You know what I think?"

"What?"

"You're making this way too hard, my friend. It's like you're trying to talk yourself out of love." He hesitated before clearing his throat. "I'm gonna be straight up with you, my friend. Usually, Amish folks don't encourage their own to marry outside of the faith. That's not something I'd normally do. There aren't many of us, and we want to ensure our beliefs carry on to the next generation."

Marcus watched his pensive expression.

Ben narrowed his brows. "Joining the faith would

take time and it would require total commitment." He lifted his chin a notch. "But if you decide to go that route, I'll be there with you every step of the way." A long silence ensued before he added in a soft tone, "And Marcus?"

Marcus glanced at Ben to go on.

"Old Sam used to say something that might help you through this. He said that if *Gott* takes you to it, He'll get you through it."

Chapter Thirteen

Where was Marcus? Hannah was surprised he hadn't come by to check on her. Monday evening, at Amish Edibles, the last group of customers finally cleared out of the shop. Hannah expelled a sigh of relief, stepped to the entrance to lock it, turned the sign to "Closed," and stepped toward the back room.

As she glanced at her nearly finished quilt, she smiled a little. She took in what appeared to be chaos in front of her. But in reality, she had everything organized. To the right of the piece of fabric was a pile of eight cut squares in between a pile of thimbles and several reams of blue thread.

A small sound prompted her to glance at the corner, where Scarlet stretched her front paws. "Sorry, I forgot about you, munchkin. I'll go grab you some milk."

Hannah bent in front of the feline for the round plastic bowl, poured a bit of powdered milk into it from the nearby Carnation box, added water from the half-full bottle on the work desk, and gave the mixture a quick stir with a plastic spoon. She returned the full bowl to its place, stood, and gingerly crossed her hands over her chest. "There ya go, girl."

As the cat lapped the white mixture, Hannah reflected on the day and the past weekend. While she enjoyed the break from customers, she acknowledged that her relief wasn't because she was now free of selling her jelly and other items.

It was because she was free from answering questions about the robbery at Lapp Furniture. It seemed as though people couldn't get enough of the phone call she'd made to the 911 operator and that she'd hidden in the bathroom until the police had arrested the intruder.

Her pulse zoomed every time she relived the sequence of events that had led to her calling and awaiting help. *I've lived through my very own adventure story. And I never want to do that again. But while I was waiting for the police to come save me, I realized something very important. Something I must tell Marcus as soon as possible.*

Before she left for the night, she pulled the light blue thread from its spool, put the end between her lips, and squinted to get it between the eye of the needle.

She pulled two squares, dark blue, and one that was a shade lighter, and began sewing them together. As she took in the beautiful hues of the mixed blues, she smiled a little. Then, she put down her work and began readying the shop for tomorrow morning.

She needed to get home for dinner. This morning, after collecting eggs and cleaning the animal stalls, she'd placed a pork roast with cabbage in the oven. Maemm was to keep an eye on it and turn it off.

After checking the locks on both doors, she hitched Miracle to the buggy, stepped inside, and started home on the blacktop. In front of her, the setting sun melted into the horizon.

She expelled a breath of awe. Sunsets had always fascinated her. Sunrises too. The sunrises reminded her of starting a stopwatch, and sunsets were when the stopwatch was turned off. It was as if *Gott* gave them so much time to get things done. And then the day was done, and it was time to rest.

As Miracle swished his tail and made an uneven clomp-clomping sound, she reflected on the time she'd spent in Lapp Furniture on Saturday. What had happened had changed her life. At the time, she hadn't realized what the experience had done inside her, but now, looking back on the day, things that had seemed irrelevant before were now important.

For instance, she'd never really appreciated feeling safe and secure in her family store. It was something she'd taken for granted. Now, she acknowledged that security wasn't something to be taken for granted.

And she'd never really appreciated that at the end of the day, she'd eat dinner with her family. It was another thing she'd always taken for granted. Until she'd seen and heard the back doorknob at Lapp Furniture jiggle. Until she'd quickly realized that someone was trying to break in to the store.

For a moment, an ache filled her chest. As the warm summer breeze fanned her eyelashes, she narrowed her brows. The moment the doorknob in the back room had turned, she'd realized something very important. That the wonderful life she had could be taken away from her at any given moment.

What if the thief had opened the door before I got out

of the room? What if the police hadn't arrived when they did? If the man who broke into the shop had unlocked the door faster, what would he have done when he faced me? Would I even be alive to think this through?

As her home came into view, an eerie shiver crept up her spine. Her reaction was to shake her head to rid it of the unwanted sensation. *Maybe what happened was meant to wake me up to appreciate blessings I've never considered. Maybe what happened was meant to give me an answer to the question Marcus asked me at the top of Pebble Creek.*

Adventure stories had always excited her. In fact, she'd always dreamed of participating in one. *It's more fun reading them. That way, there's no danger.*

But in her life, there was another adventure story occurring. And like her adventure stories, it also involved risk. But the risk wasn't a life-or-death situation. At the same time, her real-life story with Marcus had an undecided ending. But she had the opportunity to decide it.

I've always dreamed of marrying an Amish man. I still do. But now, I'm thinking outside of the box. The dangerous situation at Lapp Furniture has made me more open-minded. And I know what I need to tell Marcus. But first, there's someone I need to talk to.

The following afternoon, while Maemm ran Amish Edibles, Hannah tied her horse next to Mary Conrad's. Outside of the Conrad home, beautiful beds of flowers decorated the large front yard. Different hues of roses bloomed on both sides of the entrance.

As she caressed Miracle's nose, the horse let out a whinny. She whispered, "I love you" to her four-legged friend and smiled. One reason was that she adored her horse. The second reason for smiling was because she knew without a doubt that she could confide in the plant guru; that was to her advantage because it just so happened that Rebecca and William's only daughter was a natural expert at offering advice, which made sense because she'd been close to Old Sam.

Grinding sounds floated out of Conrad Cabinets, which was a separate building behind their home. In the distance, their fishing pond loomed. Hannah was fully aware that Jonah Conrad loved to fish. She also knew that two young boys had come close to drowning there once at a church party.

As Hannah patted the horse between his ears, he swished his tail to rid himself of a fly. Hannah firmed her voice. "I'll be back. I'm just going to have a talk with my friend. And don't worry; I've got a sugar cube for you for your patience." He whinnied again, and she began walking toward the flower garden to the right of the large, two-story home.

As she took in the vast area of land on which the Conrad home sat, Rebecca's voice pulled her from her reverie. "Hannah! It's so *gut* to see you! Come here and let me give you a hug!"

Quick steps took her to Mary's *maemm*, where they embraced each other tightly. After they released their arms, an odd combination of regret and relief reflected in Rebecca's eyes. Tiny lines of concern crinkled around her eyes.

"Oh, honey . . ." Rebecca paused as her breath caught. "I can't tell you how worried we all were when we learned that your family's furniture store was being robbed and that you were inside."

When Hannah's jaw dropped in shock, Rebecca smiled widely and laid an affectionate hand on her shoulder. "You know how quickly word travels around here." After a pause, she laughed. "Even without cell phones!"

Hannah joined in the friendly laughter.

"We were quick to get a prayer chain going, and fortunately, our prayers worked to keep you safe. Annie, Rachel, and I were catching up when we got word that the police had been called. Rachel was telling us that one of Doc Zimmerman's horses had made a remarkable comeback from a serious infection when we heard."

Hannah looked at Rebecca to continue while she contemplated how quickly, indeed, word traveled among the Amish. An appreciative smile tugged the corners of her lips upward.

"I'm glad you prayed. Because Rebecca, I needed strong prayers. And to be honest, it all happened so quickly, there wasn't much time to think." After a slight pause, she shook her head. "All I can say is, I'm glad the police arrested the person responsible and, hopefully, our town will never be robbed again."

Hannah contemplated what had been going on while she'd been locked inside the bathroom in Lapp Furniture. She certainly hadn't realized so many people were aware of her predicament, and that they were all begging *Gott* for her safety. If she'd known, perhaps she wouldn't have felt so alone.

Rebecca squeezed her eyes closed and took Hannah's

hands in hers. She lowered the pitch of her voice to a more serious tone. "*Gott* answers prayers, Hannah. And we're so thankful you're okay." After a slight pause, she expelled a breath of relief. "But I know someone who can't wait to see you."

Side by side, they made their way to the backyard, where Mary wore a large work apron while she bent to water tall purple flowers. Without actually knowing her friend was working in the flower garden, Hannah had guessed it.

When Mary straightened up, Hannah watched her place what appeared to be some weeds into a plastic bucket at her side. Rebecca cupped her mouth with her hands and shouted, "Yoo-hoo!"

As Mary turned, she offered a wide smile and waved to Hannah. With a quick movement of her hand, Hannah returned the gesture, stepping closer to the flower garden as Mary motioned her to come join her. Rebecca stepped away and made her way back toward the house. Hannah could hear the screen door snap shut.

Water pitcher in hand, Mary met Hannah at the edge of the garden, where grass met dirt, and put her pitcher on the ground. Swatting a fly away from her face, enthusiasm edged her voice as she lifted her chin a notch.

"Hannah! It's so *gut* to see you!" Immediately, Mary stepped to her, hugged her tightly, then held her at arm's length and looked into her eyes. "Oh my friend; you don't know how *gut* it is to be right here in front of you." She gave a quick shake of her head. "I just can't believe what happened to you at Lapp Furniture."

Hannah had been questioned so many times about

the attempted robbery, by the police, her family, and by curious customers at Amish Edibles, the last thing she wanted to discuss was her narrow escape from a thief.

But Mary was her true friend. And because of that, Hannah was fully aware that the woman next to her honestly cared about what had happened. Because of that, she would patiently convey the details to the plant guru. After all, this woman was special in every way.

As Hannah smiled at her, Mary pushed her glasses up her nose. "Mary, I'll tell you all about it. But it will take me a while to spill it out."

"*Gut.*"

As Hannah took in the panorama before her, she couldn't help but appreciate the beauty of the collection of flowers, as well as the array of exotic-looking hues.

The flower garden looked so beautiful, the landscape made Hannah's breath catch. Gorgeous colors made this garden a masterpiece. Hannah was far from a plant expert, but she knew enough to identify the section of rosebushes and the hot pink geraniums. As she stepped closer, she touched a white rose petal that was outlined with a beautiful yellow hue. As she took in the heavenly fragrance, she closed her eyes for a moment.

"Those are my Chicago Peace roses. My absolute favorite." Mary pointed to the one on the end with brown on the ends of the leaves. "You see that one?"

Hannah nodded. A frown followed. "What's wrong with it?"

"I'm not sure, but it might be a fungus. But I just treated it with my miracle cure." She winked. "My potion hasn't failed me yet, so I'm expecting this little guy to perk back up by tomorrow." After taking a breath, she went on. "How 'bout a chat over a fresh-squeezed lemonade?"

Hannah offered a quick, decisive nod. "Sounds just like what I need to tell you about my adventure inside Lapp Furniture."

As they neared the house, Hannah stopped to take in the rose beds in the area in between the sidewalk and the foundation of the house.

"Here." Mary pointed to the beautiful white petals with pink on the edges. "You've got to smell this one."

As Hannah bent to take in the scent, she gently touched the soft, velvety petal. "It's so soft and fragile."

Hannah breathed in and closed her eyes in amazement. "And its smell is every bit as *gut* as its beauty."

To Hannah's astonishment, Mary carefully snipped the ornate-looking flower with her cutters and presented it to Hannah with a smile of satisfaction. "Here. It's yours."

Hannah's jaw dropped as she held the gorgeous stem in front of her.

"Inside, we'll put it in a vase, and then I'll wrap it so you can take it home in the buggy."

Hannah grinned as she gently brought the petal to her nose again. "I see why you like to work with plants. I wish my entire house smelled like this."

Mary laughed. "It would. If you were a florist."

Hannah joined in the friendly laughter.

Hannah immediately sensed a great feeling of appreciation for her friend's green thumb. "I'll never question why you love growing things."

"And only *Gott* can create this beauty, Hannah." She let out a breath of awe and stretched out her hands in front of her. "All I do, really, is plant the seeds and water them." She lifted her shoulders in a small shrug. "Just look at this. All I can say is . . ." She breathed in. "This is a miracle. And it's here for us to enjoy."

Hannah glimpsed a white plastic bucket next to the entrance and turned her attention to her friend. "You're pulling weeds?"

Mary rolled her eyes and winked. "*Jah.* Unfortunately, like anything in life, there are always going to be weeds." She had lowered her voice to a more confidential, serious pitch.

Hannah stepped closer for fear of missing anything her friend said. Mary was wise beyond her years. *Gott* had blessed her with an uncanny ability to look at a difficult situation and immediately put things into perspective. And that's exactly why Hannah was there.

"Hannah?"

Hannah returned to reality.

"Are you okay?"

Hannah lifted her palms to the sky in a helpless gesture and gave a slow shake of her head. "Not really, Mary."

An affectionate touch warmed Hannah's shoulder, and Mary whispered, "It's okay. My, you're doing much better than I would have predicted." After a few steps, she glanced at Hannah. "I know what happened was shocking, and it might take you some time to fully recover." After a slight pause, she let out a breath. "My friend, I'm lucky to be standing here with you. But let's talk things out. I certainly don't have a counseling degree, but I can use common sense. And trust me, I'll do whatever I can to make sense of what happened to you."

Hannah smiled a little. "I'll tell you all about it, Mary. But amazingly, the robbery at Lapp Furniture is only part of what's weighing heavily on my mind."

Mary parted her lips in surprise as she held Hannah's gaze. "There's something else?"

As the women stepped inside the side porch, Hannah glimpsed Rebecca heading to the barn. That meant she and Mary would be alone. Which was a *gut* thing.

In the kitchen, Mary closed the door behind her and pointed to the glossy oak table.

Hannah took a seat and pulled the chaise close to the table while Mary washed her hands in the hall bathroom. A few moments later, Mary brought two glasses of lemonade to the table, placed them on coasters, and claimed the empty chair opposite Hannah.

"Now, you've really got me curious. Hannah, I'm listening."

After expelling a breath, Hannah started in a soft voice, "Mary, I'm going through something serious."

Mary leaned closer and narrowed her brows.

"It's about me and Marcus Jackson."

Mary started to say something, but stopped herself before any words came out. Hannah explained about how her simple, innocent friendship with the *Englischer* had turned into true love. She went on about how she'd always planned to stay Amish before revealing what had gone on in her mind when she'd locked herself in the bathroom at Lapp Furniture.

She stopped to take a sip of lemonade. Mary did the same. As they returned their glasses to the coasters, ice cubes clinked against the glasses.

"I love him, Mary."

Mary choked. As she tried to stop coughing, Hannah wondered what her parents' reaction would be if her friend was this surprised.

Mary finally composed herself and looked at Hannah to continue. "Are you going to marry him, Hannah?"

Hannah's breath hitched. She wasn't sure why. She'd thought a lot about being Marcus's wife. But actually hearing the question seemed much different from merely considering it.

"That's what I really want to talk to you about, Mary."

A short silence ensued.

"If you were truly in love with someone who was a Christian, but wasn't Amish, someone you enjoyed being with so much it pained you to say goodbye, would you choose to let go of that person to stay in the faith? Or would you go outside of your faith to marry your true love?"

Mary didn't respond. As the fan blades made an airy sound and a bird chirped outside the window, Hannah went on to explain her feelings for Marcus. She began with their meeting and went on to tell Mary about her unusual, unexpected bond with the Chicago native.

Afterward, she lifted two helpless palms. "Mary, I love him. And I know he loves me, even though he hasn't actually said so. And he's a Christian . . . though not Amish, as you're aware. If you were in my shoes, what would you do?"

As Mary sat back and folded her hands in her lap, Hannah breathed in a hopeful breath. Finally, in a soft, thoughtful voice, Mary smiled a little. "I'm certainly not Old Sam. Of course, no one is. But I knew him pretty well. To be honest, I'm not sure what he'd say, Hannah."

Mary stood and went to the fridge, where she poured more lemonade into her glass and Hannah's. Hannah drew her brows together as she tried to read Mary's thoughts.

Without saying anything, Mary returned to her chair, returned the two glasses to their spots, and lifted her chin a notch. "Let me think on this." She pressed her finger against her lips and narrowed her brows. "When I try to get something resolved, I like to be with my plants." She smiled a little. "There's something about them, Hannah, that help me know what to do. It's like . . . they inspire me." She sipped from her glass and continued holding the lemonade in front of her.

"Your situation, Hannah—I know it might seem hopeless, but actually, it's not that much different from what my parents went through before they were married. And Annie and Levi . . . you know, they faced a battle, too.

"Let me see . . . I'm trying to imagine what Old Sam would advise if he were still here with us." After a light sigh, she smiled a little.

Suddenly, a surge of relief flowed through Hannah. Of course Mary would figure out what to do.

Mary leaned forward, and her eyes lit up. "I just remembered something Old Sam used to say."

Hannah looked at her to continue.

"It may be difficult to wait on the Lord, but it is worse to wish you had."

Hannah considered the advice and finally offered a nod of agreement. Mary reached across the table and Hannah touched her fingers in mutual understanding.

"Hannah, this is something to pray about. And the answer is worth patience."

It was hard to believe the first week of August was already gone. That evening, Marcus stood out in his backyard, contemplating the Milky Way. If God could create a galaxy so complicated, so amazing, why couldn't Marcus decide his destiny with Hannah?

As an oak leaf floated off a branch and to the ground, he acknowledged that Hannah might be wondering why he hadn't checked on her. After all, he hadn't seen Hannah since right after the robbery. But there was good reason for staying out of her sight.

She might not realize it, but Marcus was in the midst of a very important decision: whether or not to join the Amish faith. And that choice determined whether or not he and Hannah would spend the rest of their lives together.

But he didn't feel guilty. *Why can't she join a different faith?* He pressed his lips together into a straight, thoughtful line, because he knew the answer. She could.

There were numerous denominations. Marcus hadn't

studied them, but he guessed that most if not all of them had the same goal. To serve God. Marcus wasn't omniscient, but he believed with a fair amount of certainty that God didn't allow members of only one faith into heaven.

He looked up at the sky, where he glimpsed a jet's puffy white trail. A large cloud appeared to open up and swallow the plane until the trail reappeared. *Where are the passengers going? Where am I going? I thought life was complicated before coming here. Now, it's even more puzzling than before.*

Follow your heart. His mother's words sounded in his head, and he pressed his palms on both sides of his face to drown out the noise. *If my dad had been Amish, would Mom have joined the church to be with him? If she hadn't, would my father have chosen a different faith in order to spend the rest of his life with her? I think so . . .*

In awe, he fixed his gaze on the brightest star, marveling at what he'd learned about the Bible this evening. The more he prayed with the Lapp family, the more he learned from them, the more he admired and respected their faith.

Tonight, as he enjoyed the cool breeze, he couldn't rid his mind of the Scripture Ben had read from the Bible before they'd sat down for dinner. Before coming here, Marcus had known a little about the twelve disciples and other followers of Jesus, but he'd never really been aware of the monumental challenges they had faced because they'd followed Him.

Marcus's chest ached as he realized the extreme pain

they'd endured to spread God's Holy Word. In the book of Acts, Stephen had been stoned to death while preaching the Gospel. Peter had been crucified upside down.

For a moment, Marcus squeezed his eyes closed and shook his head in disbelief and sadness. *What was I doing my entire life that I missed out on all this?*

Marcus contemplated what he'd just learned. *That is the true meaning of love.* That admission led to a challenging question. *Would I stand up for Christ if my life would be taken for doing so?*

He bit his lower lip. For the first time in his twenty-five years, he was acknowledging what being a follower of Christ truly meant. Without thinking of what he was doing, he automatically gazed in the direction of Pebble Creek, although he was unable to see the hill or the creek in the darkness. Suddenly, he connected the dots from the hill that was so out of place in central Illinois to Old Sam and the wisdom he so unselfishly offered to those who asked it.

Realization warmed his arms, and that very warmth spread down to his fingers. He extended them a couple of times before interlacing his fingers together in front of him.

The impact of his acknowledgment was so strong, it nearly pulled the air from his lungs. Again, he directed his gaze to the star-filled sky and drew in a deep breath of appreciation.

Old Sam was a disciple. That must have been why God placed him here. He was the leader in this area who, through his strong faith and great wisdom, had had the ability to bring the community together, through the hope chests he made, to the advice he offered to those he loved, to his obvious devotion to his wife of nearly sixty years.

Marcus closed his eyes a moment to think about the significance of Pebble Creek and Old Sam. *This place is special.* When he opened his lids, he blinked at the salty sting. In pleasant disbelief, he tried to absorb everything that had happened since his arrival at Arthur. And in one special, revealing moment, his mother's advice began to make sense.

Chapter Fourteen

That evening, Hannah's room seemed darker than usual. Automatically, she made her way to the window and gazed out at the starlit August sky. To get a better view, she shoved the light blue curtains to either side and fastened them to their hooks.

The view in front of her pulled her breath out of her lungs. Gott *created this incredible universe. How can people not believe in Him? To* Gott, *our problems must seem small.*

She smiled a little at that realization. Hugging her hands to her hips, she pressed her lips together and mentally reviewed Mary's advice about Marcus. The wisdom that had come straight from Old Sam. "It may be difficult to wait on the Lord, but it is worse to wish you had."

There it was. Her answer. Or at least it was a temporary one. It now made sense that to do nothing when uncertain was much better than doing something. A move in the wrong direction would have lifelong affects.

She glanced at the floor to the list of morning chores that needed to be done before Miracle would take her to

Amish Edibles. *I have to get up at four. But I'm dying to finish writing my adventure story because I can't wait to decide the ending.* Finally, she smiled a little. *I'm used to being short of sleep. I'm going to pen the last scene of* The Adventures of Hannah and Marcus.

Hannah pivoted and stepped to her hope chest, where she bent at the waist to open it, reached inside for her notepad and black ink pen, and closed her eyes for a moment while she took in the pleasant scent. With great care, she traced her finger around the first commandment. *Thou shalt not have any Gods before me.*

She looked up at the half moon and stepped to her usual sitting place on the rug next to her bed.

In a slow, thoughtful motion, she sat down so her back was comfortable against the bed cushion. As she opened her notepad to the last scene, she lifted her chin with confidence.

Leaving the lid open to admire the beautifully inscribed Ten Commandments, she lit the cinnamon-scented candles on the small bed tables on both sides of her. Because the only light was from the moon and her small portable battery light, which she'd clicked on. With great care, she moved the candles as close to the edges as she could to get light.

Staring at the etched-in-wood Ten Commandments filled her with such a comforting sensation, she stretched her legs in front of her and wiggled her toes. In excitement, she began to write on the lined paper.

She read the sentence where she'd left off. *Hannah had tied the man's hands.*

Moments later, police sirens filled the air. Two cars pulled into the Amish Edibles drive, and two neighbors rushed to help Marcus.

Hannah's heart pumped so hard, she feared it would jump right out of her chest. One of the officers held a set of handcuffs while the other officer put them around the man's wrists over the ones Hannah had made.

When the man was escorted to the cop car, the officer held out a hand to Hannah. "A neighbor spotted the three of you while he turned off on the blacktop down there." He motioned. "He called for help right away. Do you mind if we get some details from you?"

Hannah and Marcus nodded. They answered questions while Miracle whinnied. Afterward, the police waved goodbye, and Hannah locked gazes with Marcus. "He's scared to death. Would you help me reassure him everything's okay?"

Marcus grinned. "Sure."

After quick steps took them to the horse, Hannah stroked the long brown nose with great affection. "It's okay, Miracle."

Marcus laughed while he stroked the spot behind one of his ears. "He certainly lived up to his name." He gave a gentle pat between the brown ears. "You're the real hero, boy."

Hannah agreed. "If it hadn't been for you, our thief would never have dropped his gun."

As the four-legged beauty began to calm, Marcus lowered the pitch of his voice. "Hannah, I just realized something very important. Something we need to talk about."

"What?"

She stopped. *Suddenly, everything hit her at once.*

Marcus narrowed his brows and took her by the arm. "Let's get you home."

Together, they hitched Miracle to the buggy.

"Are you going to follow me?"

He shook his head. "No. I'll get my car later. I need to see to it that you make it home, safe and sound. Maybe your maemm *will have some chicken and dumplings made."*

Marcus helped Hannah into the passenger side. She turned and didn't try to hide her surprised expression. "You know how . . ."

Marcus gave a firm nod. "Thanks to Ben. He taught me everything about hitching and unhitching a horse."

As Miracle pulled them down the blacktop, Hannah turned to Marcus. "What were you saying? About something important?"

He turned his attention back in front of him, but he spoke with gentleness and affection. "Hannah, I realized what a great team we make."

She waited for him to go on.

And he did. "I'd like you to be my life partner. My wife."

The following evening, Marcus sat next to Ben in his buggy. As one of the Lapp family horses pulled them down the winding blacktop road that traversed the countryside's soybean and cornfields, Marcus took in the animal smell. The gentle up and down of the buggy lulled him into peacefulness. In the far distance, the setting sun created a portrait of peace and untouched beauty.

The miraculous scene in front of him should have comforted Marcus. But it didn't. Nothing could. Because turmoil brewed within him. And it all had to do with wanting Hannah but not wanting to join a faith that would prevent him from doing what most reminded him of his father: driving his Chevy.

To make conversation, he said, "The corn sure has shot up since I got here."

Ben darted him a friendly smile. "They used to say, 'Knee-high by fourth of July.'" He laughed. "But these days, it's double that tall."

"When I was young, I always dreamed of being a farmer."

"*Jah?*"

Marcus offered a quick nod. "Yeah. The first gift my dad ever gave me was a remote Chevrolet. I played with it on our front drive. Tractors, trucks, and combines followed. They fascinated me."

As the horse let out a whinny and swished its long, brown tail, Ben glanced to the right. Marcus did the same.

"Sounds like you and your dad were really close."

Marcus absorbed the statement and pressed his palms against his thighs. He turned briefly to Ben. "We were. We still are. In my heart. Right after my parents and I went to the Chevy dealership to buy my car, Dad and I took our first ride in it. That very evening, a semi hit my parents head-on. And they were gone."

Ben shook his head. When he glanced at Marcus, he took note of the moisture on his pupils. Marcus was touched. Because the man next to him seemed to truly care about him. Ben's concern and thoughtfulness toward Marcus showed in so many ways.

A long silence passed before Ben broke it. "I can't imagine losing both parents at the same time."

"It was rough. To be honest, Ben, it still is. But in my own way, I'm keeping them alive in my heart."

"How do you do that?"

"By focusing on things we did together." Marcus waved a dismissive hand. For some reason, the seriousness of the subject made him uneasy. He wasn't sure why. So he tried to end the conversation. "That way, I keep them in my life."

But to his dismay, Ben wanted to know more. "What was the favorite thing you did with your dad?"

The question made the corners of Marcus's lips tug upward into a wide smile. "Checking out the new Chevrolets when they came in. Test-driving them. And talking about which one I would purchase once I got my license. Ever since I was a kid, he and Mom helped me save for my first car. I did all sorts of things to earn money. Like stock shelves at Trader Joe's."

When Ben didn't respond, Marcus quickly added, "It's a grocery store. But back to cars; Dad helped me buy my first Chevy. He cosigned for my loan."

Ben darted him a grin before returning his attention to the blacktop.

A combination of hesitation and curiosity edged Ben's voice when he started again. "The last thing I want to do is pry, but were they believers?"

Marcus thought for a moment. He shifted on the bench for a more comfortable position. As cornfields loomed on both sides of them, Marcus focused on the question. But for sure, it couldn't be answered right away.

Finally, after using his reasoning skills, Marcus was sure he could answer correctly. "Believers, yes." He shrugged. "I mean, I'm pretty sure they were."

He was quick to catch the sudden frown on Ben's face as they pulled over to the side of the blacktop to allow an oncoming car to go by. Marcus bounced in his seat as Ben steered the horse back into the middle of the narrow road.

Marcus substantiated his claim by using his best logic. "When my brothers and I were young, we went to church. That must mean that my folks believed in God, right?" Before Ben could respond, Marcus went on. "If they didn't believe, why would they take us to worship God?"

"You know what I think?"

Marcus narrowed his brows. "What?"

"That your parents are in heaven. Our *Gott* is a kind and loving God. And of course, they must've believed if they took you to church. Maybe they never developed a personal relationship with *Gott* . . ." He offered a casual lift of his shoulders before continuing. "Or maybe they did. But by the grace of *Gott*, believing gets us into heaven. It's all because of the cross, my friend. And that's exactly why you should focus on eternity."

Marcus pressed his lips together in a thoughtful line.

Ben went on. "You know what I mean. Live each day for eternity. Not for what is here on earth."

Marcus stiffened, surprised at how a casual ride in the buggy had moved on into such a serious, deep conversation.

"Ben, you've really got me thinking."

"My brother, this earth only offers so much. And what it gives us is temporary. I'm sure it's hard for you because you miss your parents, but eternity is forever. And the Bible is clear that those who believe shall have eternal life. And you'll be with your parents again. That's reason to rejoice."

"I don't even know what to say." As Marcus crossed his legs at the ankle, the horse trotted, head held high. The Standardbred expelled a loud whinny as the clomp-clomping of hooves made an uneven beat against the blacktop.

"I mean, Ben, thank you."

"For what?"

Marcus paused. A few seconds later, he lifted his palms in the air and contemplated his response. "For voicing what I needed to hear. You're exactly right. I've been living as if I wasn't going to be with my parents again. But I will. Because they were believers. And you're also right about living for eternity. For God. Really, I guess we shouldn't get so wrapped up in what happens here on earth. Because it's temporary. But eternity is forever."

Ben's voice softened. "Eternity's what's being a Christian is all about.

"Marcus, I know you didn't ask for my opinion, but here's what I think about you and your relationship with your folks. You don't need to keep them alive in your mind. Because they are alive, in heaven. And, my brother in Christ, I wonder if, instead of thinking of everything you did together on earth, maybe you should move on and focus on what you'll say to them when you join them."

The unasked-for advice took Marcus by surprise.

"Death isn't the end, you know. Sometimes we get so worked up in our sadness, we forget about the cross."

Marcus swallowed an emotional knot. Because this conversation served another purpose. Of course, it benefited him because he missed his parents. But could this deep conversation help him decide what to do about moving forward with a life with Ben's sister?

Ben expelled a breath and lifted a confident chin as the horse picked up speed. "I forgot how exciting it was to be new to Christianity. Of course, that excitement never wears off. But there's something about being new to believing in eternal life. Something so precious and so rare. Savor it, Marcus. Enjoy every moment of getting to know our Lord and Savior."

Marcus considered Ben's statement. Especially the genuine way that his words had come out of his mouth. And Marcus had no doubt that his friend had meant every word he said.

The admission caused Marcus to contemplate how different his life would be had he been born in his friend's faith. And for a moment, he wasn't sure if he wouldn't have been better off. *Here I am with a man who doesn't have a higher education. And he's telling me things that someone with a higher education degree might not even come up with. And it's all because of his faith. And how he lives for Christ.*

"Ben, I appreciate you. I respect how you live. And

words can't even begin to say how much I love sharing your daily devotion time. And your astute perspective on life in general. Before I came here, I couldn't imagine living without air conditioning. But you're so right about eternity versus earth. Really, what do privileges matter? We don't grow because of them."

"While we're on the subject of religion, Saturday, our church is cooking out. At Rebecca and William Conrad's place. We'll have all morning to work on the barn. Want to come?"

Marcus didn't have to think about that one. "I'd love to. And thanks from the bottom of my heart for helping me to grow as a person today." Marcus took in a deep breath and expelled it. "You're an inspiration. You've given me a lot to think about. In fact, this conversation has changed me."

"When it comes down to it, my friend, it's all about sacrificing to live the way you believe you should. Bible interpretation is different whatever church you go to. But one thing's the same. Christ made the ultimate sacrifice for us on the cross. And the sacrifices we make for Him?" Ben shrugged. "They don't amount to much." His voice cracked with emotion. "Especially when you consider the pain and agony Jesus went through to save us from our sins while He bled and died."

Saturday afternoon, in Rebecca Conrad's kitchen, Hannah helped Mary pull the foil off the teriyaki steaks that were marinating in the dark sauce of Worcestershire, dried mustard, and ginger. The large blades of the battery fan tried to push enough air to compete with eighty-eight degrees. Hannah imagined how nice it would be to have air conditioning. Just for a day.

Rebecca stepped through the side door while Mary handed Hannah a large bowl of uncooked meat. "Do you mind following me out with this?" Mary motioned to a large platter of sliced zucchini. "I've got my hands full."

Before Hannah could respond, one of the Conrad clan flew by her, nearly knocking her over. He stopped to apologize. Mary looked down at the six-year-old and edged her voice with seriousness. "Outside, and I'm not going to tell you again."

Before Mary could say another word, the boy flew out the door, and two other cousins followed him. Hannah retrieved the dish in question and made her way carefully to the side door, while she stepped around the many sets of shoes that lined both sides of the wall.

Rebecca and William didn't wear shoes in the house because of the beautiful wood floors. And today, most of the kids were barefoot, with their pant legs rolled up over their ankles.

Outside, one of the children spotted the two and rushed to hold the screen open as they stepped down onto the sidewalk.

"*Denki*," Mary and Hannah spoke in unison.

Hannah followed Mary past the neatly covered tables and to the grills. As soon as they reached the gas grills, Ben and Marcus joined them to fork the meat onto the metal.

While they stepped toward the house, laughter came from a group several feet away. On the other side, kids were playing a game of Red Rover. When they were nearly to the house, Hannah pointed to the rose Mary had been nursing.

"Looks like it's gonna make it." Hannah stopped to bend and observe the brown plant, which was turning green. "Whatever did you do to this bush?"

Mary laughed and darted her friend a wink. "I told you, it's the heavenly potion I used. I call it heavenly because after I add it to the plant, I say a prayer that God will heal it."

"So calling it a heavenly potion is definitely appropriate." Hannah laughed as she pulled open the screen door. Mary held on to it as it closed to prevent it from slamming.

Mary handed Hannah another tray of meat. "Do you mind making another trip?"

"Of course not. I'm here to help."

"This time, we'll leave the foil on," Mary added as Hannah took the covered plate from her. As Mary opened the screen with one hand, Hannah moved down the steps. She stopped to wait for Mary, who stepped up beside her.

Mary lowered the tone of her voice to a confidential whisper. Although the yard was scattered with church members, Hannah didn't think anyone would hear anyway because of all the talking and laughing.

"I see why you like him so much."

When Hannah looked at her to go on, Mary nodded in the direction of Marcus, where he and Ben seemed to be engaged in conversation. "He and your brother, Ben, seem really close."

"*Jah.* It doesn't hurt that they work together, and of course, Marcus rents his house, and . . ." She hesitated a moment. During the pause, she and Mary locked gazes. "To be honest, Marcus fits right in with our family."

When Mary swatted away a fly, Hannah added in a more skeptical tone, "Just watching them talk . . ." She offered a small shrug of her shoulders. "You'd never dream how very different his life is from mine."

When they got closer to the grills, Mary glanced at Hannah. "The other day, I saw Marcus and Ben together. They were in his buggy."

"*Jah?*"

"Uh-huh."

"I guess that shouldn't surprise me. They've become pretty *gut* friends. In fact, Marcus even eats with them."

"I think it's a *gut* thing."

Hannah looked at her to continue.

"I mean, when you think about it, Hannah, Marcus is a believer. Just like us."

"I know. But we live such simple lives compared to his."

Mary drew her brows together as she studied Hannah. "I agree. I mean, driving a car is a far stretch from a horse and buggy. But Hannah . . . I know how you feel. And as conservative as I am, I certainly wouldn't stop praying for a relationship with Marcus. With *Gott*, anything's possible. And in the back of my mind, I vividly recall something Maemm told me. Something that Old Sam used to say."

"What?"

Mary threw some seasonings over the vegetables and pulled the foil closed around it. "Every miracle Jesus does starts with a problem. And Heaven's delights will far outweigh life's difficulties."

Hannah took in those potent statements and regarded her friend with interest. "Those are wise instructions, Mary."

As Mary closed the lid, Hannah did the same to her grill. "We could've learned a lot from Old Sam. But continue to pray, Hannah." After a slight pause, she added, "And Hannah?"

Hannah looked at her to continue.

"Have faith."

Monday, inside Amish Edibles, Marcus browsed the shelves of jelly while Hannah talked in the back room with a group of tourists from Indiana. She appeared to be telling them how she put her quilt together, and he could hear them asking questions.

While he checked out the new inventory, the pleasant aroma of cinnamon filled the small shop. Every once in a while, the clomp-clomping of a horse on the nearby blacktop could be heard. And although a ceiling fan and a battery fan tried to keep the place cool, the midmorning sun was just too hot for them to stand a chance at cooling the place.

Marcus was just beginning to digest everything that had happened in such a short time. Falling in love with Hannah. Getting to know the Lapp family. The robbery at Lapp Furniture and Hannah's presence there. Learning she was safe. Marcus's love for the Amish faith. And last but not least, Marcus trying to convince himself to join Hannah's faith without giving up the emotional connection to his dad.

He let out a low whistle while admitting there was an

awful lot on his plate. And the funny thing was that to most, moving and starting a new job would be as much as some could handle.

As he bent to smell a fragrant candle, he took in the vanilla scent and contemplated Ben's take that everything we give up for Christ here on earth is a small sacrifice compared to bleeding to death on a cross.

Marcus swallowed an emotional knot that blocked his throat. As he glanced at his car, he knew he had to get going. But all that Jesus had done for him tugged at his heartstrings as he approached the cash register to pay for his oversize container of raspberry jelly.

If I counted every sacrifice I've made during my twenty-five years on this earth, the total wouldn't even touch the huge sacrifice Jesus made for me. If I gave up every single day for the rest of my life, I still couldn't even come close. Ben advises to not look back to be connected to my dad. And he's right; a car surely won't play a role in getting me to heaven. Still, driving in my new car with my dad is certainly a happy memory. Look forward. Look to the cross. Imagine seeing my parents when I pass on to heaven. That's by far a stronger connection to my dad than any vehicle could ever be.

A woman's high-pitched laughter startled Marcus from his reverie. He directed his attention to the sound, but not one set of eyes looked his way. Apparently, the group of women had an interest in quilting.

Tapping the toe of his boot against the floor, he checked his watch and frowned. Unfortunately, there wasn't much time left on his break. Still, he didn't want to interrupt the conversation. And he needed jelly.

At the cash register, he decided what to do. Reaching into his back pocket, he retrieved his wallet and proceeded to pull out a ten-dollar bill. He didn't care about the change. As he placed it next to the register, the ceiling fan began to lift the bill and spin it like the wind creating a dust devil.

As Marcus took in the area underneath the fan, he noticed that several papers had been strewn about, and the blades continued to stir them. He quickly made the decision to put some sort of weight on top of his money to prevent it from being blown away.

His eye caught a stapler. As he reached for it, the fan stirred more loose papers from around the register area, and he bent to pick them up.

He stopped as he glimpsed his name written in neat handwriting. Automatically, he read the sentence in which his name was mentioned. He pressed his lips together in a straight line.

Is this a story? About us? What he'd already read indicated that the answer to both questions was yes. The last thing he wanted to be was nosy, but his curiosity wouldn't stop him from reading more. He gave a quick glance up to make sure nobody was watching.

He could tell that Hannah and the tourists were still in the back room because their voices carried to where he was. *This is wrong. I shouldn't read Hannah's story. I'm doing it without her permission.* He gave in to his conscience and stopped.

But as he evened the loose pages and placed them neatly underneath his money, he was fully aware that despite it not being his intention, he'd most likely read more than Hannah would have wanted him to. In the few seconds he'd glimpsed her neat writing, he'd read that they loved each other.

And the last thing he'd read was that the Marcus on the lined pages had asked Hannah to be his life's partner. A grin that was a strong combination of amusement and curiosity tugged up the corners of his lips.

As soon as he was assured that the neat little pile with his money on top for the raspberry jelly he was taking wouldn't blow away, he stepped to the entrance, opened the door, made his way outside as the bell above the door rang, and slipped into the driver's seat of his Chevy.

He started the engine, and as he looked both ways before pulling out of the drive, gravel crunched under his tires. But his thoughts couldn't leave Hannah's handwritten story alone. As he stepped on the accelerator and set the cruise control, he acknowledged what he'd just seen accidentally. *She's dreamed up a story about us in a real, live adventure. And at the end, I asked her to marry me.*

The more he considered Hannah's handwriting and what he assumed was her own fiction with real-life characters, the two of them, the more his grin widened. And the more curious he became about the story's ending. He'd read that the Marcus on the pages had proposed marriage. *But what was Hannah's response?*

Chapter Fifteen

Could he make a lifetime commitment to the Amish faith? Early Saturday morning, Marcus automatically made his way toward Pebble Creek. The barn raising was postponed due to more rain in the forecast for later that day.

With one deep breath, he stretched his arms to the light blue sky and smiled in relief. Last night, as he'd prayed, a new optimism had taken hold of him. He strongly believed that his prayers were beginning to take root. And his life was starting to make sense. *It's all good.*

A familiar voice prompted him to turn to his right, where Hannah stepped up beside him. As they glanced pensively at each other, the clouds above them moved.

In silence, they walked side by side alongside Pebble Creek. The water passing over the round stones made a comforting sound. Together, they stood next to the creek and watched the swiftness of the water push over the stones.

"Sometimes it's good to have a cloudy day, yeah?"

Hannah nodded. "Maybe *Gott*'s giving the sun a rest."

After absorbing her take on the weather, Marcus offered a nod of agreement.

As they turned their attention to the gurgling creek, Marcus couldn't help but think about how God had led him to this place out in the middle of nowhere. To this town that was so modest. So simple. To this beautiful Amish community where he felt more at ease than he'd ever felt anywhere else.

But today, he had a confession to make to Hannah.

She looked at him. "Sorry I missed you at the shop yesterday."

Before he could get a word in, she went on, "I found your ten-dollar bill. I owe you change."

"No worries. I didn't want to interrupt the conversation you were having with that group of women. But Hannah, there's something I've got to tell you." He pressed his palms together and locked gazes with her. "It's a confession. And I hope you'll forgive me."

She looked up at him and arched a curious brow.

"When I was leaving the money on the counter . . . the ceiling fan . . ."

She smiled a little. "You found my story."

To his surprise, calmness edged her voice. Maybe she wasn't upset about it.

He nodded, and his eyes didn't leave hers while he hoped she wouldn't be angry at what he was about to admit.

"Yeah, I did. I mean, right away I guessed it was a story when I saw my name and yours. But I was in the wrong . . . I read some of it."

While she kept her lips pressed together in a straight

line, he couldn't tell what she was thinking. So he went on. "The right thing to do would have been to look away. But my curiosity . . ."

He finally shrugged and let out a sigh. "I'm sorry."

After a slight pause, she looked up at him and lifted a curious brow. "So what did you think?"

Her question prompted his jaw to drop in surprise. Obviously, she wasn't upset with him, or at least she didn't appear to be.

"I don't know. I only read a few sentences. But I take it that your story is about us? And that it's an adventure?"

Without saying a word, Hannah turned and began taking small strides up the hill. For several thoughtful moments, Marcus stood with his hands on his hips, taking in her graceful stride and the chestnut strands that had come loose from her white *kapp*.

Right now, I can't read her. What is she thinking? Follow your heart. Life's all about making sacrifices that are on a much smaller scale than the sacrifice Jesus made for us.

Then he looked up the hill to the spot where Old Sam had hidden his sixtieth wedding anniversary gift. And to Marcus's surprise, some things that had been so confusing to him began to make sense as he tried to see the whole picture and where he fit in.

Every time he sat behind the wheel, he thought of his dad. He swallowed a lump that blocked his throat. He contemplated the Amish mode of transportation and decided that he liked riding in a horse-drawn buggy, too. *But all the time?*

Hannah's soft, enthusiastic voice pulled him from his

poignant reverie. She smiled at him and motioned. "Come on." He stepped up to walk alongside her. "It's an amazing day, *jah?*"

They brushed against each other as they went to the right to go around a bump in the ground. As their arms touched, he yearned to take her fingers in his. But he abstained.

"Hannah, you're not upset with me?"

She turned. "No. Not at all."

"Then there's something I want to ask you." He narrowed his brows. "How does it end?" After a long silence, he went on. "You know, after the part where I ask you to be my life partner?"

Several steps later, they stopped. When she turned to him, her eyes widened with a strong combination of seriousness and uncertainty. "That depends."

"On what?"

As thunder rumbled, the sky brightened a notch. As Marcus took in the somber-looking sky, he compared it to his relationship to Hannah. The sky looked undecided on whether to rain again.

Follow your heart. Mom, when I promised you, I had no idea I'd have to change my entire life to do it.

Marcus edged his voice with seriousness. "Hannah, maybe we should go back."

"A little rain never hurt anyone, did it? Besides, my *daed* says the rain's not coming till later today. And he never mis-predicts."

She paused, then edged her voice with seriousness. "Marcus, I don't know how my story ends yet. How do you think it should end? Do you want to see us together forever?" She corrected, "I mean, in the story?"

The question didn't take much thought. He offered a decisive nod. "Yeah, I do."

In silence, they continued up the incline. As he breathed in damp air, he contemplated his situation with Hannah. The question wasn't whether or not he wanted to marry her. He did. The issue was whether or not he could change his life to be with her.

He still wasn't sure he could be an Amish man. Especially when it involved letting go of the deep bond with his father. But the love of cars he'd shared with his dad would never go away. Even if he joined Hannah's faith. How much longer did he need to decide? A year from now . . . two years from now, would he know?

Stop beating yourself up. Anyone in my position would have trouble with this.

They proceeded in silence. The only sounds besides their breathing were the gentle lull of the creek that was now some distance beneath them. The sun shone bright in a cloudless blue sky, and the warmth feathered Hannah's lashes like a soft cotton blanket on a cold winter's night.

Light, buzzing sounds of an occasional honeybee competed with the sound of a bird chirping somewhere in the distance.

"I like to be in control of my life."

"Like coming here?"

He nodded. "Even more important is protecting those I care about. And Hannah . . ." His voice cracked. "I can't even begin to tell you how lost and helpless I felt when I learned about the robbery and that you were inside the store."

She smiled a little at his honesty. She tried to stop the

tears of joy that wanted to flow. "I've never had a friend care so much about me."

She swatted a fly away from her face and fixed her gaze on his visage. After a slight pause, she softened the pitch of her voice to a conciliatory tone. "While everything was happening, my heart was pumping so fast, I just focused on keeping safe. But I feel sorry for the man who broke in."

She was quick to note the surprised expression that immediately drew his brows together. "You're kidding me."

She softened her voice. "He's out of a job. If he'd had faith in God, he never would have gone about getting money by robbing others." After a slight pause, she firmed her tone. "When I'm over the shock of what happened, I'm going to talk to him, explain how different his life would be if he knew Jesus."

What seemed an eternity later, they stood at the top of the hill. At the same time, they turned to look down at the creek. Above, thunder rumbled.

Finally, he motioned to the stones. "Let's sit down and enjoy the view."

When she looked up at him, he smiled, extending his hand. "Ladies first."

She lifted the bottom of her dress enough to bend her legs and claim one of the stones. He watched as she rested her palms against the ground on both sides of her sitting place.

When she looked up at him, he took a seat on the other stone.

"I wonder how these stones ended up all the way at the top of this hill. Overlooking the best view in the world."

Hannah turned a bit toward him. "You want to hear the story?"

He smiled in amusement. "Let me guess. It involves Old Sam."

She laughed. "*Gut* try. But actually, Levi and Annie Miller, when they were just kids, carried these . . ." She pointed to the stones. "All the way up from the creek to sit on."

"Really?"

"Um-hmm."

He contemplated two youngsters carrying two very heavy stones up the hill. Marcus whistled. "They must've brought them up a little bit at a time. It must have taken them days."

Hannah threw her hands in the air and offered an uncertain shrug of her shoulders. "I don't know. But in the end, their efforts paid off, so we can enjoy this magnificent view."

"I'll have to thank them."

"So will I."

As the sun peeked out from underneath a cloud, Marcus blinked at the sudden brightness. He looked down for a moment, and when he lifted his chin, he turned so that his knee touched Hannah's.

She softened the pitch of her voice. "From what I hear, they used to talk about things up here. That this was a *gut* decision-making place."

Marcus narrowed his brows together, considering what she'd just said. As he looked down at the creek and at the two-story farmhouses scattered below, three things floated through his mind.

Follow your heart. You love Hannah. You're making it too hard.

He closed his eyes a moment, struggling to hear the soft words his mother had told him. He yearned to talk to his mom this very moment. About Hannah. About how vastly different her life was from his and that he loved her anyway.

"Hannah?" After she turned to face him, he went on. "What you heard? About this being a good decision-making place?"

She nodded.

"You're right about this being a good thinking place."

"What's on your mind, Marcus?"

He considered the question and didn't respond. Because the thoughts flitting through his mind were so personal, he wasn't sure he could talk to anyone about them. Even to Hannah.

The happiness that had filled her voice was now gone and had been replaced with concern. He had to say something.

His expression was a combination of surprise and fear. He took her hands in his and squeezed them with as much reassurance as he could.

"I love you so much, Hannah."

She leaned forward. "I love you, too, Marcus."

He drew in a deep breath of happiness. "My parents would have loved you, too."

A long silence ensued before she broke it in a soft, curious voice. "Tell me about your mother. What was she like?"

"She was everything wonderful all packed into one person. She was kind. She used to volunteer at a soup kitchen. It's funny: Growing up, we didn't have a lot. In fact, my mom stayed home with my brothers until we were all in school. She never had a new dress, but she always knew where we were." He laughed. "She loved doing laundry."

Hannah's smile widened.

"And she even enjoyed ironing Dad's shirts. Packing our lunches." He shook his head as he recalled something he'd forgotten. "She cut cartoons out of the newspaper and stuck them in our lunch boxes."

"She really loved you."

The more Marcus told Hannah about his mother, the more he missed her. "She used to say that taking care of us boys was her greatest joy."

Hannah softened the pitch of her voice. "I wish I could've met your mother, Marcus. I'd like to thank her. For you."

Hannah's statement prompted him to think for a moment. For some reason, he wasn't expecting that.

"Your mother passed you on to me. And I consider you a wonderful, unexpected blessing in my life, Marcus. In fact, knowing you has changed me."

Her statement stopped his thoughts for a moment. Because definitely, he reciprocated her sentiment. "You've changed me, too, Hannah. And I wish you could have met my parents. They'd love you." After a slight hesitation, he added, "Like I do."

At that moment, Hannah inched closer to him. A long, emotional silence ensued while they sat in silence. And as the two of them looked down at Pebble Creek, everything became crystal clear to him. Satisfaction and happiness filled his chest until he wanted to shout with joy.

His decision was made.

Suddenly, the temperature dropped a few notches, and the breeze turned cooler. Automatically, Hannah crossed her arms over her lap and shivered. But what caused the goose bumps that rushed up her arms wasn't so much the temperature as it was her indecision about a future with Marcus. She wanted to be with him.

Even more, she yearned for him to be happy. And she sensed that joining the Amish faith may be out of his reach, even if he loved her. But she kept Marcus's promise on her mind. *Follow your heart.* It sounded like something Old Sam would've said.

"Marcus, I want to make you happy."

Clearing an emotional knot from her throat, she released her fingers from his and sat up straighter on her stone. As she did so, large, fluffy clouds moved across the sky. Thunder sounded, and she was sure it would rain sooner than her *daed* had predicted. But it was important to finish this conversation. The outcome would affect the rest of both their lives. And she wasn't about to leave it on the table.

"My love for you is real. I can feel it in every breath I take. And the only way to decide my story's ending is to play it out in real life."

He stared at her.

"I'll give you my ending. But only if we replay the story."

He parted his lips in surprise before he heeded her

request. His voice cracked with emotion. "Hannah, will you be my life partner?"

She let out a breath of relief and smiled. "What your mother said . . . about following your heart . . . I truly believe she was an amazing woman to have wanted that so much for you. I'll carry out her wish. I love my faith, but there are other churches that serve the same God. There's only one Marcus Jackson. I'll give up my faith to spend my life with you."

She softened her voice. "I'll marry you."

Marcus took in Hannah's words, which had been spoken with such honesty and sincerity. What she'd just said left him without words to respond. For long, thoughtful moments, he absorbed Hannah's admission. That she would give up her faith to be with him. There it was. His solution to happily ever after. He could have everything he'd wanted. Hannah Lapp. And he wouldn't have to join her faith to spend the rest of his life with her.

At the top of the hill, Marcus stood in great contemplation. *Say something. She's just given up her entire being to spend her life with you.* She looked up at him. As he studied her, the expression in her eyes was an intense combination of jubilation and uncertainty.

Indeed, the woman had no doubt in her mind that she would give up everything for him. The look on her face was honest and true. And for some reason, he wasn't sure what to say as he looked down at the farmhouses that dotted the landscape.

In the distance, workhorses pulled farm equipment in the fields. An occasional horse and buggy could be spotted on the narrow blacktops that paved the way through the vast area of country.

Below, Pebble Creek loomed. On both sides of them, clover patches surrounded their feet.

Somewhere close by was the very spot where Old Sam had hidden Esther's sixtieth wedding anniversary gift. As the breeze caressed the back of Marcus's neck, they faced each other. As she looked up at him, his breath hitched with emotion. Because the expression in her eyes was different from anything he'd ever seen.

But something wasn't right.

Chapter Sixteen

Inside Amish Edibles, Hannah hand-sewed a corner that was too difficult to reach with her sewing machine. It was the best time of day to work on her project since the sunbeam coming in through the windows was the strongest and she could easily see her stitches.

Afterward, she took in what was nearly finished, and the corners of her lips automatically lifted into a wide, satisfied smile. She was ready to do the backing, which was the last step.

In front of her, the poly batting was pinned to the quilt to the rollers of the frame. The different colors of blue connected into one beautiful piece that looked amazingly as if it had been born that way.

The more time she spent with the quilt, touched it, gazed at the blues, the more she thought of Marcus and the blanket his *maemm* had made for him. The very fabric he'd never forgotten.

At the same time, she sensed that her own quilt represented her special relationship with Marcus. Like the pieces sewn together in front of her, parts of Marcus and parts of herself had automatically blended into one beautiful relationship. It was something so unexpected. And so amazing.

As she began to roll the frame, she looked up at the window. She glimpsed Miracle. Automatically, her thoughts drifted to the fiction she'd written and the scene where Miracle's whinny had been the turning point in capturing the thief.

As she cleaned up around the quilt, she stacked the stencils and placed them back into their plastics. The numbered pieces went into a different bag. She retrieved a few pins and stuck them into her cushion. She collected her thimbles and put them on the small table nearby.

When the work in front of her was as neat as she could make it, she thought of the last conversation she'd had with Marcus two days before. When they'd hiked up to the top of Pebble Creek and discussed where they should go from there.

For a pensive moment, she lowered her gaze to the floor and swallowed an emotional knot. *Don't be sad. I offered him what I love most so he wouldn't have to forfeit his bond with his father. And that wasn't easy. I've been praying about what to do since we met. I've been asking Gott how to tell my parents and my brothers without creating friction. I'm stunned that he didn't feel it was the right thing to do. And I'm disappointed because I thought that leaving my beautiful way of life was what would enable us to spend the rest of our lives together.*

When they'd proceeded to walk down the hill in silence, a huge void had filled her heart. And she worried that it would never go away. *But what will become of us? Obviously, I surprised him by offering to give up what I*

*love most for him. And obviously, he is having second
thoughts about being with me.*

As she gazed out at her horse, a tear slipped down her
cheek. Slow steps took her to the entrance, where she
opened the door and stepped outside. As she closed
the door behind her, the bell rang. But she barely heard
it as she went to Miracle. As her arms went around his
long nose, she planted a kiss on his brown mane and
looked into his large, hazel eyes. "I love you so much.
You managed to make it when the odds were against
you. *Gott* helped Dr. Zimmerman save your life."

Choking, she nuzzled her face into his mane and
tightened her grip around his nose. "I wish *Gott* would
rescue me from the pain I'm feeling."

That evening, after work, Marcus cruised down the
country blacktop outside of Arcola. Hannah's offer to
change for him had stopped his thoughts.

As cornfields loomed on both sides of him, he enjoyed the warm air against the side of his face. The
sunset displayed the most magnificent colors he'd ever
seen. But the thought of their discussion at Pebble Creek
distracted him from even that marvelous picture.

He slowed as he approached a stop sign. He looked
both ways and proceeded. He set his cruise control at
fifty miles an hour and rested his elbow on the sill of the
open window.

In the distance, a horse-pulled buggy traversed a four-
way intersection. In his rearview mirror, a truck headed
south. His head ached, and he dragged his right hand
down his face, struggling to make sense of why he hadn't
said yes to Hannah's unbelievable, unexpected offer.

As the smell of manure filled his car, he considered the scent that he was now accustomed to. *When I first came here, I found it offensive. Now, I realize that God has His own way of providing everything we need. And most of those things don't come in containers.*

Hannah, I'm sorry I let you down. I saw the look of disappointment on your face when I didn't respond to your offer to change for me. But I'm not disappointed in anything you did. I'm ashamed of myself.

He cleared his throat and continued onto the country road. As he passed a two-story, white house surrounded by farmland, his mother's words floated through his head. *Follow your heart.* He'd promised her. And failed. But ironically, Hannah had heeded his mother's words.

She was willing to do exactly what his mom had asked him to do. He let out a breath. And that was exactly what was wrong with the picture.

A new ache swept through him until a groan escaped his throat. At the same time, everything started to come together in his mind. As he sorted out what had happened, the pain inside him started to go away, and he slowed the car to turn it around. By the time he reached his house, reality had etched its marks inside him. *I'm overwhelmed that Hannah would leave her faith to be with me. But it would never work. And I've got to tell her. Tomorrow.*

The following morning, inside Amish Edibles, Hannah removed her quilt from its frame and folded it neatly. As she took her finished piece in her hands, she pulled it to her chest with great affection.

She closed her eyes and contemplated all the work she'd put into the quilt and that so many unconnected pieces of material could come together in a way to look so seamless and beautiful. In a way, her relationship with Marcus represented all the separate pieces.

Unfortunately, unlike the parts of the beautiful material in her hands, she and Marcus hadn't been able to unite their differences to create a Christian relationship for the rest of their lives.

Dear Gott, *please help me to accept that I won't marry Marcus. I still love him. Why did he hesitate to commit to our future? Especially after I offered to give up my beloved way of life to be with him?*

The bell on the door rang. Hannah startled as she put her quilt on the table and made her way to the front of the store, where she faced Marcus.

"Morning, Hannah."

"Morning," she replied.

To her surprise, he seemed in *gut* spirits. In what appeared to be a relaxed stride, he made his way to her and stood opposite her. When she looked up at him, he hesitated for a moment. Then, in a calm, low voice, he said, "Hannah, I've been thinking about our conversation. Could we talk?"

"Of course. But first of all, I have a gift for you." She pressed her lips together and turned. "Do you mind waiting while I get it?"

She returned, holding her present in front of her. In silence, she looked in his eyes as he took it from her.

"The quilt?"

She nodded. "It's for you. And every time you touch it, you can think of the blanket your mother made you."

She softened her voice so it was barely more than a whisper. "And you can think of me."

Saturday, in late August, after the barn raising crew had quit work for the day, Marcus went back home to bathe and change clothes. But he didn't stay inside long. Quick steps took him to his backyard, where he began making his way to Pebble Creek to meet Hannah.

On his way, he'd stopped to remove a splinter from his thumb. A squirrel rushed in front of him, and Marcus slowed his steps to avoid coming into contact with the tiny brown body. He swatted a fly away from his nose.

In the distance, he spotted Hannah. Her back was to him, and he could see her throw a stone into the creek. *That girl has quite an arm.*

A mélange of emotions flitted through his chest, and the pulse on his wrist picked up to a speed that was a strange dose of certainty and uncertainty. First of all, he owed her an apology. It was his sincere hope that she'd forgive him for the hurt he'd caused her.

However, the time and distance between that particular conversation and the one they faced this evening had made things much clearer to him. He'd reflected on their relationship. On her. On the Amish lifestyle and Hannah's love for him, which was so strong, she'd offered to leave her faith.

But he'd contemplated much more than that. Other factors had entered his mind, such as Hannah's belief that he hadn't robbed King's Bakery even after she'd discovered his stack of cash in his money clip.

He'd also given much consideration to the Lapp family—Ben, especially—and how they had begun to shape his new life. He had factored in his reaction to Hannah being in Lapp Furniture when he'd learned she was caught up in a robbery.

But where should he go from here? His answer would come from Hannah. She just didn't know it yet.

As he got closer to the winding creek that ran through the hill, he could hear soft, gurgling noises. A bird chirped nonstop. The soft rush of water that cascaded over stones made a light, wispy sound.

Every once in a while, he'd hear something move in the tall blades of grass and weeds, and he'd see a piece of foliage bend and spring back up.

"Evening, Hannah."

As he got to where she stood, she turned to him, and he took in her sad but hopeful reflection. "I hear the barn will be up soon."

"Yes, it will. We've worked pretty fast, considering the bouts of rain."

She arched a brow, and her lips curved in amusement. "What's amazing is how something like this can get done in such a short time when everyone pitches in."

He motioned her alongside him. They began to walk by the creek.

"Beautiful place, isn't it?"

"*Jah.*"

"I've been doing a lot of thinking about us, Hannah."

She didn't respond as they took slow steps, walking close to where the water met the land.

"I've been thinking, too."

"I'm sorry, Hannah, that I didn't accept your offer."

She looked up at him. He couldn't read her expression.

"Marcus, I did what I thought I needed to do. For us.

254 Lisa Jones Baker

But to make a relationship, the two involved must agree and want the same outcome."

After expelling a breath, she softened her voice. "I respect you, Marcus, for your honesty." She lifted her palms to the sky. "Your mother's advice . . . it was so simple." She smiled a little. "And I decided to follow my own heart. Because of that, I have no regrets about what I said to you."

A long silence ensued, until her voice cracked with emotion. "Follow your heart, Marcus. Only then will you find the peace you're looking for."

He lowered his voice to a serious tone. "That's exactly what I intend to do. What really surprised me more than anything was that I couldn't do what I'd promised my own mother, but you . . ." He touched her chin with his finger. "You did it. So unconditionally. So honestly, and with good intentions."

As the sun dipped in the sky, they gazed into each other's eyes. "Your brother said something to me that I can't get out of my mind."

"What?"

"That the treasures in heaven outweigh anything that we could ever experience here on earth." He stopped a moment to decide how to continue. "Hannah, I want to live for eternity. To see my parents again. Working on cars with my dad was an earthly bond. But what you did, Hannah . . . following your heart when I couldn't even follow my own . . . that's a bond between us that would be unbreakable."

She parted her lips.

"I hope you don't mind, but I've thought of a better ending for your story."

"Really?"

He nodded, bent down on one knee, and softened his voice. "Hannah Lapp, I want to be part of the faith I've come to love. I'll join the Amish church. Will you be my partner for the rest of our lives?"

Epilogue

One year later, Marcus and Hannah stood side by side at the top of Pebble Creek. As the warm August sun warmed their faces and the gentle breeze fanned the backs of their necks, Hannah looked up at him.

In a decisive tone, she spoke, planting a palm against her hip. "I like you as an Amish man."

His eyes lit up as he looked down at her and gently took her by her shoulders.

"I like me as an Amish man, too. I'm glad the bishop gave me a list of things to do before I join the church this fall. I'm sure he's testing my commitment by making me travel by horse and buggy for a year. And I understand why he wanted me to hone my German. Fortunately, high school lessons gave me a jump-start on learning the language." He chuckled. "But now I better understand the church sermons."

After a slight pause, he cleared his throat and edged his tone with seriousness. "I've been doing a lot of thinking. And there are two things I want you to know before we get married this October."

In silence, she searched his face.

"I have a confession. And a promise."

"What's your confession?"

"That I've never felt so humbled in my entire life as I am today. God has given me you. Your family. All of this." His tone softened. "And eternal life."

He extended his hands and looked around. "These are such unexpected blessings." His voice hitched. "And so undeserved."

Her voice cracked with emotion. "That's what God's grace is all about."

For long, thoughtful moments, they stood, taking in the coveted ambience. Both blinked at the salty sting of tears. Hannah stepped closer to Marcus.

"I believe that more blessings are coming your way."

He raised a curious brow.

"Your brothers." She lifted her hands and her chin with confidence. "Months after you went to see them, they called you. And that gives me faith. I think they're stunned by how God has transformed you."

He lowered his gaze to his boots before posing her a question. "Do you really think the three of them will ask God into their lives?"

She hesitated before nodding. "With God, anything's possible. I'm glad we have gotten to know Nate. All of our talks seem to have led him to the right road. If God can touch him, He can certainly reach your brothers."

As Marcus locked gazes with her, he said in what was barely more than a whisper, "Hannah Lapp, Pebble Creek . . . Old Sam and Esther . . . Levi and Annie . . . I think of all of the miracles that happened right here on this very hill. And you know what I've come to realize?"

"What?"

"That as a couple, we've inherited a very special

responsibility." He looked up at the sky. She followed suit. When he lowered his gaze to her, the smell of wildflowers floated between them. Even from many yards below, they could hear the soft gurgling sounds as water cascaded over the pebbles.

"To love each other and to covet this special place. To always look to the cross because in the end, it's all that matters." He smiled a little, and so did she. "And to carry on the traditions of Pebble Creek. And that's exactly what I will do for the rest of my life, my true love." After expelling a breath, he added, "I promise."

RETURN TO THE BEGINNING

THE HOPE CHEST OF DREAMS SERIES

Book 1: *Rebecca's Bouquet*

The last thing Rebecca Sommer dreamed her plan to marry would bring is a heart-wrenching choice. She thought she and her betrothed, William, would spend the rest of their lives in Illinois's heartland, raising a family in their close-knit Amish hometown. But when he must travel far out of state to save his ailing father's business, Rebecca braves her relatives' disapproval—and her own fears—to work by his side. And though she finds herself ever more in love with the dedicated, resourceful man he proves to be, William's growing interest in *Englisch* ways may be the one challenge even her steadfast faith can't meet . . .

Book 2: *Annie's Recipe*

Annie Mast and Levi Miller were best friends until his father was shunned by the church. Now, ten years later, Levi has returned to Arthur, Illinois, for a brief visit, and he and Annie discover their bond is as strong as ever. Spending as much time together as possible, Annie finds herself dreaming of a future with Levi. And Levi is soon dreaming of building a home on a beautiful local hillside—to live in with Annie. Yet their longings are unlikely to become reality . . .

Book 3: *Rachel's Dream*

Rachel Kauffman and Jarred Zimmerman seem to have nothing in common. She's the outgoing youngest of a large, close-knit Amish clan, and longs to raise a brood of her own near those she loves. Estranged from his family by tragedy, Jarred is a young veterinarian who trusts the animals he heals far more than he trusts people. However, when Rachel's beloved horse falls ill, Jarred's struggles to save him show Rachel he's a man who cares deeply. And the respect he feels for her gentle, warmhearted ways soon becomes an irresistible bond . . .

Available wherever books and eBooks are sold!

Turn the page for an excerpt from
Rebecca's Bouquet . . .

His announcement took her by surprise. Rebecca Sommer met William's serious gaze and swallowed. The shadow from his hat made his expression impossible to read.

"You're really leaving?"

He fingered the black felt on the brim. "I know what a shock this is. Believe me, I never expected to hear that Dad had a heart attack."

"Do they expect a full recovery?"

William nodded. "But the docs say it will be a while before he works again. Right now, they can't even guess at a time line. In the meantime, Beth's struggling to take care of him."

While Rebecca considered the news, the warm June breeze rustled the large, ear-shaped leaves on the catalpa tree. The sun peeked from behind a large marshmallow cloud, as if deciding whether or not to appear. In the distance, a sleek black gelding clomped its hooves against the earth.

Pools of dust stirred, swirling and quickly disappearing. Lambs frolicked across the parcel of pasture separating the Sommer home from Old Sam Beachy's bright red barn. From where they stood, Rebecca could barely glimpse the orange YIELD sign on the back of the empty buggy parked next to the house.

"I'm the only person Dad trusts with his business." William paused and lowered his voice. "Beth wants me to come to Indiana and run his cabinet shop, Rebecca."

The news caused a wave of anxiety to roll through Rebecca's chest. She wrung her hands together in a nervous gesture. A long silence ensued as she thought of William leaving, and her shoulders grew tense. Not even the light, sweet fragrance floating from her mother's rose garden could take away Rebecca's anxiety.

When she finally started to respond, William held up a defensive hand. "It's just until he's back on his feet. This may not be such a bad thing. The experience might actually benefit us."

Rebecca raised a curious brow. The breeze blew a chestnut-brown hair out of place, and she quickly tucked it back under her *kapp*. Her gaze drifted from his face to his rolled-up sleeves.

Tiny freckles decorated his nose, giving him a youthful appearance. But there was nothing boyish about his square jaw or broad shoulders that tried to push their way out of his shirt. Her heart skipped a beat. She lifted her chin, and their eyes locked in understanding.

William smiled a little. "One of these days, we'll run our own company." He winked. "Don't worry."

She swallowed the lump in her throat. For one blissful, hopeful moment, she trusted everything would be okay. It wasn't those simple two words that reassured her, but the tender, persuasive way William said them.

The low, steady tone in which he spoke could convince Rebecca of almost anything.

The warm pink glow on his cheeks made Rebecca's pulse pick up speed. As he looked at her for a reaction, her lips lifted into a wide smile. At the same time, it was impossible to stop the nervous rising and falling of her chest.

She'd never dreamed of being without William. Even temporarily. At the young age of eighteen, she hadn't confronted such a difficult issue.

But her church teachers and parents had raised her to deal with obstacles. Fortunately, they had prepared her to be strong and to pray for guidance. As she stared at her beloved flower garden, her thoughts became more chaotic.

The clothes on the line rose and fell with the warm summer breeze. Their fresh, soapy scent floated through the air. She surely had greater control over her destiny than the wet garments, whose fate was dependent on the wind. She and William could get through this. They loved each other. God would take care of them, wouldn't He?

She glanced up at William. The way the sun hit him at an angle made him look even taller than his six feet and two inches. He'd always been bigger and stronger than other kids his age.

The gray flecks in his deep blue eyes danced to a mysterious tune as he darted her a grin. When she looked into those dark pools, she could drown in happiness. But today, even the warmth emanating from his smile couldn't stop the concern that edged her voice. "Don't worry? But I do, William. What about . . ."

"Us?"

She nodded.

He leveled his gaze so that she looked directly at him. "Nothing has changed. We'll still get married in November after the harvest."

Rebecca hesitated. She couldn't believe William would really leave Arthur, Illinois. But his reason was legitimate. His father needed him. She wasn't selfish, and asking him to stay would be.

Circumstances were beyond her control. What could she do? The question nagged at her until frustration set in. Within a matter of minutes, her world had changed, and she fought to adjust. She nervously tapped the toe of her black shoe against the ground.

As she crossed her arms over her chest, she wished they could protect her from the dilemma she faced. Her brows narrowed into a frown, and a long silence ensued. She looked at him, hoping for an answer. Seeking even a hint of a solution.

To her surprise, William teased, "Rebecca, stop studying me like I'm a map of the world."

His statement broke the tension, and she burst into laughter because a map of the world was such a far stretch from what she'd been thinking.

"Of course, you've got to help your folks, William. I know how much Daniel's business means to him. You certainly can't let him lose it. I can imagine the number of cabinets on order."

Surprised and relieved that her voice sounded steady, Rebecca's shoulders trembled as the thought of William leaving sank in. They'd grown up together and hadn't spent a day without seeing one another.

She stopped a moment and considered Daniel and Beth Conrad. Nearly a decade ago, William's mamma had died, and Daniel had married Beth.

He was a skilled cabinetmaker. It was no surprise that people from all over the United States ordered his custom-made pieces. Rebecca had seen samples of his elegant, beautiful woodworking.

A thought popped into Rebecca's mind, and she frowned. "William, you seem to be forgetting something very important. Daniel and Beth . . . They're *Englisch.*"

He nodded. "Don't think I haven't given that consideration."

"I don't want to sound pessimistic, but how will you stay Amish in their world?"

He shrugged. "They're the same as us, really."

She rolled her eyes. "Of course they are. But the difference between our lifestyle and theirs is night and day. How can you expect to move in with them and be compatible?"

William hooked his fingers over his trouser pockets, looked down at the ground and furrowed a brow. Rebecca smiled. She knew him so well. Whenever something bothered him, he did this. Rebecca loved the intense look on his face when he worried. The small indentation in his chin intensified.

What fascinated her most, though, were the mysterious gray flecks that danced in his eyes. When he lifted his chin, those flecks took on a metallic appearance. Mesmerized, Rebecca couldn't stop looking at them.

Moments later, as if having made an important decision, he stood still, moved his hands to his hips, and met her gaze with a nod.

In a more confident tone, he spoke. "It will be okay, Rebecca. Don't forget that Dad was Amish before he married Beth. He was raised with the same principles as us. Just because he's *Englisch* now doesn't mean he's forgotten everything he learned. No need to worry. He won't want me to change."

"No?"

William gave a firm shake of his head. "Of course not. In fact, I'm sure he'll insist that I stick to how I was brought up. Remember, he left me with Aenti Sarah and Uncle John when he remarried. Dad told me that raising me Amish was what my mother would have expected. The *Ordnung* was important to her. And keeping the faith must have also been at the top of Dad's list to have left me here. Nothing will change, Rebecca."

Rebecca realized that she was making too much out of William's going away. After all, it was only Indiana. Not the North Pole! Suddenly embarrassed at her lack of strength, she looked down at the hem of her dress before gazing straight into his eyes. He moved so close, his warm breath caressed her bottom lip, and it quivered. Time seemed to stand still while she savored the silent mutual understanding between them. That unique, unexplainable connection that she and William had.

"I've always read that things happen for a reason," William mentioned.

"Me too." Rebecca also knew the importance of the

Ordnung. And she knew William's mamma, Miriam, would have wanted him to stay in the faith that had meant everything to her.

As if sensing her distress, he interlaced his fingers together in front of him. His hands were large. She'd watched those very hands lift heavy bales of hay.

"Who knows? Maybe this is God's way of testing me."

Rebecca gave an uncertain roll of her eyes. "Talk to your aunt and uncle. They'll know what's best. After all, they've raised you since your father remarried."

The frustration in William's voice lifted a notch. "I already did. It's hard to convince them that what I'm doing is right." He lowered his voice. "You know how they feel. When Dad left the faith, he deserted me. But even so, I can't turn my back on him."

"Of course not."

"Aenti Sarah's concerned that people will treat me differently when I come back. She wants to talk to the bishop and get his permission. If that makes her feel better, then I'm all for it."

"If he'll give his blessing."

William nodded in agreement.

"But we're old enough to think for ourselves, William. When we get married and raise our family, we can't let everyone make up our minds for us."

He raised a brow. "You're so independent, Miss Rebecca."

She smiled a little.

A mischievous twinkle lightened his eyes.

"Your decision shouldn't be based on what people think," Rebecca said. "If we made choices to please others, we'd never win. Deep down inside, we have to be happy with ourselves. So you've got to do what's in your heart. And no one can decide that but you."

The expression that crossed his face suddenly became unreadable. She tilted her head and studied him with immense curiosity. "What are you thinking?"

His gray flecks repeated that metallic appearance. "Rebecca, you're something else."

A surge of warmth rushed through her.

"I can't believe your insight." He blinked in amazement. "You're an angel." His voice was low and soft. She thought he was going to kiss her. But he didn't. William followed the church rules. But Rebecca wouldn't have minded breaking that one.

In a breathless voice, she responded, "Thank you for that."

As if suddenly remembering the crux of their conversation, William returned to the original topic. "I've assured Aenti Sarah and Uncle John that I won't leave the Amish community. That I'll come back, and we'll get married. They finally justified letting me leave by looking at this as an opportunity to explore *Rumspringa*."

Rebecca grinned. "I guess that's one way to look at it." *Rumspringa* was the transition time between adolescence and adulthood when an Amish youth could try things before deciding whether to join the faith for him—or herself. She even had a friend who had gone as far as to get a driver's license.

He paused. "Rebecca, I know we didn't plan on this." His voice grew more confident as he continued. "You've got to understand that I love you more than anything in the world. Please tell me you'll wait for me. I give you my word that this move is only temporary. As soon as Dad's on his feet again, I'll come home. Promise."

As William committed, Rebecca took in his dark brown hair. The sun's brightness lightened it to the color of sand. For a moment, his features were both rugged and endearing. Rebecca's heart melted.

Her voice softened. "How long do you think you'll stay?"

William pressed his lips together thoughtfully. "Good question. Hopefully, he'll be back to work in no time. His customers depend on him, and according to Beth, he has a long list of orders for cabinets to produce and deliver. He's a strong man, Rebecca. He'll be okay."

"I believe that. I'll never forget when he came into town last year to see you." She giggled. "Remember his fancy car?"

William chuckled. "He sure enjoys the luxuries of the *Englisch*. I wish our community wouldn't be so harsh on him. He's really Amish at heart."

William hesitated. "I used to resent that he left me."

Long moments passed in silence. He stepped closer and lowered his voice to a whisper. "Rebecca, you've become unusually quiet. And you didn't answer my question."

She raised an inquisitive brow.

"Will you wait for me?"

Her thoughts were chaotic. For something to do, she looked down and flattened her hands against her long, brown dress. She realized how brave William was and recalled the scandal Daniel Conrad had made when he married outside of the faith and had moved to the country outside of Evansville, Indiana. She raised her chin to look at William's face. Mamma always told her that a person's eyes gave away his feelings.

The tongue could lie. But not the eyes. William's intriguing flecks had become a shade lighter, dancing with hope and sincerity. His cheeks were flushed.

"William, you've got to do this." She let out a small, thoughtful sigh. "I remember a particular church sermon from a long time ago. The message was that our success in life isn't determined by making easy choices. It's measured by how we deal with difficult issues. And leaving Arthur is definitely a tough decision."

He hugged his hands to his hips. "What are you getting at?"

She quietly sought an answer to his question. What did she mean? She'd sounded like she knew what she was talking about. Moments later, the answer came. She recognized it with complete clarity.

She squared her shoulders. "I promised you I'd stick by you forever, William. And right now, you need me."

He gazed down at her in confusion.

Clearing her throat, she looked up at him and drew a long breath. "I'm going with you."

Inside Old Sam Beachy's barn, Rebecca poured out her dilemma to her dear friend. Afterwards, Buddy whimpered sympathetically at her feet. Rebecca reached down from her rocking chair opposite Old Sam's workbench and obediently stroked the Irish setter behind his ears. The canine closed his eyes in contentment.

Old Sam was famous for his hope chests. He certainly wasn't the only person to put together the pieces, but he was a brilliant artist who etched beautiful, personalized designs into the lids.

Rebecca had looked at his beloved Esther as a second mother. Since she'd succumbed to pneumonia a couple of years ago, Rebecca had tried to return her kindness to the old widower. So did her friends, Rachel and Annie. The trio took care of him. Rachel listened to Sam's horse-and-buggy stories. Annie baked him delicious sponge cakes while Rebecca picked him fresh flowers.

Drawing a long breath, Rebecca wondered what advice he'd give. Whatever it was would be good. Because no one was wiser than Old Sam. She crossed her legs at the ankles. Sawdust floated in the air. Rebecca breathed in the woodsy smell of oak.

When he started to speak, she sat up a little straighter. "The real secret to happiness is not what we give or receive; it's what we share. I would consider your help to William and his parents a gift from the heart. At the same time, a clear conscience is a soft pillow. You want to have the blessing of our bishop and your parents. The last thing you want is a scandal about you and William living under the same roof."

Rebecca let out a deep, thoughtful sigh as she considered his wisdom. In the background, she could hear Ginger enter her stall from the pasture. Old Sam's horse snorted. And that meant she wanted an apple.

Sam's voice prompted Rebecca to meet his gaze. "Rebecca, I can give you plenty of advice. But the most important thing I can tell you is to pray."

Rebecca nodded and crossed her arms over her chest.

"But remember: Do not ask the Lord to guide your footsteps if you're not willing to move your feet."

* * *

Rebecca was fully aware that William was ready to leave. In her front yard, she hugged her baby sister, Emily, shoving a rebellious strand of blond hair out of her face. Rebecca planted an affectionate kiss on brother Peter's cheek. "Be good."

Pete's attention was on Rebecca just long enough to say good-bye. As she turned to her father, the two kids started screaming and chasing each other in a game of tag. Emily nearly tripped over a chicken in the process. Rebecca was quick to notice the uncertain expression on Old Sam's face.

The sweet, creamy smell of homemade butter competed with the aroma of freshly baked bread. Both enticing scents floated out of the open kitchen windows. Tonight, Rebecca would miss Mamma's dinner. It would be the first time Rebecca hadn't eaten with her family.

Her heart pumped to an uncertain beat. But she'd never let her fear show. Ever since the death of her other little sister, Rebecca had learned to put on a brave façade. Her family depended on her for strength.

Rebecca's father grasped her hands and gave them a tight squeeze. She immediately noted that his arms shook. It stunned her to realize that his embrace was more of a nervous gesture than an offer of support. And the expression on his face was anything but encouraging. Rebecca understood his opposition to what she was about to do. Her father's approval was important to her, and it bothered her to seem disrespectful.

All of her life, she'd tried hard to please him. They'd never even argued. In fact, this was the first time she'd gone against his wishes. But William was her future. She wanted to be by his side whenever he needed her.

In a gruff, firm voice, her father spoke. "Be careful, Becca. You know how I feel. I'm disappointed that William hasn't convinced you to stay. You belong here. In Arthur."

He pushed out a frustrated breath. "But you're of age to make your own decision. We've made arrangements with Beth so that living under the same roof with William will be proper. We trust she'll be a responsible chaperone while you're with the Conrads. Just come home soon. We need your help with chores."

He pointed an authoritative finger. "And never let the *Englisch* ways influence you. They will tempt you to be like them, Becca. Remember your faith."

Rebecca responded with a teary nod. When she finally faced Mamma, she forced a brave smile. But the tightness in her throat made it difficult to say good-bye.

Mamma's deep blue eyes clouded with moisture. With one swift motion, Rebecca hugged her. For long moments, she was all too aware of how much she would miss that security. The protection only a parent could offer.

Much too soon, Mamma released her and held her at arm's length. When Rebecca finally turned to Old Sam, he stepped forward and handed her a cardboard container with handles.

She met his gaze and lifted a curious brow. "This is for me?"

He nodded. "I hope you like it." He pointed. "Go ahead. Take it out."

Everyone was quiet while she removed the gift. As she lifted the hope chest, she caught her breath. There was a unanimous sound of awe from the group. "Old Sam . . ." She focused on the design etched into the lid. "It's absolutely beautiful! I will treasure it the rest of my life."

"You always bring me fresh flowers, so I thought you'd like the bouquet."

She glanced at William before turning her attention back to Sam. "I'm taking the miniature hope chest with me."

Sam's voice was low and edged with emotion. "I will pray for your safety. And remember that freedom is not to do as you please, but the liberty to do as you ought. And the person who sows seeds of kindness will have a perpetual harvest. That's you, Rebecca."

Rebecca blinked as salty tears filled her eyes. With great care, she returned the hope chest to its box on the bright green blades of grass.

Old Sam's voice cracked. "You come back soon. And if you want good advice, consult an old man." A grin tugged at Rebecca's lips. Sam knew every proverb in the book. She'd miss hearing him recount them.

"Thank you again. I can't wait to start putting away special trinkets for the children I will have some day."

When she looked up at him, he merely nodded approval.

William's voice startled her from her thoughts. "Rebecca, it's time to head out. It's gonna be a long drive."

Her gaze remained locked with Mamma's. Mary Sommer's soft voice shook with emotion. "This is the first time you've left us. But you're strong."

Rebecca squeezed her eyes closed for several heartbeats.

As if to reassure herself, her mother went on. "We

hope Daniel recovers quickly. William needs you. In the meantime, God will keep both of you in His hands. Don't forget that. Always pray. And remember what we've taught you. Everything you've learned in church."

"*Jah.*"

"It's never been a secret that God gave you a special gift for accepting challenges. I'll never forget the time you jumped into that creek to save your brother. You pulled him to shore."

Rebecca grinned. "I remember."

"*Rumspringa* might be the most important time in your life. But be very careful. There will be temptations in the *Englisch* world. In fact, the bishop is concerned that you will decide against joining the Amish church."

"I know who I am."

A tear rolled down Mamma's cheek while she slipped something small and soft between Rebecca's palms. Rebecca glanced down at the crocheted cover.

"I put together this Scripture book to help you while you're away, Rebecca. When you have doubts or fears, read it. The good words will comfort and give you strength. You can even share them with Beth. She's going through a difficult time. Your *daed* and I will pray for you every day." She paused. "Lend Daniel your support. The bishop wants you to set three additional goals and accomplish them while you're gone. Give them careful consideration. They must be unselfish and important. Doing this will make your mission even more significant."

After a lengthy silence, William addressed the Sommers in a reassuring voice. "I'll take good care of her. You can be sure of that."

Rebecca's dad raised his chin and directed his attention to William. "We expect nothing less."

Long, tense moments passed while her father and William locked gazes. Several heartbeats later, Eli Sommer stepped forward. "I don't approve of my Becca going so far away. I'm holding you responsible for her, William. If anything happens . . ."

William darted an unsure glance at Rebecca before responding. "I understand your concern. That's why I didn't encourage her to come."

Rebecca raised her chin and regarded both of them. "I've given this a lot of thought. I'll go. And I'll come back, safe and sound."

Rebecca listened with dread as her father continued making his case. She knew William wouldn't talk back. And she wasn't about to change her mind about going.

"Daed, it's my decision. Please don't worry."

Before he could argue, she threw her arms around him and gave him a tight, reassuring hug. After she stepped away, William motioned toward the black Cadillac. As Rebecca drew a deep breath, her knees trembled, and her heart pounded like a jackhammer. Finally, she forced her jellylike legs to move. She didn't turn around as William opened her door.

Before stepping inside, Rebecca put Mamma's Scripture book inside the hope chest. William took the box from her and placed it in the middle of the backseat. Rebecca brought very little with her. Just one small suitcase that her father placed in the trunk.

With great hesitation, she waved good-bye. She forced a confident smile, but her entire body shook. She sat very still as Daniel's second cousin, Ethan, backed the car out of the drive. Gravel crunched under the tires. This wasn't Rebecca's first ride in an automobile. Car rides were not uncommon in the Amish community.

Trying to convince herself she was doing the right thing, she gently pushed the down arrow by her door handle, and the window opened. Rebecca turned in her seat and waved until the sad faces of her family, their plain-looking wooden-framed house built by her great-grandfather, and Old Sam, disappeared.

William turned to her. A worry crease crept across his forehead. The cleft in his chin became more pronounced. "Rebecca, your dad's right. I should have made you stay. The last thing I want to do is create tension between you two."

"It wasn't your choice. As far as my father's concerned . . ." She gave a frustrated shake of her head. "I don't like displeasing him either. On the other hand, it's not right for me to stay here and send you off to save Daniel's shop all by yourself." She shrugged.

In silence, she thought about what she'd just said. She nervously ran her hand over the smooth black leather seat.

"You can adjust the air vents," Ethan announced, turning briefly to make eye contact with her.

She was thankful she didn't have to travel to the Indiana countryside by horse and buggy. She rather enjoyed the soft, barely audible purring of the engine.

Next to her, she eyed the cardboard and pulled out the mini hope chest, setting the box on the floor. She smiled a little.

"Old Sam is something else." William's voice was barely more than a whisper.

"*Jah*. I can't wait to tell him about our trip." Rebecca giggled. "I'll miss listening to him grumble while he works in the barn. I enjoy watching him make those elaborate chests that he sells to the stores in town."

William gave a small nod. "He loves you three girls."

"Thank goodness that Annie and Rachel will be around to keep him company."

The three friends had loved Esther. Now they took care of Old Sam. He was like an uncle to them. But Rebecca was leaving the world she knew. Would she fit in with the *Englisch*?

Connect with

Us

Visit us online at
KensingtonBooks.com
to read more from your favorite authors, see books
by series, view reading group guides, and more.

Join us on social media

for sneak peeks, chances to win books and prize packs,
and to share your thoughts with other readers.

facebook.com/kensingtonpublishing
twitter.com/kensingtonbooks

Tell us what you think!

To share your thoughts, submit a review,
or sign up for our eNewsletters, please visit:
KensingtonBooks.com/TellUs.

Books by Bestselling Author
Fern Michaels

___**The Jury**	0-8217-7878-1	$6.99US/$9.99CAN
___**Sweet Revenge**	0-8217-7879-X	$6.99US/$9.99CAN
___**Lethal Justice**	0-8217-7880-3	$6.99US/$9.99CAN
___**Free Fall**	0-8217-7881-1	$6.99US/$9.99CAN
___**Fool Me Once**	0-8217-8071-9	$7.99US/$10.99CAN
___**Vegas Rich**	0-8217-8112-X	$7.99US/$10.99CAN
___**Hide and Seek**	1-4201-0184-6	$6.99US/$9.99CAN
___**Hokus Pokus**	1-4201-0185-4	$6.99US/$9.99CAN
___**Fast Track**	1-4201-0186-2	$6.99US/$9.99CAN
___**Collateral Damage**	1-4201-0187-0	$6.99US/$9.99CAN
___**Final Justice**	1-4201-0188-9	$6.99US/$9.99CAN
___**Up Close and Personal**	0-8217-7956-7	$7.99US/$9.99CAN
___**Under the Radar**	1-4201-0683-X	$6.99US/$9.99CAN
___**Razor Sharp**	1-4201-0684-8	$7.99US/$10.99CAN
___**Yesterday**	1-4201-1494-8	$5.99US/$6.99CAN
___**Vanishing Act**	1-4201-0685-6	$7.99US/$10.99CAN
___**Sara's Song**	1-4201-1493-X	$5.99US/$6.99CAN
___**Deadly Deals**	1-4201-0686-4	$7.99US/$10.99CAN
___**Game Over**	1-4201-0687-2	$7.99US/$10.99CAN
___**Sins of Omission**	1-4201-1153-1	$7.99US/$10.99CAN
___**Sins of the Flesh**	1-4201-1154-X	$7.99US/$10.99CAN
___**Cross Roads**	1-4201-1192-2	$7.99US/$10.99CAN

Available Wherever Books Are Sold!
Check out our website at **www.kensingtonbooks.com**